This Time
Around

Other Books by the Authors

Denise Hunter

The Bluebell Inn Novels
Lake Season
Carolina Breeze
Autumn Skies

The Blue Ridge Novels
Blue Ridge Sunrise
Honeysuckle Dreams
On Magnolia Lane

The Summer Harbor Novels
Falling Like Snowflakes
The Goodbye Bride
Just a Kiss

The Chapel Springs Romance Series
Barefoot Summer
A December Bride (novella)
Dancing with Fireflies
The Wishing Season
Married 'til Monday

The Big Sky Romance Series
A Cowboy's Touch
The Accidental Bride
The Trouble with Cowboys

NANTUCKET LOVE STORIES
Surrender Bay
The Convenient Groom
Seaside Letters
Driftwood Lane

STAND-ALONE NOVELS
Bookshop by the Sea (Available April 2021!)
Summer by the Tides
Sweetbriar Cottage
Sweetwater Gap

Novellas included in *Smitten*, *Secretly Smitten*, and
Smitten Book Club

MELISSA FERGUSON
The Cul-de-Sac War
The Dating Charade

KATHLEEN FULLER

THE MAPLE FALLS ROMANCE SERIES
Hooked on You
Much Ado About a Latte (Available January 2022!)

This Time Around

DENISE HUNTER

MELISSA FERGUSON

KATHLEEN FULLER

THOMAS NELSON

Since 1798

Published in Nashville, Tennessee, by Thomas Nelson. Thomas Nelson is a registered trademark of HarperCollins Christian Publishing, Inc.

Thomas Nelson titles may be purchased in bulk for educational, business, fundraising, or sales promotional use. For information, please email SpecialMarkets@ThomasNelson.com.

Library of Congress Cataloging-in-Publication Data

Names: Hunter, Denise, 1968- Summer detour. | Ferguson, Melissa (Assistant professor), Pining for you. | Fuller, Kathleen, He loves me; he loves me not.
Title: This time around / Denise Hunter, Melissa Ferguson, Kathleen Fuller.
Description: Nashville, Tennessee : Thomas Nelson, [2021] | Summary: "From three beloved romance authors come sweet and light stories perfect for lovers of Hallmark movies"-- Provided by publisher.
Identifiers: LCCN 2020056699 (print) | LCCN 2020056700 (ebook) | ISBN 9780785248767 (paperback) | ISBN 9780785248774 (epub) | ISBN 9780785248798
Subjects: LCSH: Romance fiction, American. | Christian fiction, American.
Classification: LCC PS648.L6 T463 2021 (print) | LCC PS648.L6 (ebook) | DDC 813/.08508--dc23
LC record available at https://lccn.loc.gov/2020056699
LC ebook record available at https://lccn.loc.gov/2020056700

Printed in the United States of America

21 22 23 24 25 LSC 5 4 3 2 1

Contents

A Summer Detour

Denise Hunter

Chapter 1

Allie Adams shoved the last red rose into the gaping vase and eyed the massive arrangement of blood and thorns with a scowl. The fragrance of flowers permeated the back of Blooms and Buds, reminding her of funerals, Georgia summers, and broken hearts.

"See, lookie there." Charlotte Jackson's grin lit up her rich brown face as she swept in from the storefront. "And I didn't even have to do triage this time. Or bring you a paper bag."

"I didn't hyperventilate." Allie blotted her pricked finger, the blood a bright spot against her pale skin. "I just . . . got a little woozy. And how did a flower with spikes become the international symbol for love anyway?"

Charlotte lifted a perfectly arched brow. "You tell me. And what happened this time? I told you to wear gloves, girl."

"I forgot. I was a little distracted."

"By the other five arrangements that need to be done in . . ." She checked her watch as she joined Allie at the work-table. "Half an hour?"

"Hey, don't blame me. I'm just the summer help." Allie's real job—teacher's assistant for a local elementary school—gave her summers off. She arranged the fern fronds and baby's breath to best set off the two dozen roses. Some poor guy needed forgiveness in a bad way.

"It's just this trip . . . ," Allie continued. "I'm kind of dreading it."

"Your grandparents' anniversary party? I thought your family was close. Unlike mine." Charlotte smirked as she gathered a bunch of hydrangeas and went to work on an arrangement. "No wonder my parents wanted me to be a psychologist—probably hoped I'd come back and fix them. As if."

Allie was looking forward to seeing her family this weekend—it wasn't that. Despite the fact that she had moved to Atlanta seven years ago, her parents and big sister remained in close contact. Her grandparents were wonderful—their Pennsylvanian farmhouse spacious and cozy.

"We are close. We just . . . It's hard to explain."

The bell on the shop's door jingled.

"To be continued." Charlotte set down a stem of snapdragons and went to wait on the customer.

Allie's phone vibrated in her pocket. She brushed off her hands and checked the screen. "Hey, Mom. What's up?"

"I just finished packing." A zipping sound accentuated the words. "But I wanted to call and remind you about your flight tomorrow. Have you packed?"

Allie rolled her eyes. It was a wonder she managed to brush her teeth without a reminder. "I didn't forget." Not that she'd started packing. Hadn't done her laundry yet either, but there was still plenty of time.

"Well, you remember that one time . . ."

"I was eighteen, Mom, and I just forgot about the time change."

"You missed Olivia's college graduation."

Allie sighed, then it dawned on her that her mother was just now packing. "Wait, I thought you were supposed to leave for Gram and Gramps's yesterday. Dad said he was going to restain their deck before the party."

"We were. But there was a delay with the Chevy. Your grandparents aren't happy—we had to make up some excuse. But they'll forget that soon enough when they see Dad's old girl pulling into the drive. They'll be so surprised."

For all these years the '57 Chevy had been atrophying on the property her parents had inherited from her grandparents. The restoration was her parents' surprise for their fiftieth anniversary. It had been in the works for months.

"But what about the deck? Gramps said they wouldn't host the party unless the deck was refinished."

"Well, he insists he can do it himself."

"He's in no shape for that." He'd recently had a knee replacement, and it was too hot for him to be working outdoors.

"I'm not happy about it either, but what else can we do? We can't leave the car here, and your grandma has tried talking him out of it, but you know Gramps."

Allie wished there was something she could do. But she knew nothing about refinishing decks.

A sudden thought occurred. "When will the car be finished?"

"Tomorrow morning. Your dad and I will pick it up and be on our way. At this rate we'll probably arrive after you."

"Wait, Mom. What if I picked up the car and drove it to

Pennsylvania?" She'd have to cancel her flights, but that was okay. On Sunday she could ride back to Copper Creek with her parents, collect her car, and drive back home.

She realized her mom hadn't responded. Heat prickled beneath her arms. "Mom, did you hear me?"

"Oh, honey . . . that's just . . . too much to ask. We'll be fine."

"But Gramps could hurt himself, and Dad can still get there in time to help if you leave today."

"But—the Chevy is . . . it's a big responsibility, honey. Driving through the mountains all by yourself. It's just not a good idea. I don't want to put that on you. Thank you, though. So sweet of you to offer."

What her mother meant was, she didn't trust Allie with the precious vehicle. Allie's shoulders hunched in, warmth bleeding into her face. No doubt if Olivia didn't have a husband and three kids in tow, the assignment would've been passed to her without a blink of an eye.

"Mom, I can do it. I'll be careful, I promise."

"Honey . . . you've had a lot of speeding tickets."

"I've had a total of two and none in the past five years. I'll drive the speed limit—under the speed limit. I'll treat the car like a baby bird."

She heard her dad talking in the background. Then her mom's intense whisper—somewhat muffled, yet Allie heard every word.

"She offered to drive the Chevy so we could head up to my parents' today."

"*Allie?* Drive the *car?*"

"What should I say?"

"Well, I don't know. You think of something."

"I can't say yes!"

"Are you sure? Your dad's set on having that heatstroke, you know."

"It's *Allie*, Bill. She couldn't commit to a teeth-whitening strip."

Okay, her mom hadn't said that last part, but it was clearly implied.

"Oh, that's right," her mom muttered. "Allie, I don't think you can drive the car. It has a—"

Her dad interrupted and her mom's reply was muffled.

"Mom? Mom, of course I can drive the car. Can you just—?"

Her parents were back in negotiations.

For heaven's sake. This was ridiculous. Allie cradled the phone on her shoulder and gathered the flowers for the next arrangement while her parents discussed whether or not their twenty-five-year-old daughter was up to the task of operating a motor vehicle.

When were they going to see she wasn't the impetuous girl she'd been at eighteen? Sure, she was still a little impulsive, and maybe she wasn't quite as stable as her parents might like— certainly not *settled*, like Olivia.

But she paid her bills on time (usually) and held down a job, sometimes two. (Though, okay, she switched frequently. But just because she had a short attention span didn't mean she was irresponsible.)

She'd been a volunteer at the zoo for four years running. She'd even kept a pet alive, going on two years now. Yes, Mary, Queen of Scots, was perhaps the most independent feline ever to roam the earth, but she still counted. All of the above showed commitment and responsibility, did it not?

Maybe she wasn't married with three kids and a mortgage, but she was a capable adult. She simply needed to prove it to her parents once and for all—and this was just the opportunity she'd been looking for.

"Mom . . ." Allie cut into the ongoing whisperfest. "I can do this. I'll take excellent care of Gramps's car, I promise. You don't want him having a heatstroke before his fiftieth anniversary, do you? Gram would never forgive us after she bought all those balloons." Her grandmother had recently rambled for ten minutes about the perils of wrangling three dozen Mylar balloons into a Subaru.

"She says she can do it." Her mom's muffled whisper sounded over the phone.

"Well, your dad is raring to go on that deck." Allie picked a long blonde hair from the flower arrangement as she strained to hear her dad's voice. *Blah, blah, blah*, something about Sherwin-Williams. ". . . in the nineties tomorrow."

That wasn't a no. "Mom, let me do this. For Gram and Gramps, okay? I'll pick up the car as soon as it's finished, and I'll take my time coming. I'll be pulling the car safely into their driveway before you know it."

Allie envisioned the moment. The older couple would spill out onto the porch, eyes wide, mouths gaping at the sight of their beloved old car, their precious granddaughter in the driver's seat.

"My old girl!" Gramps would say. "Isn't she beautiful?"

"Just look at her!" Gram would beam. "And Allie, you drove it all this way. Aren't you something! You've always been our favorite—don't tell Olivia."

The image faded at her mom's sounds of distress, a sort

of wheezing noise. Allie had first heard it at the age of seven when she'd made a beautiful mural on the living room wall with permanent markers.

Her mother was coming around though. "I've got it all under control, Mom. Trust me."

Allie could do this. She could deliver the car safely from Georgia to Pennsylvania, and then her parents would know they could trust her. No more reminder calls. No more pathetic assignment (napkins) when she offered to bring something to holiday meals. No more being rejected as a child care option for her beloved nieces and nephew, even when it meant canceling a second honeymoon. No more *Olivia this, Olivia that.* Allie would prove once and for all that she was a responsible adult, worthy of their time and trust.

"Well . . ." Her mother wheezed once more. "I suppose it . . . *might* be okay . . . ?"

"Wonderful!" Allie blurted before Mom could change her mind. "I'll cancel my flights and pick up the Chevy tomorrow morning. You two had best get on the road before Gramps ruins his new knee."

Chapter 2

There she was. The grand old '57 Chevy sat outside the big red barn of Collins Auto Repair and Restoration in Copper Creek. Allie was used to seeing the car dilapidated, overgrown by weeds and grass, and surrounded by piles of cement blocks no one ever got around to using.

But this . . . The antique car gleamed in the early afternoon sunlight. It sported a fresh coat of cherry-red paint on the body, and the top was crisp white, as were the wingy things on the back.

At the sight of the pristine vehicle, beads of sweat formed on the back of Allie's neck. Maybe it was just her long, thick hair and the hot summer sun. She wiped her damp palms down the sides of her shorts. No, definitely nerves. She had to drive that car through the mountains and deliver it safely 650 miles away.

She could do this. She'd had a driver's license for nine years, and she'd only had one accident. Two if you counted the fender bender at the Piggly Wiggly. And, okay, three if you counted the time she'd run over a parking bumper. *(Note to self: Avoid parking lots.)*

"Hey, Allie." Brady Collins emerged from the barn's shadow, wiping his hands on a dirty rag, a ball cap shading his face. Though they'd both attended the same high school, he'd graduated by the time she'd entered her freshman year. Several years back he'd married Hope Daniels, and together they were raising the boy from his first marriage.

"Hi, Brady." She exited her Fiat. "Wow, she looks amazing. My grandparents will be so happy."

"Can't take credit for the exterior, but the interior's a thing of beauty. I think your parents will be happy with the upgrades. I used a small-block V-8 265 and two 283s, a 2-barrel and a 4-barrel carburetor. I also upgraded to a 4-speed as your dad asked."

"Um . . . I have no idea what you just said."

Brady chuckled. "It's all on the receipt. She'll be running even better than she did originally."

Allie looked over the receipt (basically a foreign language), then signed it and handed it back with the check she'd picked up from her parents' house.

"Thanks. She's all yours." Brady handed her the keys. "I'm heading in the house for lunch if you want to join us. Hope made her chicken Waldorf salad—it's not to be missed."

"That's tempting, but I'm getting a late start, and I need to get on the road. My parents expect me to crawl at approximately eighteen miles per hour; I might arrive by next Wednesday."

Brady flashed a grin. "Enjoy yourself. And it wouldn't hurt to take it easy on those corners. They're summer tires, not a lot of grip."

"Will do. Thanks for the warning. And you're sure it's okay to leave my car here for a few days?"

"What's one more?"

He waved goodbye and headed into the house while Allie transferred her suitcase, pillow, anniversary gift, and contribution to the party—napkins, of course—into the Chevy's white leather back seat. She hadn't lied about the late start. At this point she'd be lucky to get there before eleven tonight.

The driver's door opened with nary a squeak, and Allie fairly glided onto the polished seat. The car smelled of new leather and carpet. Her grandparents would be so surprised. This was the car in which Gramps had picked up Gram for their first date. They'd shared their first kiss on this very seat. She couldn't wait to pull into their drive and see the looks on their faces—if only they could stay awake long enough to see it.

Allie dropped her purse onto the passenger seat and set her latte in the center cup holder. That's when she saw it—the chrome stick-thingy poking up in the middle.

What?

Her gaze flew to the floor, looking for the brake and gas pedal—both present and accounted for. Along with another pedal—a clutch.

Allie's breath caught in her lungs. *A stick shift?*

Of course it was a stick shift. She pressed a palm to her forehead. Her father had taught Olivia to drive a manual, but by the time Allie turned sixteen, he was working long hours and didn't have time. Mom taught her to drive in the Odyssey.

Her phone conversation with her mom came back to her. *That's* what she'd meant when she questioned Allie's ability to drive the car.

She wrapped her fingers around the skinny steering wheel and stared out the front windshield into the woods. What was she going to do now? She couldn't bail on this assignment. She had to get this car to Pennsylvania. But now was probably not the best time to learn to drive a manual. She'd have to get someone else to drive. She hated that. She wanted the credit for delivering the car. But there was no help for it now—she was going to have to share the glory with someone else.

Olivia was the obvious choice, but they'd left early this morning as she'd been enlisted to make the bulk of the food for the party. (Roasted prime rib, mashed potatoes, and home-made yeast rolls, for starters.)

Who else could Allie ask? Not Charlotte—she was all the way back in Atlanta, and she had her shop to run. Her other friends were also three hours south of here. She could hire a driver—but who? It really had to be someone here in Copper Creek, given the time constraints, but she'd lost touch with her old friends. She couldn't call someone out of the blue and beg a favor.

Why, oh, why was this happening to her? She thumped her head on the steering wheel once. Twice. Three times. Who could she ask?

As if the jarring had knocked something loose, an image of Luke Fletcher burst into her mind. Her parents had invited their next-door neighbor, but he declined, according to her mother. Probably because of Allie. He was still practically her parents' adopted son, but he made himself scarce when Allie came around—as well he should.

A tap on the driver's window made her jump. At the sight of Brady she composed herself and cranked down the window.

Even with a bad case of hat-head he was a handsome man. Lucky Hope. "Everything all right?"

"Um . . . sort of? It seems my parents forgot to mention this was a stick shift."

He blinked. "Oh. You can't drive a manual?"

"Well, I probably could, but I'm not sure we'd make it there in one piece." She gave him a cautious look. "I don't suppose you're available for the next, say, ten hours or so?"

"Oh, hey, wish I could. But I have a '67 Porsche 911 due tomorrow afternoon. It's for this guy's birthday . . ."

"No, of course, I understand."

"Sorry 'bout that. Wish I could help."

"Not your fault. I don't suppose you might know of anyone . . . ? I could make it worth their while."

He rubbed the back of his neck. "Gosh, everyone I know is working today. I'd ask Hope, but she hasn't driven a stick in years. Plus, she's studying for a big exam."

Allie squeezed the steering wheel. "Right. No, I understand. I'll think of something."

"Maybe your dad could come back and get it."

Wouldn't that be exactly what her parents expected? Instead of proving herself, she'd reinforce their belief that she was a complete and total failure.

Unless . . . she called Luke.

Her heart pounded at the thought of seeing him again. She couldn't even remember the last time she'd spoken to him. That was a lie. She remembered every detail.

"Don't worry about it." Allie dredged up a smile that was as fake as her "natural" highlights. "Really. Go on and enjoy lunch with your wife and give me a minute to make other arrangements. I'll be out of your hair lickety-split."

"Sure you don't want to join us while you work something out? There's more than enough."

"I'm sure, but thank you."

As Brady headed back to the house, Allie turned her thoughts to what she had to do. She knew for a fact Luke was home. She'd seen his old Mustang in the driveway when she went inside her parents' house for the check. Okay, *sneaked* inside the house. Those ugly hedges had to be good for something.

But, oh, she didn't want to face Luke again. And he wouldn't want to see her either. God knew he'd done nothing but avoid her since her senior prom.

She glanced around the beautifully restored vehicle. She was in a fix, and she couldn't fail at this task. She couldn't. Not even if it meant the favored surrogate son would receive half the glory.

She couldn't just go up to his door—too much like groveling. And she would not beg Luke, not for anything. As it happened she still remembered his old home phone number (it was tattooed on her heart), but he probably didn't have the landline anymore—who did?

So she would let fate decide what would happen. She'd make the call—just to prove to herself and the world that Luke Fletcher was not the answer to this or any other problem she might have. And if he wasn't . . .

She was sunk.

Chapter 3

*L*uke wolfed down the turkey sandwich on five-grain bread, his mind on the maple cabinets waiting in his garage. The customer requested a black cherry stain, but that was a mistake. Maple didn't take dark stains well. Luke still hoped to bring the client around.

He took his plate to the sink and rinsed it, then put it in the stainless steel dishwasher. Luke had upgraded the kitchen after his mother married Greg Barnes and moved to Florida, leaving Luke to assume the mortgage on his childhood home. When he was finished, he headed toward the garage, his bulldog, Walter, lumbering behind him.

The dog stared up at him with his wrinkled face and tragic brown eyes. "Ready to go back to work, boy?"

For Luke, every day was take-your-dog-to-work day. For Walter, the garage was just another place for a long nap. But what the dog lacked in energy he made up for with a big heart.

The phone rang in the living room—the landline. He reached for a work boot and shoved his foot into it. Most likely a solicitor. No one he knew used or even remembered that number anymore.

Except maybe his dad. If Luke was gut-level honest, it was the reason he hadn't dropped the landline years ago.

He paused in lacing his boots as the shrill ring sounded again. He straightened and went into the living room, telling his heart it was only someone selling windows, a credit card, or a "free" four-day vacation to the Bahamas.

He picked up the handset. "Hello?"

A pause followed and Luke waited for the recording to kick on. He should just hang up. But a longing for a man he hadn't heard from in years made him try one more time.

"Hello?" It was more of a bark, but he was impatient with himself and his pitiful yearning for someone who'd probably forgotten him long ago.

He'd just begun to hang up when a voice came through the handset.

"Luke?" A woman's voice.

He pulled the phone back to his ear. "Yes . . . Who's this?"

"It's . . . It's Allie. Allie Adams."

As if there were another Allie. His heart skipped a couple beats, then made up for it by doing double time. For the past seven years Allie had been holding what was apparently a one-hundred-year grudge that still had many years left on it. He could only think of one reason she'd call.

Her parents' trip to Pennsylvania—the anniversary party. Dread slithered down his spine. Bill and Becky had an accident in the mountains, and she was calling to tell him . . . "Your parents?"

"They're fine." Her voice was brittle.

Thank God. He released a breath, leaning against the solid chestnut cabinets.

"Sorry to call out of the blue like this, but I have to ask you a favor."

"Okay . . ." He couldn't imagine what she'd want since she hadn't willingly spoken to him in years. And he could tell by her tone that The Grudge was still in effect, favor or no.

Her heavy sigh came through the phone. "My parents restored my grandparents' '57 Chevy for their anniversary."

"I know."

"Of course you do. When it got delayed I offered to drive it to my grandparents' for them, but there seems to be a minor problem."

"And that is . . . ?" he asked when she paused.

"I'm here in Copper Creek to pick it up, and I didn't realize—it's a stick shift."

"You can't drive a stick."

"I know that." She grated out the words. "That's why I'm calling *you.*"

"You want *me* to drive the car to Pennsylvania?"

"If you can get away today—and tomorrow, too, I guess. Time is of the essence—the party's tomorrow night." She paused as if she expected an immediate answer.

But he was still trying to convince himself that Allie had actually called him. Was asking him for a favor after all these years. Besides, committing to something like this required thought. Deliberation. Possibly insanity.

"I'm willing to pay you," she choked out, as if giving an incentive pained her.

Luke knew what that car meant to Bill and Becky—they'd

been planning this surprise for almost a year—and Luke would move heaven and earth to please the couple. While his own mom had drunk herself into a stupor most nights after his dad's departure, the Adamses had been there for him.

Allie aside, he couldn't let them down, could he? He mentally reviewed his work schedule. His current customer wasn't in a hurry. Luke had other orders lined up, but nothing pressing. Nothing he couldn't handle if he applied himself over the next few weeks. What else did he have to do but build his business?

"Are you going to answer me or not?" Allie said.

"You're awful prickly for someone asking a favor."

"Go ahead and say no—you know you want to."

Oh, she vexed him. Always had. "What about you?"

"What about me?"

"Are you planning to ride along on this five-hundred-mile joyride?"

She gave a sharp laugh. "Closer to seven hundred, actually—and joy will hardly be a factor. Yes, of course I'm planning to ride along. You think I'm letting you drive that car without me?"

"I have a stellar driving record, I'll have you know. I won't be driving over any parking bumpers at least."

He could practically hear her grinding her teeth. Then swallowing her pride. And after all the snubbing she'd done, he was just petty enough to enjoy it.

"Is that a yes?" she asked.

Luke checked the time. He'd need to shower and change from his work clothes. Pack a few things. "Are you at Brady Collins's place?"

"Where else would I be?"

He rolled his eyes. "I'll be there in thirty minutes."

He set the phone in the cradle before she could respond. He needed the upper hand with her. But in reality, his heart was pounding and his breaths were shallow. This was going to be an exasperating day—an exasperating trip. She couldn't possibly pay him enough to put up with her sharp tongue for ten grueling hours.

Who was he kidding? He wasn't taking Allie's money. And her tongue—though it might be sharp—had once been good for things other than slinging barbs.

Chapter 4

*A*llie heard the popping of gravel on the drive long before she made herself turn and look. There, stirring up a cloud of dust, was the blue Mustang. She couldn't make out Luke through the glare on the windshield, but he no doubt saw her clearly enough.

She leaned against the driver's side of the Chevy, crossing her arms, striving for a casual effect. Well, she couldn't very well be sitting down when all six feet one inch of Luke Fletcher approached, could she? She was at enough of a disadvantage having to ask for a favor. She wondered how her hair looked, then gave herself a mental thump.

He pulled in beside the Chevy, and everything went quiet as he shut off the engine. The door squawked open, and he emerged, stretching to his full height in a snug black T-shirt and worn jeans. His gaze, guarded and mysterious, met hers across his car.

Allie couldn't drag her eyes from those familiar green

depths. She had only a peripheral impression of short dark hair, unshaven jaw, and masculine physique.

It wasn't that she hadn't seen him in years—they had too many common Facebook friends for that. But she still thought of him as the boy he'd been. However, now that she saw him in person, she couldn't deny that the boy had only been a shadow of the man he'd become. Just the sight of him made her heart tick up a notch. She scowled at the realization.

His lips quirked and a mocking light entered his eyes. "Allie."

"Luke." She dragged her eyes away, looking pointedly at her watch, even though he was right on time.

He missed the impatient gesture, as he was getting into the back of his car—for his overnight things, no doubt.

Overnight. Jeez Louise. What had she gotten herself into?

A squat, hairy beast lumbered around the back side of the Mustang. Bulging brown eyes dominated the bulldog's brown-and-white smashed-in face. Even though it was walking, it looked as if it might drift off to sleep any moment.

Even so, it was a *dog*. She shrank into the car. The terrier that had bitten her when she was six hadn't seemed threatening either—until its jaws were clamped around her ankle. She wasn't able to shake it off until her dad came.

Allie frowned at the beast. "What is that?"

Luke shut the door, and the car beeped as he locked it. "Allie, meet Walter."

"He is not coming on this trip."

"I don't have anyone to leave him with. Anyway, Walter's well trained. He won't be any trouble. Will you, buddy?"

Walter flopped down in the gravel, apparently unable to

bear another step. His jowls drooped low as if God had accidentally made too much skin and not enough face.

Allie glanced at the beautifully restored Chevy. "You can't put your"—she looked down at the animal—"*dog* on these new leather seats. *White* leather seats."

"Relax, I've got it covered." Luke—bearing a sleeping bag, she saw now—was opening the Chevy's back door. He spread it across the seat. "He doesn't have accidents."

"I didn't plan on having a dog along."

"Well, I didn't plan on driving to Pennsylvania today," Luke said from the back seat. "But here we are."

She wanted to put her foot down. But . . . beggars and choosers and all that. There was no one else she could ask to drive—if there had been, Luke sure wouldn't be here. Looked like she was stuck with them both.

She stared up to the heavens. She so deserved brownie points for this.

Allie scowled down at the mongrel, whose pink tongue was now out and lolling beside a pointy fang. She didn't relish the idea of him sitting behind her. What if he went for her carotid artery when she least expected it?

Walter peered up at her as if asking if it was time to get up yet. After a moment passed he gave a slow blink and rested his head on his paws.

Allie rounded the vehicle and got into the passenger side while Luke loaded the dog. "How old is that thing?"

Luke spared her a look. "*Walter* is seven."

"He moves like an old man." With hip replacements. She took out her phone and opened the road trip playlist she'd made just for the drive when she'd been feeling optimistic about the assignment—songs from the fifties, in honor of the Chevy, of course.

Luke stowed his things in the trunk and got into the car. The spacious interior seemed to shrink to Fiat proportions. She was grateful for the console between them, at least. Of course, if there were no console, there would be no stick shift—and no Luke.

He took a moment to appreciate the leather, his gaze flittering around the pristine interior. "She turned out real nice. Your grandparents are going to be thrilled."

He said something else, but Allie couldn't take her eyes off his hands, now stroking the large white steering wheel with its chrome center and spokes. His skin, already summer brown, was marked with a new scar or two. Long fingers tapered down to blunt-cut fingernails, stained around the cuticles from his job. A workingman's hands.

Hands that had once held hers. Hands that caressed her face so softly it made her ache inside. At one time she'd believed they were made for each other. That he was her soul mate, that they might share a lifetime of love.

But that had just been a foolish girlhood fantasy.

The engine roared to life. Allie dropped her gaze to her phone, starting her playlist, and the peppy melody of "Rockin' Robin" filled the car.

Chapter 5

It hadn't quite been love at first sight for Allie, but it still seemed like she'd loved Luke her whole life. Soon after his family moved in next door, when Allie was nine, Luke's dad left.

Mrs. Fletcher turned to drinking, leaving Luke at loose ends. He often mowed the lawn for Allie's parents or helped her mom carry in groceries. He was a frequent guest at their dinner table. Olivia treated him like a brother, but that role never felt quite right to Allie, even though Luke often ruffled her hair and called her kiddo.

When she was fifteen a boy on the bus began picking on her, making rides to school stressful. When Luke found out he insisted on driving her the remainder of the year—even though he was a senior and she a lowly sophomore.

That was when Allie fell head over heels in love with Luke. They talked on those rides about school and life and her current passion—art. Luke rarely talked about his home life, but he was more open when they were alone. Each morning and afternoon Allie's stomach wobbled as she got into his car. Her heart softened when he looked at her.

Alas . . . Luke had continued to ruffle her hair and chuckle as she shared her adolescent problems or waxed poetic about the impressionist movement. She hid her growing feelings by calling him hotshot and giving him sisterly slugs.

Before she knew it, Luke, seventeen and graduated, was off to the University of Georgia on a full scholarship. (He'd skipped fourth grade.) She mourned the loss but hid it well, dating other boys and going out often. She rarely saw Luke over the next couple of years. He hardly bothered to come home, and when he did, she was often busy with friends, drama practice, or one of her jobs.

The fall of her senior year he came home for Thanksgiving to meet his mother's fiancé. He joined the Adamses for their holiday feast.

Despite his long absence, despite all the other boys she'd dated, Allie's feelings for Luke hadn't diminished one iota. Her heart fluttered as he took a seat across the table, and her stomach was full of hyperactive butterflies.

When she opened her eyes after her father said grace, she caught Luke staring at her—the strangest expression on his face. His green eyes were fixed on hers—was that a flicker of male appreciation?

Allie's pulse jumped. Her face heated. Had he noticed her new haircut? Or that, after years of being a tomboy, she was wearing makeup and dressing like a girl?

After the meal she told herself she'd just imagined it. She put it from her mind—or tried to—until Christmas break, when he came home for his mom's wedding.

Allie was arriving home from theater practice when movement next door caught her eye. Luke was pulling his duffel bag from the trunk of his Mustang, his muscles bulging under the sleeves of his Georgia Bulldogs T-shirt. He walked over, meeting her beside the Odyssey. The intense look in his eyes made her heart pound like she'd just taken the stage on opening night.

His smile inching upward made her heart buckle. "Hey, Allie."

"Hi." Her voice was breathless because he hadn't called her kiddo and because . . . that look.

He drew her into the usual hug, but it didn't feel usual. It felt gentle and stirring, and he lingered an extra beat as if he didn't want it to end either.

When he drew away, Allie's tongue seemed stuck to the roof of her mouth, but it didn't matter because she couldn't think of a thing to say. His gaze drifted over her face, seeming to take in every detail before he looked away.

"Got all your Christmas shopping done?" His cheeks were a little flushed. Maybe just the chill in the air. It was December, after all.

"Haven't even started yet."

He gave a throaty chuckle. "Sounds about right."

Her dad pulled in the drive just then, and things went back to normal.

The next day Allie wondered again if she'd imagined the whole thing. Wishful thinking—she was a pro by now. But she'd gone on many dates and had even had two short-term boyfriends. She couldn't be wrong about that look in his eyes. Could she?

Christmas Eve found her on the back deck, overlooking the

shadowed woods. It was unusually balmy for late December—just a jacket was needed to keep her warm. The stars twinkled in an inky-black sky. There was nothing like a Copper Creek sky. She swore they burned brighter here than anywhere else. The scent of wood smoke hung in the air, mingling with the fragrance of pine and possibility. There was just something special about this time of year.

A breeze rustled the treetops, and the glider squeaked quietly as she rocked. It was almost midnight. Her family was already in bed, but she'd always been a night owl.

A noise nearby made her jump.

"Just me." Luke's voice scraped low as he stepped up onto the deck, a mere shadow in the darkness.

"Hey." Her dopey heart stuttered as he approached.

He settled next to her on the glider even though there were plenty of other seats. She was suddenly conscious of their thighs touching. Of the familiar spicy scent of his cologne. Of his big hands, resting in his lap.

She'd left the porch lights off to better view the stars. She was glad they were cloaked in darkness because she was certain her face was flushed. She'd only seen him a couple times since he'd come home a few days ago. Once across the family dinner table and another time when a date brought her home.

"Who was the boy the other night?" Luke asked as if reading her mind.

"I don't think you know him—Derek Jameson. He's in my class."

"He have an older brother named John?"

Allie lifted a shoulder. "Don't know. We didn't talk about his family."

"He didn't kiss you good night."

"It was a first date." She tilted her head and used the flirty tone she'd practiced with some effect on other boys. "What's with the inquisition, hotshot?"

Tell me now, Luke. Tell me you don't want me going out with other boys. Tell me you want to—

"Just taking care of you, kiddo." A smile suffused his tone. "Someone's got to look out for you."

Disappointment washed over her like a tsunami. *Stupid, stupid girl. He's not interested in you. Never was.* Luke would never see her as anything but his surrogate kid sister. How many times did he have to call her kiddo for her to figure that out?

Her face flared with heat. "I'm not a kid anymore, Luke. And you're not my big brother." She'd never spoken so harshly to him. She suddenly needed to escape before the stinging sensation behind her eyes turned into tears.

She started to jump from the glider.

"Wait." His hand caught hers.

She paused on the edge of the seat, heart beating so hard he could surely hear it. If he warned her off Derek or gave her some big-brother lecture, she was going to scream. Or burst into tears. She wasn't sure which would be worse.

"Don't go," he whispered. He tugged her hand until she settled back in her seat.

Their shoulders touched once again, and she felt the warmth of him through her jacket.

She stared at him in the darkness, wishing she could read his face. But it was shrouded in shadows. His hand felt big and warm around hers—he hadn't let go.

Don't be stupid. Don't start hoping again. But her heart missed the memo. Her lungs struggled to keep pace. The warmth of his breath brushed her lips, making them tingle with want.

"I know I'm not your brother," he said softly. "I used to think of you as a kid, but . . . I don't anymore."

What did that mean? Hope swelled, despite her best efforts to tamp it down. They were only two years apart, but the three grades between them had made it seem like more sometimes.

"Allie." He shifted toward her. "When I saw you at Thanksgiving . . ."

Her breath ceased, her heart halted, waiting. He sounded nervous and flustered, and she'd simply die if he didn't finish that last sentence.

"What?" She didn't dare move for fear the moment would evaporate.

"You looked . . . different. All grown up. I went away to college, and you grew up and now . . ."

His thumb stroked hers, stirring every cell to life, making her dizzy with need. "Now . . . ?"

"I—I see you differently," he finished softly.

Moonlight glimmered in his eyes, and though she couldn't read his expression, she felt the intensity of his gaze. Something hummed between them like a live wire, making her buzz.

Allie wasn't sure which one of them leaned in. But then their lips were touching, and his were moving over hers so softly. Reverently. Like maybe Luke wanted this kiss as badly as she did.

He pushed back her hair, cradled her face. The arm she'd slugged so many times was warm and hard under her palm.

The kiss was long and slow and growing more passionate by the second.

This was no boyish, fumbling kiss. It was a sensual exploration, a masterful onslaught against any reservations she might've had. A mewling sound escaped her lips just before he broke off the kiss.

He leaned his forehead against hers, his eyes opening lazily. Their breaths mingled between them.

He could probably feel her heart pounding against his, but she didn't care—because his was beating just as hard and fast. She could feel it under her palm. The wonder of that thought made her breath catch.

It was finally happening. Finally, after all this time.

"Allie . . ." Luke's exhale was loud in the stillness. "It was driving me crazy . . . being away at college, thinking of you. Knowing you were dating other guys."

He was jealous of those immature, ridiculous boys? Silly him. "I was just having fun."

He took her chin and gave her a look she felt to the tips of her toes. "Have fun with me."

Her hopes and wishes had come true. Luke liked her. Luke had *kissed* her. He wanted to be with her.

A smile she could hold back no longer unfurled on her lips. "Okay."

The door behind them slid open. Allie wasn't sure who jumped away, but suddenly a cold canyon stretched between them.

"Allie?" Dad called. "You out there, honey?"

"Yeah, Dad. Me and Luke." Even she heard a new softness in her tone when she spoke his name.

"We're just, uh, stargazing." Luke leaned forward, elbows on his knees, putting more space between them. "Want to join us?"

"No, that's okay. I just had a call and noticed Allie wasn't in her room." Her dad took his pediatric duties very seriously. Every parent in his practice had his cell number.

Luke shifted. "She's safe and sound, sir."

Dread spread through her veins at his big-brother tone. Her dad said good night and slid the door closed. Did she imagine the new chill in the air? The new distance between Luke and her that had nothing to do with proximity?

Her mind spun. Did Luke think she was too young for him? That her parents would be angry if he wanted to date her? She seemed to wait an eternity for him to speak.

"Listen, Allie . . ." He turned toward her, his voice rumbling low. "Maybe we should keep this between us for now."

She searched his face, but darkness hid the answers she sought. "Why?"

"It's just . . . this is new and . . . I don't want the pressure of your family knowing. I'd rather just keep it between you and me for a while."

Then he sat back in the chair and cupped her face, his thumb gliding along her cheek, and she could think of little else.

"Our little secret," he said softly. "All right?"

She wanted to shout the news to the world, but it was a small thing to ask, and right now she only wanted his lips on hers again.

She leaned closer. "Just for now?"

"Just for now." And then his lips were on hers, and Allie couldn't think at all.

Christmas break went too fast. She and Luke found bits of time to be together, late at night on the deck or at his house when his mom was gone. They drove around town, looking at Christmas lights, and one night they sat in his car at Murphy's Park and made out until the windows fogged over.

Sneaking around was kind of fun. But also, Allie longed to tell someone. She confided in her best friend, who'd known about Allie's long-lived crush on the boy next door.

But before Allie knew it, Luke was headed back to college and said he'd keep in touch. He would come home for spring break, he promised. But that seemed like eons away.

They texted often and talked on the phone when Allie got a quiet moment. In February Luke found out his mom was moving to Florida with her new husband. Allie could tell this troubled Luke. And it worried Allie, too, as he'd no longer have family in Copper Creek. Not that his mom had been much of a parent.

Allie was relieved when he accepted a job at Mitchell Construction for after graduation. He'd move home and assume the mortgage on his mom's house.

But soon Allie noticed he was texting her less. They went days between phone conversations, and sometimes he didn't even answer when she called. But it was his last semester, and he wanted to finish well. Allie was proud of him for earning a bachelor's degree in only three years.

Besides, he'd soon be home for spring break. And she was busy with senior activities, her own grades, and her job at the Mellow Mug. There was little time to sulk as prom approached. Two weeks before the big dance she bought a silver dress that made the most of her curves and complemented the "winter wonderland" theme.

But when she mentioned the dress to Luke on the phone one evening, he went quiet. She hadn't brought up the prom before now, but he knew it fell during his spring break. She'd assumed . . .

A shudder of dread coursed through her at his sudden silence.

"Who are you going with?" he asked finally.

She blinked as her stomach dove for her feet. "I—I thought I was going with you."

"Allie . . . ," he said after a beat.

When he didn't complete the sentence, she found her own words. "What, Luke? Aren't we seeing each other? You knew my prom was coming up. You'll be home that week and everything."

"Yeah, but . . . we're keeping everything low-key, right? Like we said?"

She gritted her teeth. "It's my senior prom, Luke."

"I know, but . . . can't you go with your friends?"

She gave the phone a withering look, wishing Luke could see it. "My *friends* are going with their boyfriends." And she'd turned down two offers from other boys.

Another long silence passed. Allie wanted to hit something. But the sting of tears behind her eyes warned her that if she didn't get off the phone, she was going to embarrass herself.

"Never mind." Her words were clipped. "It's fine. I have to go now."

"Allie, please understand . . ."

Feeling a sob rise in her throat, she said goodbye, disconnected the call, and promptly broke into a flood of tears.

She didn't hear from Luke for two days. He sent her a text

saying he wouldn't make it home for spring break after all. Some school project. Over the next couple days a few stilted texts went back and forth, wherein Allie acted as if she were fine.

Then there was nothing. No texts. No calls.

Allie grieved the loss. She couldn't eat. Couldn't sleep. What had she done wrong? She lost six pounds and dressed in her old, sloppy clothes to hide the weight loss. She convinced her family she wasn't feeling well and ended up at the doctor's office (diagnosis: senior blues).

Jared Wallace, a mutual friend of Luke's and hers who attended UGA, came home on spring break, and Allie ran into him at the Rusty Nail. In the course of their discussion he mentioned seeing Luke around campus, often with the same pretty girl.

Allie thought her heart would break in two. Luke had found someone else and dropped her like a hot potato. Luke had stayed on campus with *her* rather than coming home to take Allie to prom.

The night of the dance she dressed up in her silver dress, curled her hair, and applied makeup. She faked her way through pictures, then drove straight to a friend's house, where she spent the night.

Clearly she and Luke were over, almost before they'd begun, and she didn't even understand what she'd done to push him away. Senior year ended in a mixed fog of celebration and phony smiles.

Luke returned home and took possession of his mom's house. He didn't come around the house as often, but Allie saw him coming and going.

She couldn't stand the awkward pauses and false cheer when her family was around. So when a sudden opportunity arose in Atlanta for a spot in a summer chef class (cooking being her newest interest), Allie jumped at the escape.

And when it was over, she stayed. She hated living so far from her family. Hated living away from Copper Creek. But she had to stay away if she was ever going to get over Luke Fletcher.

Chapter 6

The boppy sounds of Allie's music were getting on Luke's last nerve. He was a firm believer in a driver's music privileges, but it wasn't worth provoking her by claiming them.

Following her GPS's instructions (and grateful for the brief interruption of "Tutti Frutti"), he turned onto a road that would take them deeper into the Blue Ridge Mountains.

He hadn't blamed Allie for being upset when things had gone south between them seven years ago. He'd never forget seeing her with fresh eyes that Thanksgiving, all grown up. Time had stopped when he kissed her, and for weeks he could think of little else.

So, yes, he'd freaked out a little at the idea of her parents finding out. What if something went wrong between them? And didn't something always go wrong eventually? How would that affect his relationship with the Adamses? That thought only made him more anxious since his mom had gotten married. And when she moved away, the thought of being alone brought a cold trickle of fear.

Maybe if he'd found the words to explain that to Allie . . . but he didn't quite understand it himself. Besides, he'd been young and afraid she'd talk him out of his decision—it wouldn't have taken much. One look into those brown eyes, and he would've been a goner. So he just kind of let the relationship drift away.

He'd thought things would return to normal when he finished college and moved back home. But Allie was furious. She hid her anger around her family. But when he caught her alone, she responded with withering looks and stubborn silence. When he went out onto his deck, she went back inside. When he ran into her at the Mellow Mug, she took his order as if he were a stranger—and he was pretty sure she'd done something to his drink.

His attempts to apologize were met with flinty looks and twisted lips.

He'd hurt her, and she was hurting him in return. If only she knew that the breakup had gutted him. That losing her had left a hollow spot inside. Why couldn't they just try to get back to normal? He missed her rambling excitement over her interest du jour, missed the way she jumped from one topic to another without skipping a beat, missed the way her eyes went to half-moons when she laughed.

But he hadn't found the words to tell her. And then she'd moved to Atlanta.

Luke still had his surrogate family. He wouldn't trade them for the world—or apparently for the love of his life, who was currently staring silently out the passenger window due to the many years left on The Grudge.

A terrible, familiar odor filled the car, and he reached for the window crank.

"*Ugh.* What is that smell?" They were Allie's first words in two hours.

Luke began rolling down the window.

"Don't. It might be outside."

Luke glanced back at Walter, who was sleeping through the outrageous stench. "Oh, it's definitely not outside."

Allie gave Walter the stink eye. "That is downright foul."

"He's got tummy troubles."

"Does he have any redeeming qualities?"

"Yes, he bites animal haters."

"I don't hate animals—you know I was bitten as a child." She sniffed, her chin notching upward. "Besides, I'm a volunteer at the zoo, and I do have a pet of my own."

"What kind of pet?"

"A cat. A beautiful gray cat—Mary, Queen of Scots."

"You named your cat after a queen?"

"She was just a stray, but her royal bearing made me feel like I should immediately genuflect. So, yes, a queen."

A grin tugged at his mouth. That sounded just like the Allie he remembered.

A sudden downpour had Luke flipping on the wipers.

"Slow down. You're going too fast."

But the shower had apparently been going on in the mountains awhile. The ground was muddy, and water puddled in the low-lying parts of the road.

He slowed, taking the next curve with caution.

Allie's phone dinged and a moment later she gave a dry

laugh. "Mom says, 'Drive carefully and slow, and for heaven's sake don't run out of gas on those mountain roads.' And Dad says, 'Don't strip the gears.' Clearly I haven't told them you're driving."

He couldn't miss the bitter tone. He didn't know if it was because she was the baby of the family or because her older sister was her polar opposite, but her parents seemed to favor Olivia sometimes.

"They obviously trusted you with the car," he said.

Which meant they were now trusting him with the car, technically. What if something went wrong? What if he wrecked the car? Allie was family—and he was not. His shoulder muscles tightened at the thought, and he eased off the accelerator.

Thunder clapped, reverberating through the mountains, as they passed a crossroads.

Luke glanced in the rearview mirror. "Weren't we supposed to turn back there?" he asked over the song blaring from her phone.

Allie checked the GPS. "I lost cell signal. But I think you're right."

He slowed down at the next turnoff and headed back to the road.

"Do you know the way without the GPS?" he asked. The roads through the mountains were like a maze, but Allie had been to her grandparents' quite a few times.

"I think so." She lifted her chin and sniffed—to let him know that, yes, she was conversing with him, but she was still miffed. Probably even more so after her parents' texts.

It was going to be a long trip.

Luke turned onto the correct road, then checked on Walter—still fast asleep, despite the storm, loud music, and rumbling engine. The rain continued, the conditions deteriorating with each mile.

"You're going too fast."

Allie was being overly cautious—totally unlike her. But, hey, no one wanted to keep the car safe more than he did. He eased off the accelerator again.

The wipers, even on the highest speed, could hardly keep pace with the deluge flooding the windshield. The road was windy, the mountain rising on one side and dropping off on the other. Rain pummeled the roof and thunder cracked nearby. At least the ruckus drowned out that ridiculous music.

As if realizing that herself, Allie shut off the playlist.

Luke drove on, one slow mile at a time, as Allie stared out the passenger window. He kept his gaze glued on the pavement, navigating the winding road carefully, fully aware that if anything happened to this perfectly restored car, the blame would fall squarely on him. He hadn't fully considered that when he'd agreed to this little road trip. His palms grew damp, sticking to the steering wheel.

One mile turned into twelve. This uncomfortable silence would be the death of him. Maybe he should attempt a civil conversation. Keep it neutral.

"So . . . your grandparents have been married fifty years, huh? That's something."

"They argue like two kids in a sandbox." Her fond tone contradicted the words.

Her grandparents were great, and they visited often. "Yeah, but then your grandma brings him a cuppa joe, and he pulls her down on his lap, and she tells him she's too old to be pawed at like a teenager—"

"And then they're off to the races again," Allie finished.

Silence settled in once again, the conversation having reached a dead end. Luke gave it another go. "So, how's Olivia doing? I don't see her around town very often."

"Busy with the kids and fund-raisers and field trips."

"Have you babysat lately? Evan must be in kindergarten by now."

"He is. But Olivia hasn't let me babysit since the Cocoa Puffs incident."

He tore his gaze from the pavement to glance at her. "What incident?"

"Don't tell me you haven't heard. I thought everyone in the entire tristate area knew by now."

"Not me, I swear."

Allie was quiet so long Luke thought she was going to drop the whole thing.

Then she spared him a look. "One night while I was babysitting over a long weekend, Evan decided to put Cocoa Puffs up his nose while I was changing Emma's diaper. Ella saw him do it and screamed for me. But when I got to the kitchen, I couldn't get them out, not even with tweezers. I knew he could breathe through his mouth, but still . . . I guess I freaked out a little.

"I drove him to the ER, totally frantic, reminding him to keep his mouth open. Emma screamed the whole way because it was time for her bottle, and Ella kept asking if Evan was going to die."

Luke's lips twitched.

"At the hospital a nurse came into the room as I was searching for Emma's bottle and dialing Olivia to break the news. The nurse gave me this condescending look as she gave Evan's nose a hard pinch and told him to blow. Then he started wailing—just as Olivia picked up the phone, of course. Turned out he was crying not because the procedure had hurt, but because his Cocoa Puffs were 'broked.'"

Luke held back a laugh he knew wouldn't be appreciated.

"Try telling Olivia that though. She and Spencer came right home from their weekend getaway, and I haven't been asked to babysit since."

His humor drained away. Olivia had always been Miss Responsibility while Allie was . . . well, she was Allie. She was impulsive and changeable and fun, which made her a great aunt. And he couldn't help but be annoyed with Olivia for taking that away from her.

Chapter 7

Allie couldn't believe she'd just relayed that stupid story to Luke. Reliving her Cocoa Puffs faux pas made her feel vulnerable, and that was the last thing she wanted to feel around Luke.

"Anyway . . ." She hoped her upbeat tone glossed over her hurt. "I still get to spend time with the little rugrats, of course, and Evan learned not to block his breathing pathways with cereal."

"She overreacted. You didn't do anything wrong. Just give her a little time."

Allie let out a humorless laugh. She wouldn't hold her breath. The rain continued to pound the roof of the car, and a crack of thunder split the air. She glanced in the back seat for the hundredth time to make sure the dog wasn't about to pounce. He was fast asleep, jowls sagging to the side.

She continued staring at the passing landscape. They hadn't passed a car in ages. Seemed like no one else wanted to meander the mountain roads during a thunderstorm. Go figure.

Luke slowed the car. "Oh boy."

Allie's gaze followed his. Up ahead a one-lane bridge spanned the river, water rushing over the roadway. It must've been raining for days up here.

"Should we chance it?" he asked as they came to a stop, the car idling loudly.

The water seemed only several inches deep, but still. "They say not to do that."

"Do you know another way around?"

"No, but I don't want to get washed away in a flood either." Her voice was, perhaps, a little too sharp. More importantly, she didn't want the car to get washed away in a flood. She could see the headline now: "Family Grieves Antique '57 Chevy Washed Away in Flood (Daughter Missing)."

"We'll have to go around," she said.

"We'll have to get over this river eventually, and all the other bridges may be flooded too."

"We have to try. Maybe your phone has a signal."

He took out his phone and checked. "Nothing. Not even a map."

Allie stared at the muddy water rushing over the road. "Well, we don't have much of a choice. We can't go that way."

He looked back at the bridge as a gust of wind shimmied the car. "All right."

He turned the car around on the narrow road and went back to the next crossroad, turning to make their way around. The road wound around a bit, then finally dead-ended at the river. "This might be harder than we thought."

"We are not going over that bridge. Go back to the main road. We'll try another route."

But the next road wound around the mountain, going every direction. There were no roads to turn onto, and when the road finally straightened, Allie had no idea which direction they were going. By the time they arrived at her grandparents' it would be the middle of the night. This whole trip was shredding her nerves.

"This isn't working," Luke said. "We're headed west and we need to go northeast. Maybe we should go back, take our chances with the bridge."

"And if the car gets washed away, are you willing to accept the blame?"

"If the car gets washed away, neither of us will even be here."

"A pleasant thought. Just turn around. We'll try another road."

When he came to a place with a pull-off, he did as she suggested. They continued on until they were on the winding part of the road again. A small hill rose to one side, and a short meadow descended on the other.

Something pinged the windshield. She looked out the window, her gaze sharpening on the ground. "Was that . . . ?"

Another ping sounded, this one hitting the roof.

Luke looked as dismayed as she felt. "Hail."

The car. The beautiful, refinished body. The perfect paint job. Another ping sounded. "Quick, get under something!"

"Sure, I'll just pull into the nearest garage."

She pointed ahead. "The trees."

"That's not enough—we need a building."

"Gee, I think we're fresh out of buildings."

"Did you even check the weather before we left?"

"Could you *please* hold off the lecture long enough to find a safe spot for my grandparents' prized car?" Her volume escalated with each word.

The pings were coming closer together now, the hail bouncing off the pavement—off the hood of the car. Allie scanned the area for some kind of shelter. *Come on, come on.* Where was a gas station when you needed one?

But they'd passed the last signs of civilization long ago.

The pinging intensified. Allie groaned, her stomach churning. "They're going to kill me."

Luke slowed, turning onto a one-lane road they might or might not have already driven down.

"What are you doing? Our chances are better on the main road."

"I think I saw a shelter down here."

"We haven't passed so much as a mailbox in over an hour. Go back."

"There was a lean-to or something down here on the left. I'm sure of it."

"A lean-to. Great. I'm sure that'll protect this mammoth-sized car from this hailstorm from hell."

But just ahead she saw it. Sitting back off the road in a grove of trees and scrub was a three-sided shelter, big enough to park a car.

Thank God. Allie breathed a sigh of relief. "Hurry!"

It seemed to take forever to navigate the muddy lane and pull under the shelter. As soon as Luke shut off the engine, Allie jumped out. Holding her breath, she searched the car for damage.

A minute later she exhaled. The car looked fine as far as she could see. She met Luke around the front.

He ran a hand over his face. "No damage on this side."

"Hard to tell under all this mud."

She sagged against the wooden studs holding up the shelter, the weight of responsibility easing off her shoulders one brick at a time. If she showed up at her grandparents' with a dinged-up mess, her parents would never forgive her—or forget.

The air was ripe with tension, the sharp words they'd spoken—and, let's face it, their unresolved breakup—unforgotten.

"We'll take it through a car wash when we get closer."

Allie looked around the lean-to. Hail hammered the tin roof, creating a cacophony in the closed-in space. But the car was safe. That was all that mattered.

She stretched her legs while Luke returned to the car. By the time he unloaded Walter, the hail had changed back to rain.

"I'd better take him for a walk." Luke disappeared into the woods, Walter lumbering behind on a leash.

Allie took another walk around the car, checking for any dings they might've missed, and was relieved not to find any.

Luke returned a while later, joining her on the horizontal board along the back wall. Walter flopped at his feet and began snoring almost immediately. "How long should we wait?"

Thunder cracked and the rain picked up, pounding the roof. "It could start hailing again. We should wait until the storm stops."

"Without a weather app, we have no idea how long that'll be."

She folded her arms across her chest. "Well, I'm not risking the car."

"Okay . . . Well, we also have no way of reaching your folks to let them know what's going on."

That one hit hard. They'd think the worst, of course. Allie had driven the car over a cliff or managed to get herself abducted by aliens—car and all. She hated for them to believe she'd failed, but it would be even worse to prove them right.

"It can't be helped. Maybe the storm will pass quickly."

But even as she said the words, she stared up into the gray abyss. The air was thick with the smell of rain, and the sky seemed like it might storm for about, oh, another year or two. It was already almost five, and they still had many driving hours left to go.

She sank to the cement pad and pulled out her phone to amuse herself with *Candy Crush.* A few minutes later Luke sat down and pulled out his own phone. The rain continued, Walter snoring nearby, the wind battering the shelter.

Allie checked her watch for the hundredth time. It felt like they'd been here forever. It was now going on seven o'clock—darned her late start—and it appeared the storm might go on all night. She glanced around the space, mostly taken up by the car, where they'd no doubt have to sleep, just her and Luke and Walter.

Her stomach wobbled uneasily. The tension between them was uncomfortable, and when she'd begged the favor, she sure hadn't anticipated spending an entire night stuck in the mountains with him.

Her stomach gave a rumble, reminding her she hadn't eaten since one, but the sound of it was covered by the deluge of rain.

"The storm's not letting up," Luke said.

"At this rate we might be here all night."

"Maybe we should get settled." He looked over at her. "I found a little cabin in the woods."

She perked up. A crackling fire. Food. Bed. *People.* "And you're just now mentioning this? Was anyone home?"

"Um, no, it's empty. But there's a key on the door ledge. Under the circumstances, I think we should help ourselves."

If someone was stupid enough to leave a key, she wasn't going to argue. At least she wouldn't be trapped in the car all night with Luke Fletcher.

"Maybe there's even a phone," she said. "Or Wi-Fi."

He started to say something, then, as if thinking better of it, he closed his mouth.

Whatever. Allie stood, pocketing her phone, visions of a crackling fire dancing in her head. "What are we waiting for? Let's grab our stuff and go."

At the edge of the woods, Allie stopped abruptly, her duffel bag thunking against her leg. The structure, perched on a mound of overgrown grass, was roughly the size of a shoebox. Its raw timber walls were crudely cut, and a piece of wavy tin stretched over the top. The wonder wasn't that someone had left such easy access to a key, but that they'd bothered to lock the door at all.

She shook her head. "This is the 'cabin' you found?"

He lifted a shoulder that was loaded down with his backpack and sleeping bag. His other hand held Walter's leash. "Better than the car."

"Debatable," she muttered, then hurried to catch up. "For the record, this is not a cabin—it's a shack."

"It's a hunting cabin."

A hunting *shack*. There would definitely be no call to her parents tonight. No roaring fire—and that was a real shame because it was a little chilly in the mountains, and now she was wet.

At the door Luke reached for the key, then twisted it in the lock.

"What if someone comes and catches us trespassing?"

The door squeaked as it swung open, and he edged inside, brushing at spiderwebs. "No one's been here in a long time."

She crept in behind him, scanning the room. He was probably right. Spiderwebs hung from the rafters in abundance. The cement floor was cleanish. A wooden bed—the kind you saw at summer camp—dominated the room. An upturned crate served as a nightstand. A broom made of—straw?—was propped in the corner. A hole in the far wall was, maybe, a fireplace. At least dry kindling was piled in the grate. She would have that fire after all.

Her tomboy years were in her distant past. These days she traveled with her own pillow, and her idea of camping involved at least electricity and plumbing—speaking of which . . . She glanced around. Nope. No bathroom.

Maybe it would stop raining soon.

Luke set his things on the dirty mattress. Well, she assumed it was dirty. It was hard to tell when there was only one small window. Walter sniffed a corner and deemed it appropriate for a nap.

"Well, at least we'll be dry," Luke said.

She cautiously made her way to the fireplace and spotted a book of matches on the ledge. A fire would offer light, and she could hang her clothes to dry.

There you go. Look on the bright side. Find the silver lining. She'd get through this long night somehow and before she knew it, she'd be pulling into her grandparents' drive with a freshly washed Chevy, preening under their beaming gazes. *Olivia who?*

Her gaze drifted to the bed—the very small bed—then connected with Luke's.

"You can have the bed. I'll take the floor. Or I can sleep in the car if you'd rather."

Tempting, the idea of him squished up in the back seat with Walter. But lock or no, she didn't relish the idea of being alone out in the middle of nowhere. Besides, the cold cement floor was punishment enough.

"The floor is fine," she said stiffly.

While he unrolled the sleeping bag, she turned to the kindling. A little fire would cheer this place right up. The match lit on the first strike, and she lowered it to the sticks and dried leaves. The bundle quickly caught fire.

"Nice of someone to leave us dry kindling."

"Allie, that's not kindling, it's a—"

A large creature emerged from the sticks, hissing.

Allie jumped, backpedaling to keep from falling. Someone screamed. Maybe her.

The animal jumped from the kindling—er, nest—snarling at her.

"A raccoon! It's a raccoon!" Allie jumped onto the bed, eyes glued to the masked creature as it bared its teeth at her. Whoa, those were some pointy fangs. "There's a raccoon in here!"

"I heard you the first time." Luke scrambled to the corner and wielded the broom. He swatted at the animal, who turned and hissed at him, striped tail swishing. Luke was only making the thing mad with those swats.

"Get it! What if it has rabies?" She looked to Walter for help, but he hadn't even made it to his feet yet. She scowled at him.

"Open the door," Luke said.

The door. It was too far away from the bed. She'd have to get down—and get closer to the snarling creature. Kind of seemed like a bad idea.

"Allie, get the door!"

"I am!" Okay, she wasn't, but she was working up to it. She eased to the end of the bed, eyeing the doorknob. Two steps away—three at most.

"Sometime today, Speedy."

Allie jumped down, took the steps, and threw open the door. The movement caught the raccoon's attention. It hissed at her, then gave chase. It was right on her heels! Allie screeched as she hopped back onto the bed.

Then Luke was there, between her and the animal with the broom, sweeping it away from her.

"Get it, Luke," she called. "Get it out! Get it out!"

The creature swatted at the broom with its little paws, snarling at Luke, baring its tiny fangs. To think she'd once thought raccoons cute and cuddly.

He finally had the critter cornered. With a quick sweep of the broom he pushed it outside and slammed the door shut.

Allie was glued to the wall as far from the door as she could get. She pressed a hand to her thudding heart. Adrenaline surged through her bloodstream. Had that really just happened?

Luke's gaze met hers. His eyes were wide, his shoulders heaving. The expression on his face . . . probably looked just like the one on hers.

She recalled the way Luke had wielded that broom, like a knight wielding a sword, his feet dancing, parrying with a—raccoon.

Allie burst out laughing. A smile cracked his face. And then he was laughing too.

"Oh my gosh," she squeezed out. "The sight of you!"

"Me?" he wheezed between guffaws. "You jumped on that bed like it was home base. You do know raccoons climb trees, right?"

"Did you see the way it came after me?"

"Well, you did light its house on fire, so . . ."

She could hardly talk she was laughing so hard. "I thought it was kindling."

"Never took you for an arsonist."

More laughter. The nest was currently an impressive conflagration. "Stop. Stop, I feel bad enough already." Plus her stomach hurt from laughing.

"Do you now? I seem to remember you cheering for its demise—something about rabies."

"It was like a room-sized edition of Whac-A-Mole." That only brought more laughter.

Allie's gaze drifted to Walter, still lying in the corner, only deigning to raise his head through the whole ruckus. "Some guard dog you are. Seriously, where did you get him?"

"At the pound. I wanted a laid-back dog."

"Mission accomplished."

They laughed again. Allie's eyes burned and teared up. She

wiped them. Man, it had been a long time since she'd laughed that hard. Her laughter gradually slowed, as did Luke's.

Allie sank onto the bed. "Jeez Louise, that was exhausting."

Luke gave her a playful look. "You didn't do anything."

"I opened the door," Allie said defensively, then looked at the burning nest. "At least we have a fire."

"There's that." Luke set the broom back in the corner. "I don't suppose you packed some food. I've worked up an appetite."

As soon as he finished the sentence, an offensive smell began spreading through the shack, growing stronger by the second.

Allie wrinkled her nose at Walter. "You are a disgusting animal."

The dog rolled his bulging eyes her way, heaved a sigh, then closed his eyes again.

"Ugh!" As the smell permeated the room, she grabbed her pillow and buried her face in it. Luke's laughter floated in the air like music, and she couldn't stop her own from following.

Chapter 8

"Ho Hos? M&M's? Twizzlers?" Luke gave Allie a wry look. They'd settled in front of the fire with a grocery sack full of food. "What are you, twelve?"

"I only planned for snacks, not meals."

Since the raccoon fiasco, there was a lightness to the mood, to their exchanges. Allie seemed to have let go—at least temporarily—of The Grudge.

He was grateful for the reprieve. He surveyed the snacks and opted for the M&M's—at least they had peanuts.

"I'm so hungry." Allie bit into a Ho Ho, eyes closing as she relished the treat. She'd always had a sweet tooth.

The rain still pounded the roof, and it had grown dark. As if by mutual silent agreement, they'd settled in for the night. It wouldn't be safe to navigate these flooded mountain roads at night.

Allie had changed from her wet clothes while he faced the corner and pretended not to think about what she was doing. She did the same for him—minus the pretending, he was sure.

Their clothes now hung on a fishing line he'd found spooled in the corner.

They ate in congenial silence. He wasn't sure what Allie was thinking about, but he was afraid to ruin their truce by saying the wrong thing. Truth was, that whole raccoon debacle had made him miss the old Allie.

He'd fallen for her so quickly. Those secret kisses they exchanged kept him warm during the lonely months at college. He thought of her constantly.

How had it all gone so wrong? He'd lost Allie for good—not just the romantic relationship but the friendship too. He missed them both in equal portions.

Allie's water bottle crackled as she drank the last of it. "We should probably try to sleep so we can leave at first light."

"Assuming the storm is over."

"Right."

They cleaned up their mess, stowing the garbage. He took Walter for one last walk, then when he returned Allie stepped outside to brush her teeth and (he assumed) take care of personal matters.

While she was gone he set out a water bowl for Walter, then spread his sleeping bag over the dirty mattress. After giving the corner a fresh sweep, he grabbed his duffel bag to use as a pillow and settled on the floor. The fire provided a little light, but it wouldn't last much longer, and there was no dry wood available. Still, it shouldn't get too chilly.

The door squeaked on the hinges as Allie returned. She shut it and locked it behind her, then headed toward the bed. "Rain's slowed a little."

"Hopefully it'll be clear by morning."

"Do you think the bridge will be passable?" She stopped by the bed. "Hey . . . you should use your sleeping bag. The floor must be cold and hard."

"I'm fine. I wouldn't want to sleep on that dirty mattress."

"You sure?"

"It'll be like camping."

Allie huffed as she settled on the bed. "Yeah, on a jail cell floor. This place gives me the creeps."

"At least my cell mate isn't a murderer."

"And my snacks beat jail food any day."

They went quiet and the pattering on the tin roof blended with the snapping of the fire.

"Well . . ." The sleeping bag rustled as Allie turned toward the wall. "Good night."

"Night." Luke adjusted the duffel bag under his head and stared at the fire, already flickering low. When he closed his eyes the scene from earlier played back. The raccoon springing from the nest. Allie backpedaling so quickly she almost landed on her butt. Allie shrieking and squealing and cheering him on—from the safety of the bed, of course. Then the laughter, those half-moon eyes.

Good to know the old Allie was still alive and well. They'd had so much fun in their childhood days. She'd never been afraid to bait hooks or climb trees or pick up daddy longlegs. She wasn't afraid of much of anything—except dogs.

And angry raccoons. His lips twitched as he rolled to his side. He needed some shut-eye. He tried to clear his mind and sink into oblivion, but no matter how hard he pursued sleep, it remained just out of reach. The wind blew and a distant thunder boomed.

He rolled to his other side and thought about the cabinet orders he had lined up back home. That also failed to put him to sleep. He thought about Allie's family. He hoped they wouldn't mind his unexpected appearance. They had invited him a few weeks ago, and they never seemed to mind having him around. But he wasn't family, after all.

He thought of his mom. He talked to her every month or two when he called. She was doing all right. Still a functioning alcoholic, but Greg seemed to be treating her well. He had three grown children, and his mom seemed to have been absorbed into their family.

A while later Luke flipped onto his back. He stared at the grate where the fire had died to orange embers, leaving the room in darkness.

He thought again of Allie and their complicated relationship. Would they find themselves on solid ground in the morning, or would she default to animosity? He hoped they could be friends again.

It was his own fault. He'd handled their breakup so badly. He'd been young and not entirely aware of why their budding relationship—while new and wonderful—scared him so much.

Maybe this trip could be good for them. Maybe they could finally settle the rancor between them and come out as friends.

Only one thing stood in the way—Allie had to forgive him.

He'd never fully explained himself. Oh, he'd tried, but now he saw his explanations for the excuses they must've sounded like. He regretted hurting her—and hurt her, he had. He could still remember the choked sound of her voice when she'd let him off the hook for prom.

Yeah, he'd been a real tool.

The bedsprings squeaked as Allie turned over. Maybe he wasn't the only one having trouble sleeping. Maybe it was finally time to put this all behind them.

His heart kicked against his rib cage as he gathered his courage. "Allie?"

There was no answer, but maybe he'd spoken too softly to hear above the patter of rain.

"Allie? You awake?"

The sleeping bag rustled. "Yeah."

"Trouble going to sleep?"

"Little bit."

The wind whistled through the cabin. A log snapped. He had to get this over with. Now or never. He had to explain—he owed her that much.

"I'm really sorry for the way I handled things between us back then." The long silence seemed to expand the air around him. Maybe he'd just botched their truce by bringing it up.

"It was a long time ago," she said finally.

"Don't let me off the hook. I was a jerk. You meant a lot to me—I don't think I let you know how much." He'd fallen in love with her, but there was no need to go there now.

⌒

For the second time tonight adrenaline flooded through Allie's system. *Fight or flight?* Either of those options sounded worlds better than facing the painful past.

Did she really want to dig into this right now? Then again, this conversation was long overdue. He had hurt her.

He had mishandled the situation. Her stomach tightened just remembering her first broken heart. Okay, her only broken heart.

But if he'd cared about her so much . . .

"Then why?" The words sounded weak and pathetic, wobbling between them.

"I don't think I even understood it at the time." He heaved a sigh. "Allie, your family had come to mean so much to me. My mom being the way she was—I couldn't count on her. I took care of her more than the other way around. After my dad left—your family became the family I didn't have anymore. The family I wanted."

She felt a pinch in her chest. "I know that."

"When I saw you over Thanksgiving that year . . . I can't even explain what happened. I saw you differently. I went back to school and thought about you constantly. Thought about how grown up you'd become and how beautiful you were and about all the boys you were dating."

Her lips curved at the thought of his jealousy. If only he knew none of those boys compared. "I didn't date that many."

"I'd call your parents and they'd tell me you were out with some boy or another—and it drove me crazy. Then at Christmas . . ."

"You kissed me on the deck." The memory of it flushed heat through her body. She'd since had many kisses, of course. But that one . . . It was the one she'd measured every other kiss against. And they'd all fallen so short.

"Those four weeks were . . . They were the best weeks of my life, Allie."

She shook her head, not understanding. The darkness gave

her the courage to voice her feelings. "If that's true . . . why did you break up with me, Luke?"

"When you mentioned the prom, it scared me—doing something so public. Making a commitment that your parents knew about. I was afraid—what if something went wrong between us? You were their daughter. If I blew it . . . What if I lost them?

"And then my mom told me she was moving to Florida and—it just really freaked me out. She wasn't much of a parent, but she was all I had. And she was leaving. Your family was all I had left—I couldn't lose them too."

Allie heard the despair in his voice. Let it settle inside her. She'd always felt so bad for him. When he came to their house because he was underfoot at home. When his mom failed to show for senior night (her parents had filled in). When his mom came to graduation drunk and sloppy, insulting her parents, whom she was clearly jealous of.

"And so you broke up with me," she whispered. Only he hadn't really, had he? He'd just kind of ditched her.

"I was afraid, and I handled it like a coward and made things even worse. I've always regretted that."

It was all making sense. Finally. She still felt for that orphaned boy, and she'd known in a vague way what her parents meant to him. He'd always worked so hard to please them, mowing their grass, picking flowers for her mom, getting their mail and watering their plants when they were away. She hadn't thought too much about it back then, but she wondered now if he'd been trying to earn a spot in their family.

"What about the girl?" she said into the void.

"What girl?"

"I ran into Jared Wallace during spring break. He told me you were hanging around with some girl at school."

"There was no girl, Allie." He sounded confused but adamant. "Wait, was he talking about Sam? She was just a good friend, a study partner, but only a friend."

Sam. She remembered Luke mentioning the name, but she'd thought it was a boy.

"I wanted to take you to prom, Allie. I wanted to be with you. I—"

Had he been about to say he loved her? Probably wishful thinking. She'd been head over heels for him. Truth be told, she'd never felt as strongly for anyone else. But maybe that was just because she'd carried a torch for him for so many years.

"I was just afraid of losing the only family I had. And in the process . . . I ended up losing you."

A crack splintered her heart. Not for her own pain, but for his. He had so little in the way of family, and she'd taken a bit of that from him. She'd carried this grudge like a shield for seven years. She was finally ready to lay it down.

"I understand now, Luke. I forgive you. I'm sorry for giving you the cold shoulder all these years."

"Thank you." The rain let up, the shack going quieter. "Could we . . . ? Do you think we could ever be friends again? I've missed you, Allie."

Her lips tipped up in a smile, warmth filling her insides. "Sure. I'd like that a lot."

Chapter 9

What happened? Did you wreck the car? Oh, Bill, Allie wrecked the car!"

Allie shifted in the passenger seat, rolling her eyes at Luke. "No, Mother, I didn't wreck the car. There was a thunderstorm in the mountains, the bridge was flooded, and then it started hailing and—"

"Hailing!"

"No worries, the car is fine. We had to stay overnight, but I lost signal and couldn't text you. Everything's fine now. The storm has passed, and we got over the bridge just fine. We're almost out of the mountains, in fact."

"We?"

"Oh . . ." She spared Luke a glance. "Yeah, I, um, invited Luke along."

Even though her truce with Luke was still going strong, when she pulled up to her grandparents' place in this beautiful car, she was going to get credit for its delivery, daggonit.

Her mother's sigh of relief could be heard from the far side of Neptune. "Why didn't you say so, dear? Bill, *Luke* is with her—we were worried all night for nothing. Allie, your father hardly slept, honey."

"I'm sorry, Mom, but like I said, I lost signal in the mountains and we felt it best for the car if we found shelter. Everything is fine though. The car looks great. Perfect."

Her gaze connected with Luke's, and she winced, knowing the car was, in fact, a muddy mess. Well, it *would* look perfect once they took it through the car wash a dozen times or so.

"We're still about seven hours away." It was going on nine now, and the party didn't start until five. "We'll make it before the party starts."

"Well, we'll be outside setting up, so pull all the way around to the back. I'll make sure your grandparents are out there. They're going to be so surprised! Bill, put that table down! You're going to hurt your back again!"

Would it be awful to ask Luke to switch places once they pulled into the driveway? Maybe she could coast into the backyard—it was downhill.

She reassured her mother some more, though it seemed unnecessary now that the responsible Luke Fletcher was along for the ride.

Allie's entire day's worth of energy now spent, she said goodbye and tapped the button to disconnect. "Oh my gosh. And why is it that you persist in claiming my parents?"

Luke gave her a sideways look. "You *invited* me along?"

Allie cringed. "I invited you. Sort of."

From the back seat Walter yawned and set his big head back on his paws. They'd already stopped to let him out twice, and he'd filled the car with his special aroma three times.

She texted Charlotte to check on Mary. Her friend responded that Queen Mary remained on her throne and had called for the head of a robin nesting just out of reach under the porch eaves.

Off with her head! Allie texted. Then, because she loved her feathered friends, she added, No, really, be nice to the birdie. She has babies in the nest.

A whine came from the back seat. Walter was now sitting up, staring out the window. Then those big eyes rolled toward her, pleading.

"There's a pull-off up ahead," Luke said.

Allie sighed. "You really should have him checked for a bladder infection."

The turnoff was in a beautiful valley, nestled in the hills and burgeoning with massive pine trees. Allie walked the needle-strewn path beside Luke. (Might as well stretch her legs.) He hadn't bothered to put Walter on a leash as they were the only ones there, and Walter traveled, more or less, at the pace of a worm.

Allie drew in a lungful of the pine-scented air, perhaps her favorite smell of all time. Well, there was also that spicy cologne Luke wore. Couldn't forget that.

But no, they were just friends. Even if friends didn't necessarily notice the way jeans hugged the derriere or the way biceps bulged as they flexed.

They reached a clearing, completely shaded by the towering pines, a picnic table in the center. Somewhere nearby a squirrel nattered and a robin tweeted from a high perch. Luke settled on the table, his feet resting on the bench.

Walter sniffed the ground and pawed at something. He was really kind of okay in his own way with his sad jowls, put-upon expression, and disinterest in ripping her apart and gnawing her bones.

Allie checked her watch.

"You worried about the time?"

She shrugged. "Not really. We'll make the party in time. I can't wait to see my grandparents' faces when they see the Chevy. They're going to be so surprised."

"That'll be awesome. Really nice of your folks to do this for them."

Allie joined him on the table. "I'm so glad that hail didn't leave a mark."

"She'll look great once we get her cleaned up. I found a car wash about forty-five minutes from your grandparents' place."

"Sounds good."

The long sideways look he gave her made her aware of how close they were sitting. And just like that it was seven years ago. Her pulse raced and her palms grew damp.

"What's your life like in Atlanta? I know you live in an apartment. Olivia mentioned you're a teacher's assistant."

Her heart gave a tug. Even her mom couldn't seem to keep up with her jobs. "Yeah, for a kindergarten class at a public school."

"You were always good with kids."

"I'm a child at heart, what can I say? They're really cute at that age. Learning's still fun and exciting, and they say the darndest things."

"You've been there awhile, haven't you?"

"For the whole school year. It's just enough of same and different to keep things interesting."

"I can see that."

"This summer I'm working at my friend's floral shop—Charlotte's a super-chill boss and I like arranging flowers, so it's a good fit."

"I'll bet you're great at that, with your creativity."

"Well, she hasn't fired me yet. And your business seems to be doing well."

"It's growing. Keeps me busy."

"And you like it, making cabinets?"

"I do. I like working with my hands and being my own boss. That way when someone asks me along on a road trip, I'm free to go."

They shared a smile for a lingering moment.

"What do you do in your spare time?" he asked.

She lifted a shoulder. "Hang out with friends, go to the park, go garage-saleing. And as I mentioned before, I volunteer at the zoo. That's fun."

"They didn't teach you angry-raccoon management?"

"Strangely enough, no. The raccoons at the zoo are cute and cuddly." She slid him a smile, maybe flirting a little. Would that be so terrible?

"What about boyfriends? Seeing anyone special these days?"

She met his eyes, her smile falling, and got stuck there for a hot minute. Like, literally hot. Her skin burned and her face was probably turning twelve shades of pink.

"Um, not at the moment." Her heart rate was reaching rabid-raccoon-evasion levels. "How about you?"

He leaned forward, elbows on his thighs. "Nope, no boyfriends."

She nudged him with her shoulder.

"I was dating a girl from Ellijay for a while, but it didn't work out. We broke up a few months ago."

"Who broke up?"

"I guess I did, but I think it was pretty mutual."

Sure it was. Allie gave a wry huff. Men like Luke—capable, mature, responsible, and fun—did not come along every day.

"What was that for?" he asked.

"What was what for?"

"That huff. You huffed."

"I didn't huff."

"Yes, you did."

"Well, if I did, I've forgotten why."

Walter, having finally found the perfect spot to relieve himself, lifted his leg at the base of a pine tree. But this was just the beginning. He always seemed to have enough reserves to water several trees.

"I don't have an anniversary gift for your grandparents."

"They won't expect you to. I can add your name to mine if you want."

"That's okay. What'd you get them?"

"I had their wedding photo made into one of those canvas prints. It turned out really beautiful." She stared up past the canopy of treetops to the blue skies beyond. "Fifty years . . . can you even imagine?"

He leaned back, his shoulder brushing hers. "Yeah . . ."

At the reflective note in his voice, she looked at him. Gazing into those mysterious green eyes, she still saw the boy he'd been. But they were more solemn these days, as if life and its trials had drained away a bit of the fun. She made a note to fix that.

But something else simmered in those depths too. Something warm and inviting. Something that made it hard to breathe.

The air seemed to crackle around them, electrified. It had been this way before. But no other man had made her feel the way Luke had. All these years she'd written it off as the flush of adolescence. That magical elixir of hormones that somehow allowed a person to reach emotional levels never again achieved.

But no. It was still there, this incredible, wonderful pulling and wanting. It both compelled and frightened her at once.

His gaze dropped to her lips, making them tingle.

She'd always loved his mouth. That perfectly arched upper lip. The lower one almost too thick for a man's. Those lovely lips of his knew just what to do.

He leaned toward her, the space between them shrinking. Allie's eyes fluttered shut, the magnet of desire irresistible.

"Koda, get back here!" someone shouted.

Allie and Luke jumped apart just as a black Labrador burst into the clearing. A middle-aged couple was on its heels. Koda found Walter and clearly wanted to be best friends forever. Walter tolerated the other dog's enthusiasm with a slow blink.

Allie's eyes bounced off Luke's in one of those awkward "we almost kissed" looks. Her heart still beat out a wild tattoo.

Then she stood and greeted the couple with a wide smile as if she didn't want to hurt them just a little bit for interrupting the moment.

Chapter 10

They were only thirty minutes away from Bedford. Luke slid the gear into fourth and gave it more gas, the engine practically purring. Man, the Chevy sure did drive out nice. And now that she was sparkling clean again, he could sit back and enjoy the ride.

Beside him Allie fiddled with her playlist. The old songs were starting to grow on him—as was Allie. They'd spent the last six and a half hours catching up—and carefully avoiding mention of the almost-kiss.

Luke's only regret was the interruption. Allie got to him in a way no other woman had. She was fun and funny, and she helped him loosen up a little. Reminded him schedules could be broken and new things could be exciting.

And now that she'd forgiven him, he couldn't help but wonder if they could be more than friends. He couldn't help but wonder if the Adamses would be okay with that. Was he good enough for their little girl?

He pushed back the niggle of worry and palmed the back of his neck where tension gathered.

"Hey, mister, both hands on the wheel." Allie tossed him a smile that almost made him forget he was driving.

Allie might be fun and impulsive, but she sure was serious about keeping this car safe. Then again, so was he. He gripped the wheel with both hands, his gaze falling to the gas gauge.

"We should probably fill up. There's only a quarter tank, and we should leave it full for your grandparents."

"Good point." She started a new tune: "All Shook Up." "We'll be getting there as the party is starting, but that'll make our arrival even more exciting. There's a gas station a few minutes up the road."

The sun was low in the sky, they were surrounded by woods, and the country road wound around the hills. Beautiful country. Beautiful day. Beautiful woman in the seat beside him. She was singing along to the song, completely unaware or uncaring that she sang out of tune. The wind blew through her open window, making her hair wave behind her like a flag.

Eyes on the road, buddy. You're not home safe yet.

A few minutes later he saw Allie was right. Despite the lack of civilization, there was a mom-and-pop gas station with four pumps and a sign reading *Country Store—hunting licenses, permits, ammo.*

For such a small place, it was doing good business. One of the pumps was taken, and two cars were parked in front of the store.

Luke pulled up to a pump and filled up while Allie waited in the car. When he was finished he put Walter on his leash and took him for a quick walk behind the station.

Allie joined him a minute later. "It's pretty back here."

Her honey-colored hair was windblown, and her cheeks and shoulders were sun kissed. "Sure is."

"We're doing okay on time. I might run inside and restock my snacks."

"Wouldn't want to run out of Ho Hos."

Her eyes smiled. "Right? And you already blew through my peanut M&M's."

"I'll buy you another bag."

"Nah, you drove all this way for me—I'd say that evens things out."

Walter finally found a suitable tree and lifted his leg.

"I'll agree to that," Luke said. "But only because I got to drive a '57 Chevy."

"Through storm floods and hail. Not exactly the joyride you expected, huh?"

It had actually been so much more.

"Hey, mister!" The woman from the store came around the building. "Is that your old Chevy out front?"

"Yeah . . ." Luke walked toward her, tugging the leash.

"Some kids just took off with it."

"*What?*" Luke jogged toward the front, dragging Walter behind him.

Allie reached the parking lot first and screeched to a dead halt. "It's gone!"

"Like I said." The woman shelved her hands on her hips. "Those boys who were inside a minute ago just took off with it. They bought cigarettes and . . ."

She recited a list of goods purchased, but Luke couldn't hear any more. He laced his hands behind his head, staring at the empty spot where the beautiful '57 Chevy sat only moments ago. He tried to imagine telling Bill and Becky what had happened, and a fist tightened in his gut. Sweat beaded on his neck.

That car was irreplaceable—and Luke had *lost* it.

———

No, no, no.

Allie paced in front of the store, staring at the empty spot where the car had just sat. The store clerk had disappeared inside to call the cops. Allie couldn't believe this was happening.

She palmed her cheeks. Her parents were going to *kill* her—and she deserved it. When Luke blocked her path she stopped, dropped her hands, and met his gaze.

His jaw was knotted and a furrow split his brows. What was he so worried about? The car was her responsibility—this catastrophe her problem.

"How could this happen?" She'd only been out of the car two minutes. Could someone hot-wire a car that quickly? "How could they have made off with it so fast?"

"Do you have the keys?" A bite sharpened his tone.

"No . . . Why would I have them? You're the one driving."

"I left the keys in the car, Allie. Because *you* were in the car."

She gasped. "Well, I didn't know that! You didn't tell me."

"So you left the keys in the car."

"No . . . *You* left the keys in the car." She glared at him.

He glowered right back. "Didn't you think to check the ignition before you followed me out back?"

"Why would I do that when you haven't left the keys in the car before now?"

"Because I haven't left *you* in the car before now." He was clearly working hard at that level tone.

"Sheriff Dudley'll be right here," the pretty clerk said as she exited the building. She was eyeing Luke like he was her next meal.

Allie speared the woman with a withering look, but she was too busy making eyes at Luke to notice.

"He's a real good guy, the sheriff. You'll like him a lot." The clerk swung her gaze between the two of them, finally seeming to sense the tension. "Well . . . I'll be right inside if you need me."

"Can we review the camera footage?" Luke asked.

Allie perked up at the question. Maybe they could retrieve the car before—

"Sorry, hon. We don't have cameras. Never had a car stolen before—that's a first. Maybe a candy bar or a six-pack or . . ."

She kept talking but Allie tuned her out. If she didn't get a moment alone, she was going to scream. She wandered off and found a picnic table on the side of the store where someone had smoked about two hundred packs of cigarettes and dropped the butts in the dirt.

Her heart thudded in her chest and her palms sweated. How was she going to explain to her parents that she'd allowed the car to be stolen? Because Luke was right—the whole key thing was her fault. She was the last one in the car. She should've checked before she left it.

She perched on the table and buried her face in her hands, her stomach roiling until she felt sick. Instead of demonstrating that she was a responsible adult, she'd proven just the opposite.

The grand surprise was going to be a disappointment of

epic proportions. Her news would ruin the party—ruin her grandparents' fiftieth anniversary. How could she have been so stupid?

A few minutes of self-flagellation later, the jingle of Walter's tags made her lift her head. Luke approached, his face unreadable. He dropped the leash and sank onto the table beside her. "Sorry I got so upset."

All the fight was gone from her now. All that was left was the matchless misery of failure. "It's okay. You were right. I should've checked for the keys."

"Who would've dreamed someone would take off with it? I mean, you think of this stuff happening in the city, not at some backwoods gas station."

Even now her parents were waiting for them to pull into the drive. Allie's lungs struggled to keep pace with her heart. At the thought of facing her parents, her throat thickened and her eyes stung. "My parents are going to kill me."

"Nah. You'll maybe be sentenced to a lifetime of guilt trips. But that was probably going to happen anyway."

A wet sound erupted from her throat. She seemed to be crying. Allie covered her face.

"Hey." Luke put an arm around her and pulled her into his side. The welcome comfort only made the tears come faster.

"It's going to be okay. As much as they might value that car, it's just a car, Allie. They care more about you."

"They think I'm hopeless! They already think I'm a screwup, and now I'm going to prove them right."

"That's not true. They love you. You're not a screwup."

"You don't understand." The words burbled out of her. "They count on Olivia for everything. Need someone to water your plants and get your mail? Ask Olivia. Need an executor for your will? Ask Olivia. Five-course meal? Olivia!"

"Look, honey. Olivia's just a different kind of personality. She's very structured and prepared—a stick-in-the-mud, some might say."

A laugh slipped out just as she felt something wet on her foot. Walter reclaimed his tongue and gazed up at her with mournful eyes that seemed to reflect her pain. Okay, she had to hand it to the dopey dog—he had his good points. She ruffled his ears.

"You're spontaneous and fun and accepting," Luke continued. "There's nothing wrong with who you are."

"Tell my parents that. Know what they assigned me to bring to the party? Napkins."

His low chuckle stirred something deep inside, as did the hand that caressed her bare arm. "And while your sister's in the kitchen today, slaving away over the stove, guess who's going to be on the lawn playing tag with the kids? Guess who's going to be regaling her grandparents with funny stories from work? Guess who's going to be beating her dad in a game of cornhole?"

"Okay, okay. But this is still going to be awful. The whole reason I offered to bring the car was to prove to them that I'm a capable adult. And now look what's happened. I lost their car." The last words escaped on a pathetic squeak.

"Hey . . ." He pulled her in tighter, and she laid her head on his shoulder, a tear trickling down her cheek. "You are a perfectly capable adult. You've been on your own since you were eighteen, haven't you? You've held down a job—okay, lots of jobs, but it still counts. You have your own place, you pay your bills. You don't have anything to prove, Allie. You're perfect just the way you are."

Allie tipped her head up and their eyes connected.

"Thanks, Luke." When he brushed the wetness away with his thumb, her heart gave a squeeze.

"Allie, I—"

A siren chirped, dragging their attention to the gas station's entrance where a sheriff's car was turning in.

Allie fixed her gaze on it as she straightened, her stomach weighted with lead. "I guess we might as well get this over with."

Chapter 11

Sheriff Dudley was over six feet tall and reminded Allie vaguely of Mr. Clean. His manners were spot-on, but she was filled with so much dread she couldn't even return his smile.

It seemed to take eons to answer all his questions. Thankfully the store clerk was able to provide a detailed description of the two boys.

Once the woman tore her eyes from Luke long enough to return to her job, the sheriff turned to Allie and Luke. "Can I give you kids a ride somewhere?"

The thought of pulling up to her grandparents' house in a sheriff's car . . . "Oh no, that's okay."

Luke checked his watch. "Sure about that? We're already late, and it's not like we're going to catch an Uber around here."

"You're right about that." Sheriff Dudley nodded. "Where you folks headed?"

Allie's stomach knotted. "My grandparents' house—Lou and Vicki Stuart."

"I know them. My mother plays bingo with Miss Vicki on Wednesday nights at the community center."

Perfect.

And just like that, they were riding with Sheriff Dudley, Luke in the front for legroom and Allie in the back seat like a common criminal. She looked over at Walter on the seat beside her. He rested his big head on his paws, already on his way to another successful nap.

Once they were on their way, Allie bucked up her courage and dialed her mom. Better to give a little warning before she broke her family's hearts. But her mother seemed to have her phone off. Her dad's phone rang and rang, which wasn't unusual.

As much as she hated to, she dialed her sister. But Olivia must've had her hands full in the kitchen. Somehow Allie didn't have her brother-in-law's phone number, and her grandparents didn't believe in cell phones.

Looked like they would find out about her monumental failure in person.

"I can't reach my family," Allie told Luke during a lull in his conversation with Sheriff Dudley.

"We're almost there anyway," the sheriff said. "Just up the street."

Allie looked out the window. He was right. The knots in her stomach tightened, a sense of doom hanging over her like a thundercloud. Before she could gather herself, they were pulling into her grandparents' driveway. There was the big white farmhouse and the red barn behind it. Cars lined one side of the wide drive, leaving the other side free for passing—and that's just what Sheriff Dudley was doing.

"Oh, hey . . ." Allie leaned forward. "You think you could—"

The sheriff chirped the siren as he breezed past the house, heading to the back.

Oh, good. Now everyone would see her pulling up in a sheriff's car, in the back seat, no less, restored '57 Chevy nowhere in sight.

The crowd turned their way. It seemed the entire town of Bedford had shown up for the big event. There was Gram, little Emma on her hip, and Gramps, showing off his newly stained deck to someone Allie didn't know. Even Mom and Olivia had escaped the confines of the kitchen in time for her arrival.

Sheriff Dudley pulled to a stop, and Allie exited the car, leaving the door open for Walter. She was vaguely aware of Luke unloading their stuff, then the sheriff gave a wave and circled back out of the drive.

Her mom had approached, looking summery in pink capris and a billowy white top, her blonde hair pulled into a chic ponytail. "Allie, what in the world?" Her harsh whisper harkened back to Allie's childhood days. "Where is the car?"

"Hi, Mom. I can explain." Allie hugged her, finding the embrace stiff and formal.

Dad joined them, his dark brows pinched behind his glasses. "Where's the car? What happened?"

Allie swallowed hard as she drew back. "Mom, Dad . . . I hate to tell you this, but—"

"Allie, honey, are you all right?" Gram approached, looking beautiful with her short gray hair curled and her makeup just so. She gathered Allie in a warm, soft hug. "Did you have an accident, dear? Are you hurt?"

"Please tell me you didn't have an accident." Her mom's voice was tight.

"No, ma'am." Luke shared a look with Allie, silently asking if he should expound.

But no, this was her responsibility. Gramps had joined them, along with Olivia and Spencer. After greeting them, they all waited with expectant expressions.

Allie's heart hammered in her chest. Probably best to just get it out there. She drew in a shaky breath. "I'm afraid the car was stolen."

Her mom's gasp sucked half the oxygen supply from planet Earth.

Her dad frowned and blinked.

"What?" Gramps nudged his glasses up. "We're going bowling?"

"Turn up your hearing aid, old man," Gram yelled. "She said her *car was stolen*. Oh, Allie, you poor dear. Come inside and have a cookie."

"Not *my* car, Gram." Allie looked at her parents. "I'm so sorry, Mom and Dad. We were gassing up a while ago and I—I left the keys in the car. A couple of kids took it. We called the sheriff and filed a—"

"For heaven's sake, Allie!" Mom said. "You left the keys in the car? How could you do that?"

"Oh, Allie . . ." The disappointed look on her dad's face brought a lump to her throat.

She swallowed hard and drew a shaky breath. Luke had come to stand close to her, and his solid, warm presence bolstered her.

"You know how much that car meant to your grandparents." Mom began wheezing.

"I'm confused," Gramps said. "What happened to Allie's car?"

"Not *Allie's* car, Dad," her mom said loudly. "Bill and I had your old Chevy restored for your anniversary, and Allie was supposed to drive it here and surprise you with it. But now . . ." Her mom covered her trembling mouth. A wheezing sound escaped.

"Oh dear," Gram said.

"That was awful nice of you two." Gramps rubbed his bald head. "It was stolen, you say?"

"That car was irreplaceable, Allie," her mom said. "You promised you'd take good care of it."

A crowd had gathered and conversation buzzed around her. The snippets she heard filled her face with heat, her eyes with tears. She wanted to sink into the ground. She wanted to—

"It wasn't Allie's fault." Luke's voice cut through the clamor, quieting the crowd. "It was mine."

———

Luke felt as if his breath was stuffed inside his lungs. He struggled to draw another. He hadn't known he was going to say that. But he'd seen the disappointed looks Allie's parents were giving her. He'd seen Allie withering before him, and it had just come out.

"*I* left the keys in the car." Luke pinned Bill and Becky with an unswerving look. "So if anyone's to blame . . . it's me."

Becky's gaze toggled between Luke and Allie, finally settling on Luke. Her eyes turned down at the corners, her lips tightening, her breath raspy. The look of displeasure cut straight into Luke's heart. The cold trickle of fear returned.

Then Becky burst into tears.

Bill spared Luke a look before gathering his wife in his arms. "Now, now, sweetheart. We'll figure this out."

Well, Luke had done it now. All those years of trying so hard, and he'd finally disappointed them. He'd probably lose them over this. At the very least, things would never be the same. But he couldn't bring himself to regret it.

"I'm so sorry about all this," Luke continued. "The sheriff has a good description of the culprits, so there's still a chance they'll catch them, find the car. I'll do whatever I can to help."

But Bill was leading Becky away, and the crowd was dispersing. The hollow feeling inside would go away. Eventually.

He caught Allie's gaze and saw the gratitude shining in her eyes. "Luke, I don't—"

"Allie, honey." Her grandma hooked an arm around Allie's waist.

"It's so good to see you, sweetie," her grandpa told her, then stretched out a hand to Luke. "You too, Luke. Glad you could make it."

Mrs. Stuart looked at her husband, raising her voice. "Fetch some water for the pooch. You kids come inside and get some food. We'll figure all this out."

The three of them headed up the deck steps, but Luke hung back, watching until they disappeared into the house. His gaze flickered up to the white structure, then over the pretty property. His eyes drifted over the crowd, mostly strangers, mingling on the deck and lawn.

Bill was still consoling Becky over by the grill, Olivia must've retreated to her kitchen duties, and the rest of the party carried on as if nothing had even happened.

Chapter 12

*O*nce Allie had a cookie, she joined her mom and sister in the
kitchen where the aromas of prime rib and yeast made her
stomach turn. Normally she'd be outside keeping her nephew
and nieces out of trouble, but as Allie had just lost a prized
antique car and subsequently let someone else take the blame,
she figured she should probably make herself useful.

She helped the others carry food to the tables set up on
the lawn under the shade of the big oak tree. The sun was setting, streaking the sky with pink and lavender, and an evening
breeze beat back the heat of the day.

Her mother had recovered from her shock and was now in
the-show-must-go-on mode. Allie had to admit, they'd done a
wonderful job setting up the party. Fresh flowers and balloons
adorned a dozen round tables. They were beautifully set with
china, their white tablecloths fluttering in the breeze. Twinkle
lights draped the tree branches above, creating a space that
would feel intimate when darkness pressed in.

Allie set down a platter of corn on the cob and scanned

the crowd for Luke. She found him tossing a football with her nephew. She'd hunt him down later. He'd come through for her, at his own risk, and that meant more than he could know. She couldn't let the blame fall on him, however.

She passed the assortment of hot foods, salad, and the coolers of bottled drinks. At the end of the table, silverware was set out with cups and napkins and— *that are in the a stolen car!*

Allie did a double take. She'd brought white napkins—the really nice ones that were practically cloth. But the napkins on the table were blue.

Heat flushed through her limbs, leaching into her face. Her mom had brought backup napkins. Allie's muscles quivered and her fingers twitched. She scanned the table. But no, her white napkins were nowhere to be found.

Her mom passed with a crock of something. "Honey, can you get the candles for the cake? They're on the kitchen— What's wrong?"

"Where are my napkins?" Allie tried hard for a level tone and didn't quite succeed.

"Oh, they're inside. I saw the blue ones at the store and thought they'd look wonderful against the white tablecloth. Pretty, don't you think?"

"But you asked me to bring the napkins—and I did."

Her mom blinked at her. "Well, sure, honey. We can put them out, too, if you want."

"That's not the point, Mom."

Her mom set the crock down and tilted her head at Allie. "Then what is the point, dear?"

"I wish you'd just—" She struggled for the words. But now that she was trying to verbalize her thoughts, it all sounded so stupid. Besides, there was the stolen car to consider. "Never mind."

Allie turned to go.

Mom took her hand. "Honey, what is it? If this is about the car, I'm sorry I flipped out on you. But it was terribly upsetting, as I'm sure you can imagine."

"It's not the car, Mom. Or not just the car." Allie huffed, collecting her thoughts. "You don't trust me to do anything. You treat me like I'm incapable of carrying out the most basic tasks—I can't even be trusted with *napkins*."

"I just thought blue would look so—"

"This is not the first time. If I'm assigned cups you bring extra, just to make sure. If I have an important appointment, you call to remind me. I can handle basic tasks, Mom."

Her mom glanced sheepishly at the napkins.

"I know I've been a little changeable in the past," Allie continued. "I still am—that's just who I am. But that doesn't mean I'm not a capable adult. That's the reason I was so adamant about bringing the car up here. I wanted to prove to you that I could follow through. That you could count on me." Allie threw her hands up. "And now look what's happened."

Mom squeezed Allie's hand. "Well, that wasn't your fault, honey."

Allie caught a glimpse of Luke across the lawn, still tossing the ball with Evan. Ella had joined them, and Luke had taken the spot of man-in-the-middle. As far as Allie knew, neither of her parents had even spoken to him since his confession. Since they'd turned their disappointment on Luke. Allie couldn't get his stricken look out of her mind.

Allie faced her mother, her spine straightening. "You know,

Mom, it wasn't really Luke's fault—it was mine. *I* left the keys in the car. He was only being nice, taking the blame for me. And I'm really sorry to disappoint you. I'll do everything I can to get that car back.

"But you know what? You're basically the only parents Luke has. He loves you guys, and you need to let him know that you're going to love him no matter what he does—even if he loses a priceless car." Allie's throat tightened and the words constricted.

Her mom's face softened, her lips going slack. She gave Allie a long, speculative look. "And maybe you need that, too, honey?"

Allie's eyes burned. She blinked back tears.

Her mom squeezed her hand again. "You know, part of being an adult is accepting responsibility. And you did that today. In fact, if I consider the past few years, you've been doing that all along. I guess I've just been too blind to notice."

"I know I'll never be like Olivia, Mom. I'll never be perfect."

"Oh, honey." Mom chuckled. "Olivia's far from perfect, and we never wanted you to be her. We don't want you to be anyone other than who you are. I'm sorry we ever made you feel otherwise. It's just . . . I still see you as my baby girl—the girl who wore two different shoes to school in the seventh grade and needed me to rescue her."

"That was a long time ago."

Her mom drew her into a hug that felt warm and welcoming. Allie settled her head on her mom's shoulder, inhaling her flowery scent.

"You're right, honey. Somewhere along the way, you grew up. I'll do better. We both will, I promise. I love you so much."

"I love you, too, Mom. Thanks." A weight lifted off Allie. She should've said something long ago. Why had she let this go so long?

Over her mom's shoulder, her eyes caught on Luke as he made a show of missing the football, which was well within his grasp.

Allie pulled back, meeting her mom's gaze. "And you and Dad will talk to Luke?"

Mom's blue eyes sharpened on her, probably seeing far more than Allie intended. "Of course we will, honey." She cradled Allie's face. "And now we'd best gather everyone around before all this wonderful food gets cold."

The meal was finished, the cake had been served, and the sun had set. Allie's dad had made a sentimental toast that brought tears to her grandparents' eyes. After supper Allie played two rounds of tag with her nieces and nephew and one round of Chase the Mean, Hairy Monster—Allie being the monster, of course. She had grass stains on her pants, leaf chips in her hair, and a smile on her face.

Darkness pressed in, the twinkle lights aglow as the guests mingled on the deck, lawn, and makeshift dance floor. The sweet strains of "I Only Have Eyes for You" filtered through the air, and a cool breeze ruffled Allie's hair as she leaned on the deck railing, watching her grandparents slow dance.

They looked so sweet, rocking back and forth, smiling at the gathered guests. Gram had a bit of red lipstick on her teeth, but Gramps was so farsighted he probably couldn't tell.

When Gram said something to him, Gramps leaned closer. "What's that?"

"We haven't danced in years!"

"I *did* clean out my ears."

"No, *we haven't danced in years*!"

"We have ants in here?"

"*I said, we haven't*— Oh, never mind. Just hold me, old man."

Allie chuckled, her eyes stinging a little. A strange bubble swelled in her throat. It wasn't all rainbows and sprinkles with her grandparents, but they loved each other. Allie couldn't even imagine being with the same person for fifty years. But she'd sure like to try.

Olivia joined her at the railing, her dark braid hanging over her shoulder, looking no worse for wear after hours of slaving over the hot stove.

"Kitchen duties all done?" Allie asked.

"Spic-and-span." She scanned the lawn. "Where are my kids? If they're eating cake again, I'm gonna kill Spencer."

Allie pointed toward the back of the property where they were trying to get Walter to fetch a stick. The dog was rooted to the ground like an ancient oak tree.

"Sugar rush aside," Allie said, "I think I got them good and tired for you earlier."

"Thanks for keeping them occupied. When Spencer gets to talking he forgets to watch them." Olivia swished her drink around in the glass. "I was wanting to ask if you'd be free to babysit a couple weekends from now. Spencer has this work thing in New York, and I thought I might tag along."

Allie's lips parted. "Really? You want me to babysit?"

"Listen, I overreacted to the whole Cocoa Puffs thing. You acted in Evan's best interest." Olivia gave her a chagrined smile. "It's not your fault he likes to put food up his nose."

Allie chuckled. "I'd love to babysit, Olivia. Thanks for asking. And the meal was great tonight, by the way. Everything was delicious."

"Thanks. And in case you didn't notice . . . I switched out the napkins after Mom went through the line."

how?

Allie's gaze connected with her sister's. They burst out laughing. A moment of recognition that yes, their mother was ridiculous sometimes. But they were in this together, Olivia and Allie.

Allie's laughter hadn't yet died away when she caught sight of Luke by the rose trellis talking to her parents. He was so handsome under the golden glow of twinkle lights. He wore an attentive expression as he listened.

Dad put a hand on Luke's shoulder as he spoke with him. Her mom chimed in, smiling. And then . . . a group hug.

Allie looked on, her eyes burning yet again, something like relief filling her. Also maybe a bit of gratification at having prompted this moment. Luke deserved to know he'd always have Bill and Becky. He was family. He was accepted. He was loved. Her heart went squishy at the thought.

And that's when she knew. Somehow over the past two days she'd managed to fall in love with Luke Fletcher all over again. Her pulse fluttered as she homed in on him.

The hug ended. Her mom spoke to him, gave his hand a squeeze. And then her parents headed toward the dance floor.

Luke turned just then, and his eyes locked on Allie. Something vibrated between them. Heat flushed through her, settling in her cheeks. Even after all these years he still had her, heart and soul.

Olivia nudged her. "When are you going to do something about that?"

Allie blinked at her sister. "About what?"

"Please. I'm not blind. You've had a crush on him for years."

And here Allie had thought she'd hidden it so well.

"Go dance with the man." Olivia nudged her with a shoulder. "From the look on his face, he's just as crazy about you."

Chapter 13

*L*uke couldn't take his eyes off Allie as he walked up the deck stairs. She was beautiful, standing under the white lights, her blonde hair ruffling in the breeze, her eyes locked on his. He'd watched her from afar all evening, and he couldn't keep his distance a moment longer—not when she was looking at him like that.

He joined her at the railing and held out his hand. "Care to dance?"

"Thought you'd never ask."

Her hand small and soft in his, he led her down the deck and onto the makeshift dance floor. A poignant melody filled the night, the lyrics piercing his heart as he led her into the fray.

"Could I have this dance, for the rest of my life?"

Luke slipped his arm around her waist, his heart giving an extra thump at the slight weight of her hand on his shoulder. Allie's sweet scent wrapped around him like a sultry breeze, driving him a little wild.

Her fingers moved against his shoulder as she smiled sweetly at him. "Thank you for what you did earlier. It meant a lot that you'd take the blame. I know how you hate to disappoint my parents—as do we all."

He returned her smile. "And yet you set them straight."

"It was the responsible thing to do."

"They were talking to me a minute ago. They said some very nice things."

She glanced away. "I'm glad."

"Why do I get the feeling you had something to do with that?"

She blinked, all innocence. "I have no idea."

That talk had left him feeling light and worry-free. It had left him feeling loved. Maybe it was time to stop clinging to the unrealistic hope that his parents would become what he needed and just be grateful for what he already had.

"You know, I think I'm going to get rid of my landline."

She gave him a questioning look. "What? Where did that come from?"

"Never mind." He smiled, drawing her closer, his heart stuttering as her head settled against his shoulder. He breathed her in, hardly able to believe she was in his arms again after all these years. But there was still so much unsaid between them.

"My grandparents seem to be having a good time despite the car debacle."

In the middle of the pack Mr. Stuart spun his wife out, then gathered her close again, laughing.

"Fifty years . . . ," Luke said.

"Twice as long as I've been alive."

"They're a good match."

"Well, they're not perfect . . . but they're perfect for each other."

Was she still talking about her grandparents? The air seemed to crackle between them. His chest tightened as his heart swelled with love for her.

He wanted that for himself, fifty years of love and marriage.

And he knew with sudden certainty—he wanted it with Allie.

———

Allie breathed Luke in, relishing the feel of being in his arms again. As a girl she'd dreamed of this, and later she'd had him for a short while. But her feelings for Luke had grown and deepened. What she felt now was no longer the crush of a girl but the mature love of a woman.

Luke saw her for the way she was—he always had. She was most herself when she was with him, and she didn't worry she'd disappoint him. The thought of it tightened her chest.

"Allie?" Luke drew back, his hand sliding from the center of her back to her side.

That voice. Those hands. Those eyes. He looked at her with such intensity that her breath hitched.

"I'm glad we got to spend the last two days together." His lips curled in a smile. "I've enjoyed your company. Enjoyed getting to know you all over again."

"It's been fun—minus the rabid raccoon and, you know, the grand theft auto."

He chuckled. "You made even those things worthwhile."

She fell into those green eyes, her mouth going dry. She couldn't even think, much less speak.

"I know this might seem sudden, but somehow it isn't sudden at all." His smile had fallen away, leaving a warm and wistful look on his face. "I love you, Allie Adams—I don't think I ever stopped."

Her heart skipped a beat at his words. He'd echoed her own thoughts so perfectly. How had she gone all these years without him?

"Oh, Luke. I love you too."

The corners of his eyes relaxed, and his mouth curved as he leaned closer and brushed her lips with his. Soft and firm and gentle. Then he hovered over her for a moment, meeting her gaze, his breath a gentle whisper before he reclaimed her mouth.

He gathered her closer, and Allie wound both arms around him, her fingers finding home in the soft dark hair at his nape. She forgot to dance. Forgot to breathe. Forgot everything but the man in her arms. The man who'd always felt like hers.

When he finally drew away, he captured her face between his hands and gave her an intent look. "Best. Detour. Ever."

She chuckled, warmth spreading its languid fingers throughout her. She caught her mom's eyes across the floor where she danced with Allie's father.

Mom gave her a wink.

"Um, I think they're on to us," Allie said.

Luke followed her gaze, then looked back to Allie. "I hope they approve. Because I intend to kiss their daughter a lot more."

Allie gave him a saucy look. "Is that a fact?"

"Oh, it's a fact." He leaned toward her, and her lips tingled in anticipation.

But the chirp of a siren captured her attention. Darn those stupid sirens.

A sheriff's car rolled to a stop in the drive—and right behind it was her grandparents' shiny red '57 Chevy.

"They found the car!" Allie said.

"Your old girl!" Gram said from across the dance floor.

"Your cold pearl?" Gramps said.

"No, your *old girl*!"

"You told Earl?"

"Look, old man!" Gram pointed to the Chevy.

"My old girl!" Gramps headed toward the car, dragging Gram along behind him.

Allie's parents followed, as did the rest of the crowd. Allie started to follow, but Luke tugged her hand, pulling her back into his arms.

She looked up at him with questioning eyes.

"You know . . ." His mouth slid into a crooked grin. "As long as they're occupied . . ."

Allie smiled and leaned in closer, love for him swelling like the grand finale of a concerto. "I like the way you think, Luke Fletcher."

Epilogue

*A*llie had no idea where she was going tonight, but she knew what she was wearing. She slipped into her dress, pulled up the zipper, and glanced in the mirror. The dress was a gift from Luke and was a little, well, froufrou for her taste. But the pale pink complemented her skin tone, and let's face it. She'd wear a burlap sack if he asked her to. She had no idea where he was taking her tonight; he wouldn't give her even a hint.

She found her heels easily enough as she'd been making an effort to stay organized since her move back to Copper Creek. Long-distance dating had grown old quickly, and when a job had opened up at the local elementary school, Allie decided to move back home.

She'd started in late August and now, almost four months later, she was in love with her job and the little munchkins in her kindergarten class. She'd recently been asked to help the high school theater department with their production of *A Christmas Carol*. They were gearing up for opening night.

Best of all, working at the school, she got to see her niece and nephew on a daily basis. Olivia, too, as she headed up the PTA and volunteered for every fund-raiser and field trip.

She missed Charlotte, but the two of them had already met up twice, and they texted and called each other frequently. Allie was busy making new friends and reacquainting herself with old ones.

Her parents had really come around in the trust department. For Thanksgiving Allie had been asked to make the turkey. Just kidding. But she had been assigned the sweet potato casserole, which was the second most important dish. Okay, third. Whatever—it was better than napkins. Also, she'd made pumpkin pies with Olivia. Or rather, Olivia had made pies while Allie kept the rugrats occupied.

As she slipped her feet into the heels, Mary, Queen of Scots, slithered along her leg, back arching high. The cat had given her the cold shoulder for a solid four weeks after moving, but they were on good terms once again. Well. On queen-subject terms anyway.

"Well, hello, Your Highness." Allie stroked Mary's soft fur. "How do I look, huh? Fit for a six-month anniversary? What do you think?"

Mary turned indifferent eyes toward Allie, blinking slowly.

"If you're nice, I'll bring Walter over soon."

Strangely, the furry beasties got along well. And by "got along well" she meant Walter napped in the corner while Mary pranced around, claiming the rest of her kingdom.

The doorbell rang, and Allie glanced at the clock. She was running a little late. She grabbed her glittery earrings and put them on as she walked to the door.

On the second ring she flung the door open and went mute

at the sight of Luke in a navy suit. His dark hair was carefully combed, his jaw freshly shaved, and the look in his eyes made her lean in close. She brushed his lips with hers.

Mine. He's all mine.

"You look beautiful," he said against her mouth. Then he drew away, scanning her face as if to appreciate the view a little more.

She fingered the collar of his crisp suit coat. "And look at you. This must be some restaurant you're taking me to."

"We're celebrating, after all."

She smoothed her hands over her hips. "Thank you for the dress."

"You look perfect. Are you ready to go?" He waved gallantly toward the parking lot. "Your chariot awaits."

Her eyes fixed on the car, gleaming in the last light of the day.

Allie sucked in a breath, her gaze darting back to Luke's. "I can't believe they trusted us with it again."

"I promised I'd keep the keys on my person at all times," he said wryly.

Allie chuckled. "There's not a storm on the horizon, is there?"

"The weather is clear—I checked."

"Let's go, then." Allie grabbed her purse and wrap off the table. "Be good, Mary," she called, but the cat was already sauntering away.

Allie locked up and drew her wrap around her against the cool evening air. She followed Luke to the car where he assisted her into the passenger seat.

"I have got to learn to drive a stick shift," she muttered as he walked around the car.

Once Luke was behind the wheel, he started the engine and off they went. They chatted as he drove, about family and his business and her job. Conversation always flowed easily between them. Soon they were passing through downtown. Evergreen garlands spiraled up light poles, ornate wreaths adorned shop doors, and twinkle lights shimmered against picture windows. Good ol' Copper Creek.

She thought he was perhaps heading toward the Blue Moon Grill, the town's fanciest restaurant. But he passed the pull-in and continued, turning instead onto a road that led to the small town of Chatsworth. What in the world?

"You've really got me stumped now." Allie shifted toward him. "Where on earth are we going?"

A smile played around his mouth. "You'll find out soon enough."

"Or you could just tell me . . ."

"That wouldn't be nearly as much fun."

Allie huffed. "But the suspense is killing me."

"Patience, sweetheart. We're almost there."

Almost *where*? Only the endearment and, okay, the adoring look in his eyes kept her from pressing him. That look had earned him more than compliance over the past several months.

He slowed the car and turned into a parking lot.

Allie frowned. "This is my school."

"Indeed it is."

"We're . . . eating at the school?" The parking lot lights were already beating back the encroaching darkness. As could be expected this time of night, there wasn't a single vehicle in the lot. "I don't understand."

"You will shortly." He pulled the car into a slot and shut off the engine.

"But what are we doing here?"

Luke said nothing as he exited the car and came around to help her out, an enigmatic smile on his face.

"You're not going to tell me, are you?"

He took her hand, placing a quick kiss on her lips. "For the love of Pete, you are the most impatient woman I've ever known. Come along."

Allie followed him up the sidewalk. He headed not toward the elementary building where she worked but toward the high school, set off to the side.

The high school? "Does this have something to do with the play? But no one's here. Opening night's not until— Did Olivia—?"

"Hush, woman." He spared her a smile, squeezing her hand.

When they reached the side door he pulled it open and ushered her inside, his eyes sparkling. The hallway was dim and filled with the familiar smells of old books, sweaty lockers, and lofty aspirations.

"This way." Luke led her a short way down the hall and stopped at the gym doors. He pushed them open.

Allie stepped forward, and her breath froze in her lungs at the sight. White lights twinkled all around the darkened gym, and snowflakes of all sizes and shapes hung from above as if suspended in midflight. The floor glistened white, and dots of light seemed to be falling from the sky in some sort of snow effect. The gym had been transformed into a winter wonderland.

Allie pressed her hand to her chest. A lump formed in her throat, thickening until it cut off anything she might say. She looked at Luke, her eyes burning. She couldn't believe he'd done this for her.

"I thought it was time I took you to your prom."

"Luke," she breathed.

He led her deeper into the room, and she took it all in. A soft ballad played from somewhere, and a single table, clothed in white and laden with food, sat in the middle of the room.

"I can't believe you did this."

"I should've taken you the first time. I'm sorry I didn't." He produced a corsage he must've hidden behind his back.

She laughed, holding out her hand, and he slid the spray of pink sweetheart roses onto her wrist. "You've thought of everything."

He kissed her hand, his expression growing intense. "I've thought of nothing but you for the past six months, Allie."

She fell into his soulful eyes. What this man did to her. "Oh, Luke. It's been the best six months of my life."

He gave her a long look, as if assessing something. Then his mouth relaxed in a smile, as if he'd made up his mind. "I was going to do this after we'd eaten, but I can't wait."

He reached into his pocket, then dropped down to one knee, holding out a sparkling diamond ring.

She pressed a hand to her trembling lips as her breath flooded from her lungs.

"Allie Adams . . ." Luke's eyes pierced hers, saying so much. "More than anyone ever has, you see me for who I am, and you love me anyway. I'd like nothing more than to spend the rest of my life with you, taking road trips, getting lost together—and finding each other over and over again. I love you so much, Allie. You're my home. Will you marry me?"

"Oh, Luke. Of course I will. Yes!"

He beamed at her as he slipped the ring onto her finger. It was beautiful—a substantial solitaire with a band that curled and twisted in a whimsical way. It was so *her*.

Luke gathered her close and took her mouth in a kiss that matched the joy in her heart. Allie held him close, returning his affection with equal fervor. This was the man she'd held out for. The one who'd claimed her heart so long ago. And now he was hers again. Hers forever.

When he drew away their breaths were labored. A slow melody played in the background. Allie recognized it as the song they'd danced to at her grandparents' anniversary party, when Luke had first professed his love.

Luke wore a knowing look, and a smile dawned on his face. "Could I have this dance?"

Allie smiled up at him. "For the rest of my life."

And when he took her in his arms, Allie knew it was true. She'd fallen in love with the boy next door—and he'd fallen right back in love with her.

Pining for You

Melissa Ferguson

To Christine Berg,
Dreamer, Believer, Talented Artist,
and Whimsical Friend
with the Happiest Christmas Tree Farm
in the World Worth Writing About.

Chapter 1

Theo

*T*hree weeks into dating, and already odds he'd marry this woman were approaching 45 percent.

It was a spontaneous though not unexpected thought, flickering in and out as quickly as the votive between them. After all, here he sat: Theodore Watkins III, bachelor of thirty-five years, financial adviser who lived by facts and figures. He was well aware of the statistical odds of discovering an eligible woman within ten or so years of his own age in Abingdon, Virginia, town of eight thousand. Aware even more, as he looked into the blazing blue eyes of one of the most beautiful women he'd ever encountered, of the slim chance of stumbling upon one so poised and intelligent. Compatible. Charming.

Absolutely perfect.

Although, yes, the last time he walked into her home he'd discovered an unnerving number of framed photographs of her previous boyfriend lining the hallway. One was so candid of the man walking to his car, sunglasses on, you could almost, *almost* wonder if she'd snapped it from across the street. And sure, judging the bizarre shift in neckline from blue to green in that framed snapshot at the end of the hall, you could almost, *almost* be led to believe she'd photoshopped him into the family Christmas photo, Santa hat and all.

But what was photoshopping a person into a photo besides a noble desire for inclusion? And what was snapping a photo in broad daylight without the subject's knowledge but one mere step beyond affection? Skew it a bit one way and it might require a restraining order, sure, but skew it the other and she was the world's best girlfriend.

Right now, she was the world's best girlfriend. Theo couldn't think of one person he'd rather be sitting with at this moment.

Well, one. But that person was fourteen years and 2,629 miles away, and he had learned a long time ago how to carry on with a good life despite the ever-present memory of her in the back of his mind.

Ashleigh glanced up from the menu and caught his gaze. Her lips, pink as the roses decorating the tables, parted slightly. Her cheeks warmed as her eyes slipped back to the menu, no doubt attempting to hide similar thoughts behind her long black lashes. But the secret was out, had been out for a few dates now. She was enjoying herself as much as he was, and neither of them was interested in playing games.

At this rate, they'd be shopping for rings by June.

"You know," Theo said, placing the menu and its lines of French descriptions on the crisp white linen tablecloth. "*Fiddler on the Roof* is opening on Saturday. I wondered if we could watch the performance, take Bree and Chip out after the show to celebrate her role as Golde—"

"You mean voluntarily sit beside our exes so we can re-experience at what precise moment Chip lost interest in me?"

Ashleigh delivered her polished words with nothing but serenity as she gazed at the menu, although he could've sworn he saw her left eye twitch.

She set her menu down and reached out to give his hand a lighthearted squeeze. "I will be forever grateful to those two for setting us up, Theo, but that doesn't mean I can forget so easily. You, however, are a wonder."

She held his hand until he bowed his head with a nod.

"Of course. My apologies. I brought it up too soon."

He hadn't lied. By *soon*, he just meant relative to the life span of a two-hundred-year-old bowhead whale.

It had been more than a year since Chip and Bree had said their "I dos," almost two since Theo and Ashleigh each had to endure "the talk" with their former significant others. Despite the unpleasant conversation, Theo had understood Bree, both then and now. The heart wanted what it wanted. Openness to heartache, unfortunately, came with the dating landscape. Through it all, Theo had maintained a friendship with both Bree and Chip. The weekend prior he even celebrated with them at their baby shower.

Baby steps. Ashleigh just needed to take baby steps.

Like removing the framed photographs of her entwining her arm with someone else's quite-possibly-photoshopped husband. That would be a good start, particularly before any unfortunate incident whereby Chip or Bree happened to see it one day.

Theo's pocket vibrated just as the waiter stepped up to the table. The man gave a short dip of the head. "Good evening, ma'am. Sir. Are you ready to order?"

"You go ahead, Ashleigh," Theo said as he slipped his hand into his pocket and peeked discreetly at his phone. His occupation often leaked into his life after hours, but he did his best to remain courteous in the company of others. Especially Ashleigh.

But one glance at his phone and he paused.

The name hovering on his screen wasn't from Harris, calling about the upcoming company merger, or from gubernatorial candidate Lee, wanting reassurance about how the investment into Quicken would affect his future and reputation. It wasn't even his frequent after-hours caller, multimillionaire Hardy, announcing he'd "accidentally" purchased another Jaguar while on vacation and needed to hide the diminutive expense on the account report from his wife.

No, it was a name much more important. One that caused him to do something he'd never done in the middle of their meals—slip from his seat with a "Forgive me, I have to take this" to Ashleigh and the waiter.

The caretaker of his family's Christmas tree farm.

The caretaker himself.

Skye's father.

Chapter 2

Skye

*Y*ou have to go to the hospital." Skye struggled to keep hold of her father without hurting him further as she eased him into his recliner. Carefully she undraped her arm from his shoulders. "This is going to be one of those nonnegotiables. Like paying taxes. Stopping at crosswalks." She waved a hand at his slumped shoulder. "Seeing a doctor when part of your body has been crushed into a thousand tiny fragments."

He looked at her as though she'd just pushed a three-weeks-expired crab cake into his mouth. "Nonsense. It'll heal itself—"

Skye glanced down to his shirt. "Is there something poking *out* of your arm right now—"

"My arm's just like a starfish—" her father continued.

"Dad? Is your *bone* coming out of your *body*?"

"It's made to grow back on its own."

"That is *incredibly* inaccurate. You are welcome to look at any amputee as a living example—"

"Just need to give it time." He exhaled sharply as he pulled the lever with his good arm and the recliner popped back. He nodded to her. "You go look it up, honey. You'll see. I'll not be wasting my time on a bureaucratic system trying to take my money." He picked up the remote and flicked on the television. "Won't fall into their trap . . ."

Skye threw her hands out as she spoke over the television. "Sure. I bet all those doctors hard up for money were just lying in wait to push your tractor over while you weren't looking. It's probably some grand ploy happening all over the country. The headlines will be splashed across the news tomorrow: 'Desperate Surgeons Discovered Hiding in Cornfields from Sea to Sea.'"

He nodded, his eyes on the TV. "Now you're starting to think."

Skye bit her bottom lip to keep from wasting her breath on a fruitless response. It was time to get her mother.

She'd been inside her parents' house almost every day for the past three months; before that, years had passed since she left her childhood home. The strangest thing about being gone and coming back, however, wasn't how much things had changed. It was how much things hadn't.

The blue-and-white wallpaper, the pale-pink couches, the old flamingo table lamps—these were all as they had been when she left for Seattle fourteen years ago. The same lemony Pine-Sol smell permeated the air. Even the flickering television, boxy and crying out to be used as a prop on some set for an *I Love Lucy* musical, was the one she had watched through high school. Everything in Skye's life had changed in the past fourteen years. But for her parents? Nothing.

Well, nothing except for the dozen landscape oil paintings covering every square inch of wall space above the couch.

Skye's eyes drifted to the glimmer of a poker chip on the shag carpet, now visible beneath her father's reclined chair. She frowned. Frowned deeper as she picked it up and the words *Bristol Casino* glinted against the lamplight. A one-hundred-dollar chip.

Terrrrrific.

Nothing here had changed *at all*.

Her father's attention and expression shifted as he realized what she held. He started to reach for it, winced, and settled back again.

"Now how'd that get there?" he said gruffly, eyeing it as if it had slithered in like a lizard and taken post beneath the chair of its own accord. "Must've slipped out of my pocket and been stuck in this chair for ages."

Sure. Because her mother—tidiest woman in all of Appalachia—would've let a single *day* go by without vacuuming under the furniture.

No, if that coin was under the chair, he'd gone today. Maybe last night.

She'd only recently come to terms with the reality of her parents' extreme financial situation. It was the very reason she'd packed up her successful, vibrant Seattle life three months ago and headed back to Whitetop, Virginia, population 412—now 413. At the moment she was going to have to remember the stubborn man was missing some very critical functions in his limbs.

Medical attention first, Skye. Kill him second.

"I'll take that." He held out his hand, grinning at her as though she were a kindergartener who'd accidentally picked up a cigarette.

"Don't you worry about it," Skye replied with a tight smile, clamping the coin deep inside her fist and then shoving it into her back pocket. She gave his knee a heavy-handed pat as she spoke. "You. Just. Leave. It. To. Me—"

A rapping on the front door cut her words short. Skye's eyes moved from the door to the clock on the wall to the blank expression on her father's face. Her parents always had their little church group over on Thursdays, but who would be knocking on their door at 8:00 p.m. on a Friday night?

"Are you expecting someone?" Skye said, crossing the old, familiar carpet. She opened the door. *"Theo?"*

The television in the background dimmed as Skye spoke the name she'd refrained from speaking for just about as long as the carpet beneath her feet had been in existence.

The yellow porch light shone on the man who wore a two-piece suit as if he were entering a fine establishment instead of her parents' double-wide. Mist settled on the broad shoulders of his beige overcoat. He belonged in a boardroom, not on a porch with green outdoor carpet and aluminum chairs.

And yet his clean-shaven chin still carried the lightning scar where he'd fallen off that log and into the creek years ago. Whereas the world beyond was matte black, his skin beneath the porch light was shades of elm-wood brown. His eyes, onyx and wide as they looked down at her, were the same ones she'd looked into the whole of her childhood.

And in those eyes, one very clear expression.

He was just as shocked to see her as she was him.

"*Skye*." Her name was a whisper before he cleared his throat and tried again. "Skye . . . I . . . didn't expect to see you. How is he?"

Despite asking about her father, his eyes stayed on hers, probing, as though he expected her to vanish at any moment.

They'd done their best to avoid each other for fourteen years. And yet here they were. It had finally happened.

"He's . . . good." She shook away the bombarding thoughts and questions as she pulled the door open wider and waved a hand to showcase the man in the recliner. She could do this. She could act normal.

"Theo," her father said, looking just as startled as Skye as he scrambled for the remote.

"Considering he got knocked over in a tractor without a seatbelt while isolated out in the middle of nowhere, then dragged himself the length of the farm to get home, he's okay. A bit delusional, believes he's some type of arm-growing starfish who doesn't need medical care. I expect it'll take about two, maybe three days tops for him to bleed out."

"What?" her father said.

"Hm?" she replied.

It was bizarre. She was actually managing to keep a cool tone, as though years hadn't lapsed since she'd seen Theo face-to-face. As though she hadn't wondered a hundred times in the past three months—as she looked out the airplane window at the blanket of clouds, as she dusted off the mantel of her new fireplace, as she unpacked each cardboard box and set each book in its place—how this precise moment would go.

The moment she bought the plane ticket, she knew she was going to run into him eventually.

Theo swiped a raindrop off his brow as he stood on the mat. "Bleeding out. How unfortunate."

"And unnecessary. Come on in." Skye pressed her hand to her rib cage to still her nerves as she stood back.

"Theo. I didn't expect you." The recliner creaked as her father pulled the lever, lowered his feet, and attempted to stand, his elbow supported by his other hand. Her mother appeared and pressed him back into the chair.

"Ralph, sit down," Skye's mother said, pushing gently on his good shoulder until he dropped back down. "I called him." She shot a sugary smile across the room to Theo.

Both Skye and her father held the same expression as they watched her cross the room to land a peck on Theo's cheek. *Why?*

As if hearing their question she continued: "Under Section 3A of the Workers' Compensation policy, employees should notify employers of personal injury—both to self and property—within a reasonable timeframe. And of course"— she slipped off Theo's overcoat—"Theo would *want* to know how Ralph was doing, wouldn't you? Now, dear, how was the circuit? I know you must be so relieved to get tax season behind you."

Theo touched his freshly exposed cufflinks with a bit of a startled smile. Her mom, quick as a flash, had settled his coat on the hook and was standing before him, waiting patiently for his reply.

"It was . . . tedious, I have to admit." He smiled around the room, his eyes landing on Skye's only for the span of a blink.

"Mr. Calhoun didn't try to pull the wool over your eyes again, did he?" Mom said as though she spent her nights and weekends handling the finances of Southwest Virginia's elite.

Theo laughed.

Skye's mother laughed back, then went into the nearby kitchen.

"I'll be glad to get my weekends back, I'll say that much. It looks like I've missed quite a bit. How are you holding up, Mr. Fuller?"

"As I told Maggie a hundred times, I'm *fine*. Just a bit of bruising." He grunted as Skye's mother returned and dropped an ice pack onto his shoulder. "You needn't have come all this way on account of me."

Skye felt the old unease rising in her stomach as she watched her injured father try to wave away the ice pack and struggle to stand. Her chest tightened as she watched his eyes rove every crook and cranny of their small living room, checking for anything amiss, things Theo might notice. He pushed several magazines into a neat stack, moved the can of beer onto the coaster beside it. It was behavior her father rarely displayed, behavior she loathed almost as much as the casino coin in her back pocket.

He was ashamed. In his own home. The one Theo himself—charming as he may be—was responsible for.

How everyone in this house acted oblivious to this fact was the most infuriating thing of all. Or possibly worse: nobody in this house knew she knew the truth.

She was alone in her mother's kitchen last December, sore from neck to fingertips as she stirred the fifth batch of snickerdoodle cookies for her parents' church's annual Christmas banquet. The scent of hairspray wafted down the hall as her mother sprayed her curls in place. Her father was finishing up another long day at Evergreen Farm, loading some of the last trees onto cars for the season. The dough was giving Skye such fits that the old wooden spoon cracked clean in half. As she looked for a replacement, she almost didn't open that last drawer—what would traditionally be called the junk drawer in other homes but was too immaculate for such a slur. And yet on impulse, she did. But instead of a stirrer, the item that caught her eye, folded neatly beside scissors and tape and sewing needle, was an open piece of mail with the letterhead of Evergreen Farm—glinting just like that coin in her pocket—and a statement of her father's yearly salary typed neatly in the body of the letter. The low number was jaw dropping.

At the bottom of the cover letter was Theo's signature.

She packed up her bags in Washington and moved back to Virginia the following week.

Be calm, Skye. Be cool.

"Have a seat, Theo," her father said. "Let me get you a drink—" He let go of his arm and made to push aside a couple couch throw pillows, then groaned as he gritted his teeth and doubled up his grip on his elbow.

"Sit down, Dad." Skye moved around the coffee table and lowered him to the couch before he could protest. The firmness in her own voice must've startled him enough to obey. She sat on the edge of the coffee table, eye level. "That's it. You're going to the hospital. Now."

"I'm fine—"

"You're not fine. You're clearly not fine and if it's broken you'll need a cast, maybe even surgery—"

"Oh, and I'm sure you would've thought my knee needed surgery fifteen years ago, too, but look at 'er now."

Skye squeezed her eyes shut as he slapped his knee, the same knee with the torn ACL that slid out on occasion and caused him to fall and roll on the ground like an NFL player with—well, a torn ACL. "All it needs every now and again is a little tune-up—"

"Rubbing Vaseline on your knee every six months isn't a tune-up, Dad. If I had a word to express how *unhelpful* that is—"

"*Inutile* would serve well, I believe," her mother chimed in as she passed them, handing Theo a cup of lemonade, then moving toward the closet.

"You bet your bottom dollar it isn't helpful," her dad said, giving it another slap. "In fact," he said, struggling once more to rise, "I think I'll give it a little tune-up right now . . ."

Skye felt the groan growing within her, threatening to erupt any moment. She clenched fists and teeth as her body tightened. She was going to have to do it. She was going to have to haul this man over her shoulders, throw him into the truck, and drive him down the mountain. Or worse, call an ambulance.

"Mr. Fuller, did you get a chance to pick up that Lowe's order I requested?"

The crackling in the room faded.

Skye and her father peered at Theo.

Her father frowned. "What Lowe's order?"

"Oh, you know. The one for the lumber for the new tree shed. I believe I called it in last week."

"Last week?" Her father's frown turned urgent. "You made an order at Lowe's last week? Well, I didn't—they've had it a *week*?" He started reaching behind him, feeling for the "going out" jacket so often laid on the back side of the recliner.

Theo, cool as a cucumber as he sipped the lemonade, watched Mr. Fuller rise from his chair. "Well, if you haven't gotten to it, I could run down myself—"

"Maggie!" he called, stretching his neck toward the kitchen.

"Right here, dear," Skye's mother said, standing at the front door, raincoat on and a duffel bag over one shoulder. She held open a second raincoat for Skye's father. "Skye, I've switched over the laundry, moved the Crock-Pot into the fridge, packed an overnight bag, and made some sandwiches for the ride. Can you be sure to lock up after we leave? Theo, do you mind assisting Ralph to the car? It's slick out there."

He nodded. "Certainly."

They passed a smile to each other as she turned toward the door after her husband. Skye could practically see the high-fives they were making with their eyes. Lowe's was all the way down in Abingdon, quite conveniently all but next door to the hospital. All her mother had to do at this point was stop at the hospital and throw the passenger door open beneath the emergency-room sign while hospital staff handled the rest.

"Oh, and Theo?" Her mother turned as if a thought just occurred to her.

"Yes, Mrs. Fuller?"

"The seedlings came in today and a heat wave is expected next week. Those seedlings, as I'm sure you're aware, will need to get in the ground immediately."

Theo looked slightly startled. "Oh. Yes. Of course."

"And the tractor will need to be seen to."

Theo's uncertainty deepened. "Oh, sure. Right."

She flapped her hand. "But I'm sure you can handle an up-turned tractor."

Theo swallowed.

Skye's mother let the silence linger, her smile making a panoramic move around the room until it landed on her daughter. "Although even the hardiest of farmers would no doubt appreciate a second pair of hands for the job."

Skye's eyes narrowed.

Do not say it. You do not have to say it.

You are a grown woman who is perfectly capable of not saying it.

"I'll help." Skye shut her traitorous mouth the second the words flew from her lips.

Her mother gave a short nod, as though she was the conductor of this little play and her flautist performed the solo right on cue. "Terrific. Now that it's settled, Theo, I went ahead and turned up the heat in the cabin and slipped an egg casserole in the fridge for you in the morning. Let's be off, then, shall we?"

Theo's startled gaze turned from her mother to Skye, and Skye did her best to avoid his eyes.

If Skye wasn't so peeved at the turn of events, she would've laughed.

Instead she followed her parents and Theo outside and stood on the gravel driveway, watching her parents' truck swing onto the road and the taillights fade until they disappeared. Her all-consuming thought was that she was exactly in the one place she had told herself she never wanted to be.

Alone. On a mountaintop. Beside the man who broke her heart fourteen years ago.

Chapter 3

Theo

She was exactly as he remembered.

Her hair was shorter now, the thick auburn waves curling around her chin instead of trailing long past her shoulders. The loose sweater ornamented her natural attributes; the olive color offset her brown irises. She used less eyeliner now, but the subtle black line framing her almond-shaped eyes highlighted her best feature in a more refined way than it had in those days of oversized plaid shirts and ripped jeans. She looked . . . positively radiant.

Skye stood in the driveway watching the road, both hands tucked in the back pockets of her slim jeans. That stance. Another thing that hadn't changed about her.

The full moon and a thousand stars hung directly over-head. A few were blocked by the occasional cloud, but the sky was free of light pollution and the air was thick with dew from the rainfall. Theo inhaled, feeling as though his lungs were being purified. The gurgling creek on the other side of the road was the only sound for miles. Nothing but forest lay behind them. The single road in front of them took the occasional traveler up and down the mountain on either side, and to Evergreen Farm ahead.

Where rows and rows of Fraser firs and white pines glinted in the moonlight.

A rush of wings overhead caused Theo to wonder if the pounding in his chest was so loud it had caused the bird to flee.

He took a step forward. "Skye."

Skye dropped her head and turned. Smiled, but it looked forced. As though he was blocking her way. As though she had been trapped and now she had no choice but to converse. "So. Exploiting a man's weakness for his own good. Nice play. Tell me, are you actually planning on building a new shed?"

Theo smiled slightly as he kicked at a piece of gravel. "We are now."

Everyone knew Mr. Fuller was one of the most hardworking men around, but he had a classic weakness: he always worked alone. This worked splendidly as he single-handedly managed "his farm" throughout the year, but during the Christmas season, the very presence of part-time staff—with their jingle-bell hats and ho-ho-ho attitudes—was enough to give him hives. Theo couldn't count the number of complaints he got each year about the "cranky old man getting in the way" while the staff tried to sell trees and hot chocolate. At this point, the complaints were practically a Christmas tradition.

A genuine smile drifted like a whisper across her face, then a cloud seemed to cover her again. She started moving toward the trailer.

Theo slipped both hands into his own pants pockets. He waited for several seconds as the creek filled the silence and the distance between them grew. But his question grew, too, with every second that passed. "So . . . I can't help noticing it's not a holiday and, unless I'm mistaken, there's no memorable occasion going on at the moment. What brings you back to Virginia?"

Skye paused, her hand on the door handle.

For the first time that evening Skye's eyes brightened as she looked back at him, and she tipped her head toward the dilapidated stone cottage bordering the farm across the road. The old, abandoned shack held quite a few of their childhood memories—

Theo frowned.

The house was covered in shadows by the overhanging trees, but as Theo squinted he made out the simple frame of the cottage. And the bulky object parked beside it.

Theo squinted even more and the compact form of a Prius evolved. "Is that . . . a car?"

"It's my car."

"You? But why"—he ignored the growing pressure in his chest, the sense of something about to unfold he wasn't quite prepared for—"are you parked there?"

"Why? The only reason why. Because I live there."

Theo whipped around from the house to her. He took a step toward her. Then back toward the house. "You *live* there? *Here*? In *that*?"

Skye's smile slipped from her face as she tugged the door open. "Yeah, well, I know it's not as *grandiose* as the cabin you have up there—"

Her eyes darted to the Evergreen Farm sign swinging oh so slightly above the long gravel driveway where, at the end, the Watkins family cabin nestled in a stand of pines.

He'd offended her. But honestly, how she could have been offended was unfathomable. The old cottage was at least a hundred years old; it had been uninhabited for more than fifty. There was a reason they'd snuck in there for wild adventures as kids: it was deserted, every window was either cracked or shattered, and half the floor was missing.

But then something else startled him as he pulled his gaze away from the house.

She had moved back. Here. To Whitetop.

Skye was *back*.

The realization hit him like a tidal wave.

"How long have you been here?"

"Twelve weeks," Skye said, reaching inside and flicking off the light switch. The living room blackened, leaving only the porch light above her head to illuminate them.

The door creaked as it shut, and she turned the lock with her key.

"Well, thank you for coming," Skye said in a perfunctory way, hopping down the stairs instead of stopping to look him in the eyes. She spoke like she was passing a mailman on the way to the mailbox. "I've gotta get some things sorted out if I'm going to spend the next week running the farm."

"You mean helping me run the farm."

Her foot hovered over the bottom step. For a long moment she was silent, her silhouette tipped downward as she stared at the mud-slopped grass. Then, with a determined jerk of her head, she looked up. "Look. I appreciate you"—she seemed momentarily stuck as she waved her arms around—"coming out here to check on Dad . . . but . . . I think we can go ahead and give up this illusion about you running the farm. We both know this is about as far out of your arena as humanly possible, and anyway . . . I'm sure you have plenty of . . ."—she indicated his coat, again seeming to search for words—"duties of some sort to handle with your life in Abingdon, so I'm going to make it easy on you. I know how to handle a tractor. I know how to put the seedlings in. Frankly, this will all be easier if I handle it myself. Consider yourself off the hook."

Theo stood rooted. He heard everything she had said, but the words and sentiments flew by faster than he could snatch them. He wanted to speak, felt the need to speak, but also felt the sneaking suspicion that if he didn't choose each of his words wisely, he'd miss an opportunity he couldn't identify. Frankly, he needed to get alone and think.

After several seconds ticked by, she jutted a thumb behind her. "Well, my shack is calling. I'd better run. Good night, Theo."

Theo nodded, which she seemed to take as release from the conversation, and began walking down the driveway and across the road.

He watched her figure slowly disappear beneath the overhanging trees as she stepped onto the small bridge leading to her—most unbelievably enough—new home.

A single car and its beaming headlights momentarily lit up the road between them on its trek up the mountain.

There was so much to process.

Skye had returned. Half a lifetime had passed since their last conversation. They had no doubt changed since their last meeting. He was in a steady relationship with a woman who brought more life and joy to his days than he'd experienced in years.

It was clear Skye wanted him to stay out of her life.

But at the bottom of all the mess and complication was one thing Theo realized the moment she opened that door. One thing he could not deny when he saw her face after all these years.

She was the one person in the world he had never, ever, stopped wanting to see.

Chapter 4

Skye

She was halfway across the short bridge over the creek before she took a breath.

So she'd been a little hard on him.

No, Skye. That's the lie you're supposed to feel. Keep your grip.

She knew better. If her parents wouldn't admit it, accept it, and deal with it, she would. This was why she came back. To fix it.

And by *it* she meant her parents' undeniable life situation.

Proof one: the slowly dilapidating double-wide behind her. There was no denying that for all his flaws, her father was one of the hardest working, loyal men in all of Whitetop, perhaps the state. He'd watched over Evergreen Farm for the past thirty years as though he owned it. He treated the land and business with such respect, frankly, he *should've* owned it. Heaven knew he was the only one who kept the farm alive and well all these years. Whereas the Watkinses liked to "play country" and roll up on the occasional weekend in their flawless, spun-by-Norwegian-mountaintop-villager-where-bells-chime-across-the-town-announcing-every-vegan-sweater-finished outfit to make s'mores over their granite-top fire pit, her father was out there in blizzards or heat waves, rain or shine, keeping that farm going. Getting it done. The Watkinses owed the success of Evergreen Farm entirely to Ralph Fuller.

And yet a sixteen-year-old babysitter would be offended if offered the salary rate she'd seen on that piece of stationery.

Signed by Theo himself.

Theo was the Fullers' employer, and despite all the fond memories of Skye's childhood, despite his undeniable charm and the care for her family he *appeared* to show, her parents needed to grasp the truth: *he* was the reason they lived this way. *He*, with his luxury cars and tailored suits, who for several years now had been capable of providing a living wage but didn't.

Forget the grievances of two decades ago.

That experience may have pained her enough to run away to Seattle, but this? This was a whole new brand of infuriating.

He could try to fill the gaps with platitudes, but since he didn't back them up with action, they were only empty words.

In the meantime, she had a farm to run.

She stepped into her yard, and the honeysuckle bushes overtook the scent of Theo's cologne. Following the cobblestone path, she slipped the key out of her pocket, then moved onto her slate porch step.

"Skye, wait."

Skye pressed her lips together.

Forced herself to turn.

Theo stood at the head of the path, surrounded by heady earth and dimpled leaves collecting teaspoons of mist, alien to her world in his pressed tie and the beige overcoat swaying lightly at his calves. If he thought he could possibly handle her world . . .

"Do you think the old path is still there?"

"What?" She followed his nod toward the swath of trees between the back of her cottage and Evergreen Farm. Beyond it, at least half a mile away, stood the dark silhouette of the Watkinses' cabin backing up to the foot of the ridge. She didn't want to say it. Right now, she didn't want to remember the memories they'd had. But the silence grew.

"It's been a long time," she said at last. "I doubt it."

He started loosening his tie. "I'll give it a shot anyways."

She blinked. "You're . . . going to give it a shot. Walking into those woods. At night."

A smile played on his lips as the tie uncurled and slipped off his neck. "At night," he repeated.

A few seconds passed as Skye tried to hold her firm expression in place. She would *not* bite. She would *not* take the bait.

In fact, she would walk into her cottage right then. Say *Suit yourself* and shut the door.

But even as she edged toward the door, she couldn't help watching him stride over and stop at the perimeter of the woods. Her frown turned to a squint as he began stretching one arm over the other.

She suppressed the bucking smile trying to escape as he began doing squats.

After he started taking what appeared to be practice steps

into the black woods, only to step back in search of another entry point, she couldn't help calling out, "Theo, what are you *doing*? The last time you attempted to walk through those woods in the *daylight* it took you two hours."

A stick tapped his ankle and he jumped back a solid three feet into the safety of her yard.

She rolled her eyes.

"I recall," he said.

"You came out the other side all but *naked*—"

"The memory haunts me."

"—covered in mud and leaves like a thirteen-year-old girl covers herself in glitter—"

"I had no choice but to camouflage myself."

"Theo." She leveled her gaze at him. "You came out carrying a whittled stick like you were fighting for your life in *Lord of the Flies*." Her sweater fell off one shoulder and she tugged it up before pointing at the woods. "I don't know what you're trying to prove right now. And I don't know all the ways you've changed, but I do know there is *no way* you are going to walk through those woods in the pitch-black dark. So why don't you just go on home?"

"In my defense," Theo said, turning to face her properly, "the bear was *hunting*. In the woods. For me."

She threw a hand out. "For the millionth time, it was a bear. A tiny, adolescent *black bear*—"

"A rabid beast cloaked in deceivably adorable fur," he replied.

"Well, maybe if you'd listened to me and hadn't doused yourself in that ridiculous fruity concoction you liked to call cologne—seriously?" Skye put her hands on her hips as he began rubbing dirt over his glinting cufflinks. "Why are you doing this?"

"Simple," Theo said. "It's been months since I've been back, and I would be remiss if I didn't take the opportunity to enjoy the spoils of a fine evening like tonight—"

As if on cue, a thick raindrop landed squarely on Skye's head. She looked up to see one of those little ominous clouds anchoring above their heads. "It's raining."

"It's *misting*," Theo replied, holding his palm upturned toward the sky with a smile. "'As dew leaves the cobweb lightly threaded with stars'—"

"Aaand there he is," Skye said, turning on her heel. She raised a hand over her head as she walked toward her door. "Well, you enjoy that good old-fashioned poetry walk. Let me guess. Your favorite little guy, Sterling?"

"Teasdale," he replied, clearly suppressing a smile at the fact she so easily remembered his most annoying high school habit of reciting poetry at every leaf and stump like some afflicted peasant of the 1500s. "'Dew.'"

"I'll see you around."

"Bright and early," Theo called back, turning the flashlight on his phone toward the forest.

Skye felt the grinding of wheels in her stomach but forced herself to ignore them.

"Wait a moment. What is this? This is new."

Skye turned. The beam of Theo's phone flashlight fell upon a building twenty yards off and moved slowly up and down its glass walls.

Strips of moonlight passed through the overhanging trees and glinted off the new windows. A dozen hanging flower baskets cluttered the awning. A couple of old easels stood propped against one wall.

He took a step toward it. His eyes lingered on empty paint bottles on their sides by the door.

Protectively, Skye took a step toward it. "It's my greenhouse. And . . . studio."

His eyes lit up at the word. "May I see?"

For only a moment, Skye wavered.

She looked at him standing there with both hands in his trouser pockets as he gazed at the greenhouse. His skin nearly melted into the dark forest behind him. He was only a sliver of a silhouette as he took in her new and greatest treasure, his expression clear. He wanted to see it. Part of her, the old part of her, wanted to show it off to him.

She turned away. "I'll see you tomorrow."

Before Skye closed the door, she watched his shadowy figure move into the forest with the small beam of light guiding the way.

She wouldn't let him get to her. He could try to cozy up all he wanted, reminisce about old times, but she wasn't going to forget—not what happened then. Not what was happening now.

But as the flashlight blinked and flashed as it moved deeper into the forest, she couldn't help calling out, "Oh, and watch out for the brown recluses! There was just an infestation of them at the greenhouse."

The flashlight's beam shook and sputtered toward the sky just as Skye grinned and shut the door.

Chapter 5

Theo

*T*here were a hundred things to do. But first, a shower.

Theo all but tore off his clothes as he entered the code into the cabin's security system and entered the two-story foyer. He slid out of his shoes and his jacket as he moved up the stairs. As he entered the hallway he unbuttoned his top collar. The house was still on the cold side, the thermostat showing a slowly rising fifty-four degrees. Honestly, *how* had Skye's mother known he was going to stay, and *when* in those twelve minutes he was at their house had she snuck away to turn on the heat? He went directly to the master bedroom.

Must. Get. Into. Shower. Immediately.

Theo dropped his dirt-encrusted cufflinks onto the porcelain trivet and flicked on the bathroom light. His feet were cold as he stepped onto the tile, but chilled feet were the last thing on his mind at the present moment. No, the most pressing matter was the spiderwebs. The dozens of spiderwebs he had encountered as he trod through Skye's forested backyard to get here.

All for the sake of a conversation.

A tickle crept along his neck and he slapped at it before turning the shower knob.

So, he still had a little problem with spiders.

Any sane person aware of the three thousand species of spiders in the United States, most particularly the two *fatal* ones local to the area, would have a problem with spiders. He hastily worked the buttons on his shirt, and with increasingly concerning tickles covering at least five areas on his chest and back, he gave in and finally yanked it off. The two remaining fastened buttons made a distinct *snap*. They *pinged* as they bounced and then scattered across the tile floor.

He was *not* arachnophobic.

Everybody else in the world was just, in his mind, absolutely insane.

He stepped into the still-icy shower, well aware of all he'd been called since he was a child. Everything from a simple "scaredy-cat" and "chicken" to the diagnosis at one point given by the child psychologist: "entomophobic."

But what befuddled him was that there was no name for those who *voluntarily* put their lives on the line by making sleeping outside a *sport*. Boy Scouts. Campers. Those absolutely out-of-their-minds hikers who walked through the town every year with their fiddles and tin cans in their six-month-long, 2,200-mile trek of the Appalachian Trail.

Insane.

Who would *choose* to cocoon themselves into sleeping bags like saucy enchiladas for every Lyme disease–bearing tick, leg-amputating brown recluse, rattlesnake, mountain lion, bear, or serial-killing maniac to discover?

Somebody needed to write *that* condition in the book of psychological disorders.

In truth, Skye had been right to question him when he volunteered to help out over the next few days. She was right to doubt his interest in turning tractors and clearing land and planting seedlings in a minefield of undesirable experiences. But she wasn't right to doubt his interest in turning tractors and clearing land and planting seedlings *with her*. When you find yourself suddenly face-to-face with your life's greatest regret, you don't walk away. Even with the threat of spiders.

So yes, in a moment of bravado, he walked through those woods and hiked between rows of firs beneath a dewdrop sky.

Yes, he had regretted every moment since the first blind *slap* of the spiderweb hit his face.

Yes, every square inch of his body had begun to itch by the time he emerged from the woods.

Yes, he was very aware that after he dressed he was going to have to walk the length of the farm again, this time via the safe, wide berth of the long gravel driveway, to pick up his car from the Fullers' driveway and make the forty-five-minute drive to Abingdon for some belongings.

But in exchange for real conversation, he had cracked Skye's concrete demeanor with the topic of his own weakness. Was it worth it?

Absolutely.

Whatever it took.

Theo's headlights followed the zigzagging road that clung to the side of Whitetop Mountain. The second he hit the halfway spot down the mountain and was back in service, his phone started beeping with notifications. Glancing at the screen, Theo caught one name repeated several times. He wasn't surprised.

He took a breath, then pressed the Bluetooth button on his steering wheel. "Call Ashleigh."

The phone made it through one full ring before she picked up. "Theo. I'm sorry—I know it's late. You just had to leave so quickly—"

"No, I'm the one who needs to apologize. Believe me, that's not customary for me. I've never walked out in the middle of a date."

"Well, I've never had anyone walk out on me in the middle of a date, so we're even."

Theo heard the shy smile in her tone and felt the corners of his lips turn up.

But then he remembered where he was, and where he was about to return.

His headlights shone on another deep turn in the road, and Theo turned the wheel. "I would've called back sooner but I just got down the mountain enough to get service."

"You're still up there? With your employee?" The surprise in Ashleigh's voice was understandable, but Theo frowned slightly at the almost imperceptible tone of disapproval. But then, when he'd explained the situation as he broke off their date and dashed out the door, the barrage of questions revealed she hadn't quite understood then either. *"You're driving up to Whitetop to visit someone who takes care of the farm? At his home? Tonight? Now?"*

"I was. It's going to take longer than expected to deal with the situation up here. I need to gather some supplies back in town before heading back."

"You're staying?" This time the disapproval was clear as crystal. "*Why?*"

He recalled the image of Skye in her slouchy sweater opening the door. The millisecond of shock in her deep brown eyes. The emotions that swirled in her irises the moment before she blinked and the concrete mask dropped into place. He saw no hate or bitterness. Neither did he see blankness, as though she had removed him from her life and forgotten him.

Quite the opposite.

The look—a momentary, millisecond look—suggested she had seen someone she cared for in the deepest, most secret parts of her soul.

If he was wrong, if he had only seen the reflection of his own desire in her shining eyes, then, well, it didn't change a thing.

"Theo? You still—there?"

"Sorry," Theo said, "I'm about to hit another dead spot."

"Why are you going to stay at the Christmas tree farm?" The threat of a lost connection heightened her urgency.

He knew his answer.

But here, now, with the voice of the woman who'd been a constant source of companionship these past few weeks filling the car, he found himself pushing the brakes on the words that had formed in his head. Felt himself turning in another direction to answer her question in another true, if indirect, way.

Theo grinned. "Why, to return to my heritage. To be a farmer," he said, just as the line went dead.

Chapter 6

Skye

Someone was on her porch.

It was six fifteen in the morning, and someone was on her porch.

The sky was only just starting to break through the linen curtains over her window when she wrapped her robe around her and followed the sound of the creaking porch swing to her front door. When she opened it, there was Theo, clad in what appeared to be knockoff Carhartt pants, still crisply creased in that hadn't-been-washed-yet way, holding two cups of steaming coffee. He wore an ill-fitting orange flannel as his shirt of choice, the crisscrossing plaid of blue and orange so bright it would no doubt glow in the dark.

He was just breaking off a sip of his coffee, looking toward the creek with one ankle resting on the other knee, when he heard the sound of the door opening.

Seeing her figure in the doorway, he dropped his boot to the ground. The porch swing creaked. "I realized last night we never set a time."

"Honestly, I'm surprised you made it out of the woods alive." Skye's voice was hoarse, making her wonder what shape the rest of her was in at that precise moment. She wrapped her robe around her tighter. "But good grief, Theo, I would've gone up and gotten you."

"Would you have?" A somewhat challenging smile lifted the corner of his mouth. He returned his gaze to the babbling brook. "Anyway, I don't mind the wait. It's nice sitting out here. I have my coffee. I made you some if you'd like it. Very peaceful." But even as he spoke the last word, a branch snapped in the distance, and she could see his neck tense.

Her eyes almost missed the black sedan sitting in the grass beside her Prius.

"C'mon in," Skye said, opening the door wide as she moved into the living room. "We don't want you to get mauled by the blood-hungry bears following the scent of your organic Peruvian-roasted coffee beans."

Theo followed her without further prompting.

"I see you brought the car today. Didn't feel like a poetic stroll this morning?"

He laid one hand casually along the mantel. "Oh, I got a refreshing stroll in much earlier. Went through the woods a good two or three more times. Communed with the bears."

"Yeah?" Skye said, taking the second cup from his hand. She raised a brow at the mantel. "There's a spider crawling toward your hand."

She smiled as he snatched his hand up so quickly the daddy

longlegs skittered in the opposite direction. "I'll be a few minutes."

Though she acted cool and collected, she found the coffee cup tremoring slightly as she shut the bathroom door. But then, in three minutes she'd gone from a dead sleep to drinking coffee with the ghost of her past. Her heart hadn't adjusted quite yet.

"I can hardly believe it," Theo called from the living room. "This house is unrecognizable."

"Believe it," Skye called back, her heartbeat slowing enough to allow her to take a sip of coffee and turn on the water. "This renovation took me every bit of the past three months."

"*You* did all this yourself?"

The question was both infuriating and complimentary. It was the same fiery comment of his last night that made her want to dunk his head in the creek. She splashed some water on her face and called through the door, "*You* don't think I could?"

"Given how it was before, I didn't think anyone could, not single-handedly."

Her annoyance eased as she splashed her face a second time.

The floorboards creaked as Theo moved from room to room.

Skye rubbed face wash into her cheeks.

It had taken quite some time, but she'd determined last night how to handle him—more specifically, how to handle herself around him. She was not going to be rude. She didn't *hate* Theo. Well, when she'd watched her mother at Food City scraping pennies at checkout last weekend, hate had crossed her mind. But she was not going to let hate lie there useless. No, what she was going to do was use that particular experience to fuel her behavior over the next few days.

There was nothing to gain by acting furious at Theo, and there was potentially everything to gain by treating him exactly like he wanted: as an old friend. So she would do that. She would remember the good ol' days. For the sake of her father she would help Theo, because left to his own devices, he'd plant the seedlings sideways and drive the tractor into the creek. And when the opportunity came, she would act like the mature adult she was and communicate with him about her dad's pay. Not overtly, of course, but in a subtle way, so that when the time was right, she would bring up a point that would make him pause and rethink the course of his actions. That would make him realize how unjust he was being.

How had the mother said it in *My Big Fat Greek Wedding*? She would let him think he was the head of his own decisions, but all the while she would be the neck that turned his head in any direction she wanted.

This wasn't going to be about what happened fourteen years ago. This wasn't going to be about *them*. It was just going to be about ensuring her parents got what they deserved.

Honestly, this was a golden opportunity.

All she had to do was avoid hating the parts she hated about him, appreciate the parts she had at one time truly appreciated about him, and to be sure, above all, not to let her heart get in the way.

"How's your dad doing?" Theo called.

She cracked the door open an inch and peeked at the man standing in her dining room. Running his fingers down the length of the dining room table, one hand resting in his pants pocket. The same jawline. The same broad, if not broader, shoulders filling out his shirt.

He had taken the best features of his youth and improved on them.

Frankly, it was irritating to see.

Skye closed the door and rummaged through her makeup bag for something to cover up the dark circles beneath her eyes. "Broken collarbone and some bumps and bruises all around," she called back.

"Will he need surgery?"

"They don't think so. He's just going to have to take it easy awhile."

"I'm sure that's killing him."

Skye opened the foundation case. "Mom caught him trying to sneak out to the tractor at 3:00 a.m. You have no idea."

A few moments went by in silence.

"You don't keep any paintings for yourself?" Theo called.

Skye stilled. She'd been an artist for twelve years. For the last six she'd done well enough that it supplied her whole income, but still, his words surprised her. A small secret revealed: he kept up with her life. Even though she hadn't been around, he knew about her art. Did he *want* to know? Did he seek out information about her, keep tabs on her all these years?

Skye shook her head. Of course her parents would mention her life from time to time. Of course it would come up on occasion.

"I can't stand it actually. I just have the itch to take them down and keep working on them." Skye clicked the foundation case shut as she thought she heard him murmur, "How unfortunate."

"Come again?" she said, raising her voice as she leaned against the sink toward the mirror and pulled out the mascara wand.

"Do you feel the same when you see your own work around town?"

"Like where? I've never had a chance to find out."

"Surely the Martha would. You're a local fine artist. You're a newly returned regional treasure."

Skye laughed. It was a childhood dream of hers to be featured at the Martha Washington Inn one day, but the dream held no value now. She was better known on the West Coast—and pleasant enough, in a few regions of English-speaking Europe—than here. "The Martha doesn't know my name from Adam. No, I dropped that dream a decade ago."

"This kitchen is stunning," Theo called, his voice more distant. "I never would've imagined these bold colors would work so well together, and yet—" His voice ticked up a notch with renewed admiration. "Where did you find this island?"

She smiled as she ran the mascara brush through her lashes. Of course he thought it was stunning. Her own father had walked through the house, grunted, and said, "An orange kitchen. Never seen one o' those before," before focusing on the more pressing point—why was there no TV? But no, this was Theo. "It's a dresser I found at a yard sale," Skye said, moving on to the other eye. "I just did a little rehab on it and—"

"And put butcher block on top. So clever," Theo said. "You could go into business as a designer."

She imagined him running his fingers over the butcher

block of her deep-teal dresser island, analyzing, processing. In fact, she would bet anyone a hundred dollars he was actually doing that right at that moment.

"Are you touching my butcher block?" Skye called out.

There was a guilty pause. "Did you not want me to?"

Skye smiled to herself as she dropped the mascara into the bag and gave one last look in the mirror. Well, she was no anti-aging Theo, but her brown eyes looked larger and rounder now, and the blue-tinted bags beneath them were concealed. Her cheeks carried a subtle pink pop, and with a few brushes through yesterday's untamed curls, she looked as presentable as she was going to get next to Idris Elba out there. Two minutes and a paint-clad pair of pants, sweatshirt, and pony-tail later, she was slipping into her work boots at the back door. Meanwhile Theo stood at the copper farmhouse sink, looking like a kid in a candy store.

"Want a banana or something before we go?" Skye said, ripping off one for herself from the bunch on the counter.

Theo gave a startled turn. "I ate some of that casserole your mother somehow providentially baked and managed to drop off at the cabin during the ten-minute span we were all together."

"Ah. She is a crafty one, isn't she?" Skye replied. "And let me guess. You managed all this—the 5:00 a.m. poetic stroll, the slow-morning breakfast—just after your morning workout?"

Theo's brow lifted. "There's a Peloton at the cabin, and yes, I did so happen to make use of it for a few minutes. How did you know?"

"Well for one thing, you are the one person on earth who has actually improved with age." She put up a hand as his brows rose. "Don't take it personally. It's a fact, and I'm trying not to hate you for it. And second, you are the most meticulous, self-disciplined person I know." Skye waited for him to pass and then shut the door behind her. "I once left you unattended in Dad's toolshed and came back to find you'd reorganized the whole thing alphabetically."

"So? I like organization. Everybody likes organization."

"Yeah, well, we were six," Skye replied. "Anyway, I imagine that level of neurosis as an adult equates to having one of those commercial rotating racks of color-coded ties in your smudge-free, floor-to-ceiling mirrored closets and jogging religiously every morning before dawn. Am I right?"

As she moved to turn the lock, he shifted his back against the railing, their bodies suddenly compact on the back porch covered in empty pots facing the greenhouse and woods beyond.

"So, you think I've improved with age, eh?"

She pressed her lips together as she dropped the key into her pocket. "I also called you neurotic in the same breath. But sure, if that's what you want to focus on . . ."

Theo's eyes were bright. "It's the orange flannel, isn't it?" He tugged on the cuffs, which were about three inches too short.

"Yeah. Speaking of," Skye said, hopping down the steps, "you really went a bit overboard with that good ol' country boy outfit."

"Forgive me," he said, following. "I wasn't exactly brimming with options at ten o'clock at night."

She stopped and turned to face him. Put up a finger. "Wait a minute. You honestly drove all the way down the mountain last night to enter a store two hours shy of midnight? To buy that? You honestly don't own a single pair of pants that can get dirty?"

Theo rubbed the back of his neck.

When it was clear that his nonanswer would be his final answer, she laughed and turned toward her car. "Seriously. You haven't changed at all."

Both her breath and foot caught on the last word.

With effort, she planted her boot and kept walking.

She was losing herself so quickly, forgetting valid resentments in favor of childhood memories. Sure, he hadn't changed at all. She was right to have said he hadn't changed at all. Because he hadn't. He was just like he was fourteen years ago.

Her eyes flitted over to the tallest Fraser fir in the center of the field. She'd given her heart to him then, on that blanket beneath that tree and a midnight sky. They'd whispered their first pronouncements of love to each other—not like the thousands of times they'd said it before, like the burst of a laugh before you take another's hand and hop the creek, like friends. No, they'd peeled off the bravado that night, slowly, in layers, until they were looking into each other's eyes and saying it with all the sincerity they could pour from their lungs. Bare before each other. Vulnerable. She had, for once, let herself be vulnerable.

And then he left for UVA.

The calls came every day that first year.

Then every other day the fall semester of the second.

Then every weekend.

Until one day, one brisk January day of his junior year, he held her hand once again as they walked along that long driveway, the wind nipping at their feet and flurries swirling between trees, and she was just beginning to breathe again as he poured out all the fantastical stories of college memories and friends. She listened while quietly stacking away the insecurities and fears that had built up over the months, squeezing his hand until there was no space between their fingers at all. Months of tension in her shoulders and the consequential headaches started to ease.

And then, the growling of the gravel driveway. Both of their heads turning in surprise.

The white BMW packed with girls, halfway up the road, suddenly skidded to a stop.

The music poured out of the car as one girl, with rippling blonde curls, stepped out of the car to face the sweetheart of a boy she had driven so far to surprise. The wind stripped her neck of the white scarf she was just wrapping around herself and sent it flying, yet no one moved.

So Skye would remember that Theo hadn't changed. After what she had seen of her father's salary, she was certain of it. He was charming and said all the right things. He had an aptitude for appearing so loyal you'd trust him with your life, but when push came to shove, where was he?

He was Theodore Watkins III. Savvy financial adviser whom clients entrusted with all their money. Beloved employer whom employees slaved away for on a dime. Light of her childhood, best friend of her youth, man who collected hearts.

She needed to remember what was true. That he hadn't changed.

She grinned suddenly, making for the Prius as she pulled out her phone and began tapping. She knew just the way to remind herself.

Chapter 7

Theo

The air shifted and he had no idea what he'd said to cause it.

One moment they were reminiscing and laughing; the next she was jabbing the car keys with her thumb and telling him quietly to get in.

He didn't get it.

She even noted that he had aged well. Sure, she said it like the fact was a nail in her shoe, but still, the words were there. He'd heard them.

But then suddenly she was pivoting on her heel, furiously tapping out a text on her phone and charging toward the Prius with fresh determination.

Whatever was going on, this was a classic Skye move.

For all Skye's gifts, communication was not one of them. Not when it came to something serious. Fun things, funny things, what to eat for dinner, or whether she liked your present—Skye could give you a thousand reasons for her honest opinion.

But the raw things? The real things? The matters hidden deep within the heart? Well, you'd have better luck recovering gold from the 1715 Treasure Fleet in the middle of a hurricane than getting her to admit you hurt her feelings.

He knew that fact all too well. She'd once moved as far as she could across the country for that very reason.

The Prius rumbled beneath them as Skye pulled the gearshift into reverse and the car started moving backward. Theo hesitated. "And . . . is there a reason we are using the Prius instead of walking to get to the tractor?"

"I thought you didn't like walking through the woods," Skye retorted, gazing intently into the rearview mirror.

"True, yes," Theo said, his knees knocking against the glove compartment. "But if I'm not mistaken, your gaze possesses a somewhat villainous flair, and your Prius doesn't have four-wheel drive. Wouldn't it be easier to walk?"

Skye squinted as she turned her head to the back window, moved one arm to hold on to the back of his headrest, and whipped the car around his Tesla.

"*Skye.*" He inhaled sharply as the side mirror of his own car came into view—more specifically, came into view an inch away from hers.

He threw his shock her way. "Did you pick up getaway-car driving skills while in Seattle?"

She knocked the gearshift into drive, and the gravel beneath them sputtered as her car swerved toward the road.

Theo clutched the seat with one hand and pointed with the other. "You can't be serious. There's a bridge."

Skye glanced over. "You're trying to hit an imaginary brake. My mother does that."

"Eyes on the *road*!" With one hand pressed against the roof and the other against the passenger window, he pushed himself off his seat. His head knocked against the ceiling. The ledge of the rickety wooden bridge was all but beneath her right tire as the wheels spun. The jagged rocks in the creek below peered up at him in the glow of dawn. He squeezed his eyes shut. "Your mother is the most commonsensical person in your family," he cried out. "Have you ever considered that she is right to question your driving skills?"

Theo felt the bump, then heard more spitting gravel, then felt his body collide into the passenger door as Skye swerved left onto the road. It took several seconds for him to lower back down into his seat and let go of the roof.

When he opened his eyes, Skye was grinning at him like a madwoman. "Good thing you were holding that roof up to protect us. Otherwise, we would've been goners for sure."

"Road!" he called, clenching his teeth as they approached one of the many, many swift turns.

Skye cackled. "Theo, how many times do you think I have driven down this mountain?"

"Don't try that on me," he replied through gritted teeth. His grip on the passenger door was nothing short of ironclad.

He couldn't be sure—he wasn't willing to risk looking away from the road—but he thought he sensed her shifting. A moment later, he felt the car slow.

His grip loosened reluctantly, his hand stiff and aching. He clenched and unclenched it before folding his hands together.

For several minutes, Theo watched the trees whip by out his window. "So," he said at last, "care to divulge where we are going?"

"Not at all." She was pleasantly upbeat as she turned the wheel around another switchback. "We're going to Luke's."

"Luke's?" It took a moment, but then the name rang a bell. "Ah. Luke's."

Skye raised a finger, clearly enjoying herself too much. "That's the one."

So that's what she was up to. The pieces were starting to come together.

At least now he knew the rules of this game. "I do recall meeting him that one time and receiving the rather unfortunate experience of a broken nose. Did you know that led to reconstructive surgery?"

"I did not," Skye said, not even bothering to hide her upbeat tone as she turned the wheel.

"Which led me to miss the Mediterranean trip that was a required piece of my spring course," Theo continued, "and as such, required that I find another class to fill its place." He turned to her. "Only every class was full at that point. But one."

He let the silence linger until she surrendered and turned her head his way.

"Which was?" she asked.

"*Basket weaving.*"

Skye barked a laugh. "I hope you got some great baskets out of it."

"Oh yes," Theo replied. "While my friends returned from Athens and spent the spring semester reading ancient Greek literature aloud while taste testing brizola, I sat in a circle with eighteen females under rather clangy wind chimes and labored over a basket that would end up looking like a deranged duck.

For the record, it was the only class at university in which I got a C."

Skye pressed her hand to her heart in the most unconvincing manner possible. "Oh, poor you. That must've been awful."

Theo swept an invisible thread off the bulky plaid sleeve. "Yes, well—"

"Really. That, of all things that could've possibly happened that semester, must've been *the worst*."

Theo exhaled. Took a moment to consider the timing of what he was about to say. He would've done things differently, waited until they had spent more time together, but because she was bringing it up . . .

"For what it's worth, I deserved it. After everything that happened—"

"And here we are," Skye interrupted, her cheeks pinking. She jerked the wheel into the parking lot.

So, Skye had simply wanted to poke the fire, blow and stir the ashes just enough to make the embers glow. It made sense. This would be their dance, he suspected: shuffling closer, then breaking from the heart of the matter again and again, more and more, until one moment, one unexpected moment, she was ready.

And for him? He had waited fourteen years. He could easily wait a little longer.

The car slid into the first available parking space beneath the gas station's sign: *Luke's*.

Skye popped her door open and Theo followed suit.

As for Luke, Theo had a theory. And it was time to test it. "I'm guessing Luke is still that same lovable, easygoing man I had the pleasure of meeting?"

On that fateful night fourteen years ago, Luke was 280 pounds of pure muscle who had a keen enjoyment of watching martial arts videos and practicing in his living room. He was part of Skye's long-running friend group and apparently had been waiting for a heroic opportunity to put his homegrown skills to use. Hence, after Theo had made that fateful mistake of running to Skye's friend's house to try to talk to her, the broken nose.

Skye's eyes twinkled as she grabbed hold of the front door. "You nailed it."

So there it was. Luke was Skye's attempt at a bit of revenge.

Theo grinned.

The doors jingled as they entered and slipped past rows of chips and chocolate bars, ATM machines, and quarter slots for M&M's. They walked toward the man behind the register. He was holding something up to a customer, and as the customer stepped aside, Theo saw all of him. The gas station's logo on the lime green T-shirt was stretched across his chest almost to the point of being unreadable. The chiseled jaw was gone, replaced with baby-face cheeks, victim of a recent sunburn. The bowl cut was gone, replaced with much fewer, tender-looking hairs. A single gust of wind could cause them to fly off like dandelions in spring. But the most startling change of all was his face.

His wide, positively buoyant face.

Luke caught their eyes and stretched out his arms. "Theo! You came just in time."

Chapter 8

Skye

If Skye's confusion grew any stronger, the contortions of her forehead would seal her eyes shut. As it was, she barely managed to follow Theo as he walked up to the register.

"Luke," Theo said, reaching across the glass and giving him a shoulder pat. "It's good to see you."

Luke beckoned to Skye. "Come see this. I need both of your opinions."

It took a few moments, but Skye forced herself to shuffle forward to form the strange triangle of people. Luke rested his elbows on the counter and leaned forward. He tapped the envelope as he spoke in hushed tones. "I have . . . in my hand . . . at this very moment . . . the secret to the baby's gender."

Well, it wasn't the super, ultrasecret, undercover plan to save the world, but it was still something.

Skye's eyes widened. "I thought Tracy didn't want to know."

Luke waggled his eyebrows. "She doesn't. Just got back

from the doctor yesterday. She had him write it on a piece of paper and seal it up so we could take it to Blackbird Bakery and get a cake made for the shower, you know, pink in the center if it's a girl, blue if it's a boy." (To his credit, Luke looked like he was about to burst out of his shirt with excitement.) "Anyway, she forgot she had a highlighting appointment for one of her clients, so she gave this to me and made me promise I wouldn't look." He looked at the envelope in his hand like it was a treasure map. His blue eyes shone like a baby's. "And I'm keeping my word." He pushed it in Skye's face. "Read it."

"No way." Skye threw up her hands and took a step back. "Your wife would kill me."

"C'mon," Luke urged, leaning farther over the counter to push the envelope her way. "Read it."

"Absolutely *not*," Skye said, moving behind a row of candy bars for good measure.

"Aw, c'mon, Skye, I can't read it myself. I made an oath."

"So you give it to everyone else who comes in here and try to figure it out by their reactions? Heck no. I've experienced the wrath of a pregnant woman. And that was over the one time I accidentally threw away her *yogurt*. Can you *imagine* what she'd do to you—to *me*—if she found out we knew the sex of her *baby*?"

Luke, who was looking more like the retired version of Mr. Incredible by the moment, put his fist on the counter and dropped his head. But a moment later, he was popping back up, smile back in place. "Theo. I know I can count on you."

Theo put up both hands. "You know I'd love to—"

"You won't even have to *say* it out loud," Luke pressed. "Just read it to yourself."

The corner of Theo's mouth tugged upward until it formed a wry smile. "Why? To see if you can guess by my expression?"

Luke pointed to Theo. "*Exactly.*" He looked down at the scribbled back of a receipt. "So far I have three eyebrow raises and two winks."

"Which leads you to believe . . . ?" Theo said.

"It's a girl. Naturally."

Theo shook his head. "Well, a fifth girl would be eyebrow raising for sure. I look forward to hearing the official word in due time. But in the meantime, I believe we are here for a reason." Theo glanced toward Skye. "Right, Skye?"

What was going on? Who were these people? In what parallel universe had she landed?

She shook herself back to the matter at hand. "Right. We're here to pick up the tractor."

Luke reached beneath the register and tossed her the key.

"Thanks, Luke," Skye said, closing her fingers around it. "It'll be back by dinnertime."

"Take your time," Luke said, already back to staring at the tally marks on the back of the receipt.

They had just reached the door and opened it when Luke called out, "And Skye?"

Skye turned at the sound of her name. "Yes?"

Luke grinned. "Good to see the Evergreen Twins back together again."

Chapter 9

Theo

Theo couldn't help smiling as he reached out to catch Skye stumbling off the curb. They walked toward the tractor parked beside two dumpsters.

For Luke to have called them by the name they'd been tagged with two decades before was the perfect finale to the perfect conversation.

"I don't . . . how does he—know you?" Skye said, shuffling her words as poorly as her feet.

Theo shrugged. "It's Luke. It's also the only gas station in town. I'm up here a lot."

"And . . . you just became friends."

"Well, he hasn't invited me over to grill out in his backyard . . ."

Skye nodded as though this was obvious.

"Since last year," Theo continued, "but sure, I'd say we're

friends." He tipped his head thoughtfully. "He is, after all, one of the only people to appreciate my lasagna."

"You make him lasagna," Skye mumbled, more to herself it seemed than to him. She stepped up to the tractor. "Sure you do. Sure you do."

Theo tried to slip his hands into his pockets, but the insides of both felt like the outside—sandpaper. "So." He looked up to the tractor behind her. "What's next?"

Skye popped open the glass door and took a step up. "You take the Prius. I take the tractor."

As she settled inside, she tossed a set of keys at him.

Theo caught them. Looked at them. "Ah. See, I believe I forgot to mention I've never driven a stick shift before—"

"You'll be fine." Skye put the key in the ignition. "Just be sure to press the clutch all the way to the floorboard with the gear shift in neutral first."

"The clutch," Theo said uncertainly. "Right. And that is the . . ."

Skye's brow creased as though she both could, and couldn't, believe the man before her. "Left. The little pedal on the left."

"Right." Theo nodded.

Skye pointed up the road. "We only have to take it those five or six miles, but the road will be steep, so you're going to have to keep it firm in second and be careful not to let it stall out."

He nodded again. Stalling out. On a mountain with woods on one side and a cliff-like drop-off to rocky crags on the other. "You know, I am actually very good at jogging—"

At last, Skye cracked. "Oh my *gosh*, Theo. You are not going to jog next to the tractor for six miles in your . . . your"—she frowned as she glanced down at his feet—"absolutely hideous cowboy boots that look three sizes too small."

Theo looked down at the overly ornate, gold-threaded black boots. "Two. But it was all they had."

"*Come here.*"

He raised a brow and took a step forward.

"You'll ride with me." She stepped down from the tractor and waved impatiently for him to get in.

Theo hesitated, then glanced up the road.

"*Get in.*"

He felt momentarily helpless, unable to drive not only the tractor—which, given his occupation and lifestyle, was at least understandable—but a standard-transmission vehicle as well. Had he known, however, that she had expected him to drive her car, he could've driven his own, dropped her off at the gas station instead—

"You first."

Theo's thoughts dissolved as he peered inside. "Can this handle both of us?"

Skye gave him a look as if to say, *Did your eyeballs just see Luke? What are you trying to imply about my weight?*

"But of course we'll fit," Theo said. "With you being so petite, the tractor will need me simply to keep us grounded."

"For heaven's sake, Theo, *just get in.*" Theo felt her two hands press against his shoulders and push him forward. He scrambled up the steps and, careful to avoid touching any gadgets, sat on the cracked seat. The weathered steering wheel was large and tilted toward the sky. Numerous dials and switches were arranged beside the armrest to his right. Glass surrounded him.

Skye dropped all of her weight on his knee. He nearly

grunted but managed to hold it in. "Ah. So that's how we'll fit. That makes perfect sense."

She frowned at him and turned the key. The engine rumbled.

Skye flicked the switch and turned the vast wheel, and the massive tires of the tractor began to move. Theo's world slowed as the wisps of her hair tickled his cheeks. While trees flickered by in his periphery, his breath caught on the scent he had almost forgotten. After all these years, her hair still smelled of strawberries and cream.

He lifted his voice to match the grumbling noise of the tractor. "You use the same shampoo."

Skye jerked the wheel and looked over her shoulder. "Try not to sound like a creeper while I'm stuck in here with you. And . . . I can't believe you remember that."

He didn't reply, but instead looked out the window. Only then did he realize just how quickly the trees whipped by. "How fast does this tractor go?"

"Twenty-five." She looked back, noticed the car crawling behind them, and pulled closer to the creek-side edge. She pushed the window open and waved them on. Theo watched the tire creep over the white line and inhaled sharply before looking the opposite direction.

But as he watched her intent posture, her alert gaze, the confidence with which she handled the wheel, he remembered another thing he hadn't called to mind for years: the way he used to trust her. Blindly trust her, really. Always eager for the next adventure.

"Do you remember the time I let you drive me around in that four-wheeler?" Theo said, his voice barely audible above the rumble.

There was a pause. Then a laugh. "The ATV? I was grounded for three weeks. How could I forget?"

Theo smiled to himself. "It was so cold that night. Do you remember how cold it was?"

Though her face was half obscured by her loose curls, he saw her wistful smile. "My fingers nearly froze clicking that flashlight so many dang times. I thought you'd never see it."

He chuckled. "Oh. I always saw it."

She didn't respond, no doubt because she didn't need to. They both knew he did. By the time they were teens, every weekend, every summer break, every chance he could convince his family to pack up and drive to Evergreen for a reprieve, he always went to bed keeping one eye on his window, just in case he'd see that blinking flashlight. Their code.

"It just took a while to see it coming from the barn," he continued.

The tractor rolled past Skye's cottage, the roof dappled with sunlight that spilled through the leaves of the great maple.

The sign for Evergreen Farm came into view, and Skye turned onto the gravel. "The snow was coming down too thick for you to see from my bedroom, and besides, I had to rig up the four-wheeler. I was coming for you whether you were sleeping or not."

He grinned as they progressed along the bumpy gravel driveway between the trees. He recalled the energy, the adrenaline high, of spotting her blinking flashlight through the heavy snowfall. How he'd bounded out of his bed. How quickly he'd slipped into his warmest boots and bibs, barely snatching up his toboggan before cracking open the heavy front door and sneaking outside. He never had any idea what Skye planned; he was only certain there was nowhere else he'd rather be.

That evening, Skye screamed and laughed as she whipped the four-wheeler in figure eights beneath the midnight storm on the snow-covered field. Theo gripped the sled for dear life and laughed along with her. Screamed and laughed. Screamed and laughed. Until they saw her father in the distance, stalking out of the woods.

Theo blinked toward that empty field, now filled with rows of adolescent trees. "That was by far the most fun evening of my life."

Her eyes flickered almost imperceptibly to the thirty-foot Fraser fir standing in the center of the field. The one in all this time he'd never cut down. "The most?"

He pressed his lips together. He could never forget the night before he'd left for UVA.

"The most *fun*. Another evening has its own category for simply being the most."

She let go of the wheel with one hand to pull her hair behind one ear. Her large brown eyes gazed back at him. The corner of her mouth turned upward. "The most. You have a category where one evening wins for being *the most*. If that isn't the most grammatically incorrect thing I've ever heard from you—"

Her hair slipped from her ear and covered one eye. Without thinking, he returned it to its place.

Suddenly they both stopped. Words stopped. Theo felt the tractor slow to a stop. And what was in her wide brown eyes welled, brimming with emotions, questions, memories.

His breath caught in his lungs, a heady strawberries-and-cream scent encapsulated by four walls of glass.

But then one word came to mind. *Ashleigh.*

"You know, I forgot I needed to make a few calls before we got started," Theo said. He nodded to the cabin not so far in the distance. "I'll just hop out here and meet you at the tractor."

"Good plan," she said, only too eager to push the door open and move down the steps before her sentence was finished. "It'll take me a while to get the rachet straps on anyway."

While the tractor continued puttering in the opposite direction toward the ridge, Theo took his first clear breath. Put his hands on his hips as he strode up the gravel driveway and then made his way to the cabin's wide porch steps.

He couldn't pretend anymore.

It was time.

Theo slid the landline phone off the counter. Picked it up and began tapping.

Before eight thirty yesterday evening, he had been happy. He was in a relationship with someone who was as eager to be with him as he was her. If their relationship were a flower, it'd be a sunflower growing six inches a day. They were thriving.

But then the woman he once loved more fiercely than his own life had returned, as if from the dead. And maybe she didn't care a whit about him. Maybe he didn't have a chance, but he couldn't go for it this time without giving his all.

And he wouldn't—ever—try to build the foundation of his relationship with Skye on a lie.

He had fallen before for a girl at UVA, a friend who'd somehow, without clear definition, turned into something more over the course of months.

He wasn't even sure how it had happened all those years ago. He started dating Skye mere hours before he left for UVA, and then, through five more long semesters, he lived apart from her. Day in. Day out. Making friends. Memories. Growing a whole life apart from her. Trying his best to make a life out of calling every night, visiting on the infrequent weekend. But with every passing semester the workload grew, the hours hunched over those books lengthened, and the calls shortened. It got harder to deny the bond growing with Chloe as they pored over books and met with friends. Just before winter break of junior year, they'd taken one step too far. Then Chloe, with mutual friends in tow, had hopped in a car during winter break to surprise him at Evergreen.

And it all went horribly, horribly wrong.

He'd realized the lines had blurred then and, without redrawing them sharply, he just let them bleed.

He would not do that again.

"Hello?"

Ashleigh's voice came on the line and he took a breath, lifting his gaze to the row of oil paintings lining the living room wall. His eyes traced the small cursive script in the corner of each one: *S Fuller.*

"Ashleigh . . . there's something I need to tell you."

Chapter 10

Skye

She had to pull herself together.

Skye gave the toe strap one final yank at the anchor point of the overturned tractor and hopped off the tire. Already she could see Theo walking toward her in the distance, although to be fair, people in a plane seven miles up could see his blazing orange flannel.

They hadn't been reunited even twenty-four hours and already her emotions were getting in the way. She had to remember the issues at hand and not even *think* about making out like teenagers in Daddy's tractor. The fact of her father's abysmal pay remained. And while Theo was and always had been a master wielder of words, his actions were indisputable: he was a man driving around in a hundred-thousand-dollar Tesla while paying her father, who had been the farm's faithful employee more than thirty-five years, a *quarter* of that. *A quarter.* That was a fact. Along with the fact that while Evergreen

Farm's eight-seater hot tub and Peloton bike waited shiny and ready for the occasional Watkins weekend visitor, her parents were living with the same furniture in the double-wide of her youth. These were facts.

She needed to focus on getting *that* figured out instead of doing something she regretted.

She wiped her dirty hands against her pants, then shaded her eyes and watched Theo move into the forest. Her lips turned up in a smile.

"Theo, what are you doing? You look like a chicken."

Theo's casual gait had turned into something else. He was lifting his knees unusually high and slow as he stepped over broken tree limbs and moved cautiously around thickets. A long, slender branch stood before him and he carefully pinched it between his fingers and pushed it aside to pass.

"I don't know what you're talking about. I look like a sensible man who is aware that three to 384 spiders—two of whom live in our area and are fatal—exist within one square meter of you at any given time. You, on the other hand, look like a Neanderthal."

"Well, this Neanderthal would outlive you by a hundred years if we got stuck out here, so how about you give walking like a human a try?"

As he stepped over a thick log, she turned back to Luke's tractor.

"C'mon, you can help me run this strap to the hitch." As she stepped over snapped limbs, she worked to undo an unruly knot in the toe strap. "Once we get the tractor upright, we'll need to keep the tension on it so I can get it over that mound without flipping it again. I'll need you to move the—"

"Skye!"

Skye barely had time to turn her neck his way when she felt Theo's chest crash into her body and then, a moment later, was swept off her feet. Literally swept. Followed shortly by a branch slapping her across the face as he began barreling through the woods.

For a moment, all she could do was hang on to his neck for dear life. And notice, despite herself, how firm his chest was. *Good grief, it's just like a marble chessboard. Like the hardest pillow you've ever slept on in your life. Like asphalt. If I just press my cheek against it . . .*

She jolted at the thought and pulled her neck as far away from him as she could, which, given the circumstances, wasn't very far.

"Theo! *What are you doing?*"

Skye yelped as Theo high-kneed into her back as he ran.

"Stop, you crazy man! *Stop!*" She felt like she was trying to command a runaway horse to yield. "*Theo!*"

It was time for another tactic. Her cheek scraped against his orange flannel as she put both arms around his neck and began pulling herself up. *Good grief. How is the man not getting hives from this material?*

She yanked her legs out of his arms like the pair of them were in a swing-dancing act and swung back until her boots hit ground.

They dragged against twigs and dirt for a moment, her arms still locked around his neck, his arms wrapped tightly around her rib cage.

To his credit he didn't tumble; instead, Theo slowed to a stop. He looked down at her feet as though to ensure she was securely grounded, his clean-shaven chin brushing her fore-head. A tingle crept up her spine as he let go.

For a couple moments they just stood there, inches apart, the wind dancing on newly sprouted leaves as it passed through the trees.

And then, most awkwardly, she realized she hadn't let go.

"Your shirt is *horrible*," Skye said, letting go of his tree-trunk neck and half expecting her cheek to have been rubbed raw. She touched it and looked up at him, partly wanting to laugh, partly wanting to ask if he'd just gone clinically insane.

"There was a snake," he said through breaths. He pointed behind her. "There was a snake."

Skye blinked and took in the man, like a poor alien in this place called Earth. "So you hoisted me up and knee-highed me out of there."

She smiled, her tone lighthearted, but the world in her periphery was shifting subtly. The blanket of trees and their leaves gained a more vibrant green hue. The sunlight peeking through the dimpled leaves shone a more golden yellow.

The man deathly afraid of snakes had stepped into striking distance to save her. Was willing to put himself in front of his greatest fear in order to help her escape. It was touching. Ab-solutely crazy and ridiculous and paranoid, but also . . . touching.

"A rattlesnake can strike up to half its length in distance," he continued. "And given the rattlesnake typically can get as large as six feet—"

"There's no way you just saved me from a rattlesnake, or any lethal snake for that matter," Skye said, putting a consoling hand on his shoulder. The stiff, itchy fabric bit her hand and she immediately retracted it. "I'm sorry, Theo, I really do hate to break it to you after the heroics and all, but black snakes are a dime a dozen out here."

"It wasn't black."

"I'm sure it was—"

"It wasn't."

"I'll bet you anything that's what it was."

"You'd bet dinner?"

The words came out of Theo's mouth so quickly he looked almost as startled as she was that he said it. Skye looked at him for several seconds, watching for clues in his expression. For regret in his words.

But his onyx eyes only grew steadier as they gazed at her.

Finally, she nodded. "Dinner. Fine. If you win, you buy me dinner. But if I win"—Skye raised a brow—"I get to hand you the snake."

Theo looked as though he had just choked on his own breath. "No. Something else."

Skye shrugged. "What's the problem? You're the one so sure of this bet." She grinned, seeing the red splotches forming on his neck. "Good grief, Theo. Either you're getting hives from the idea or you seriously need to take off that flannel."

"Fine. Deal." Theo put out his hand.

Skye shook it, a smile starting to form. "This is going to be so good."

A minute later Skye was standing on the spot.

"Okay, Romeo, where is it?"

Theo, looking both incredibly uncomfortable and committed, stood in the barest patch of dirt cleared by the tractor and scanned the area. Skye, meanwhile, began stalking through the thick underbrush beneath the canopy of woods.

"There." Theo pointed, looking ready to jump on the tractor itself.

"Theo, it's a yard snake, not an anaconda. It's not going to get you twenty feet away."

Skye moved toward the base of a lightning-cracked tree.

"Stop. Not that close." Protesting spasms came out of Theo's throat with every step.

Finally, she stepped directly on the spot he was pointing at and looked up. "There's nothing here."

"*Skye Renee*," Theo hissed, pointing at the ground beside her, "*do not make me pick you up again.*"

Skye stiffened, her neck tingling at the sound of her name. Theo was so focused on the ground at her feet he didn't even seem aware of what he'd said.

"Are you sure it's even here?" Skye said, returning her gaze to the ground. "I don't see—"

A patch of grass rippled but two feet away, and she took a guarded step backward. She squatted, squinting to see through the blades. "C'mooon, black snake . . . ," she murmured. "Theo wants to hold you."

She reached forward, started to sweep aside some blades, and then—

The beady eyes of a beige snake stared at her, its body already twisted into striking position.

Skye snapped her hand away, rose, and took three measured steps backward just as Theo started to move toward her.

"Well, I'll be darned," Skye said, pushing both hands in her back pockets. "You called it."

Theo took Skye by both shoulders and moved them back five more feet. When he let go, he put his hands on his hips, looking as though he was trying to be both relaxed and smug, but preoccupied by the fact they were still in the woods. "Well, I have done quite a bit of research on snakes. Phobias tend to lend a hand in that—"

"So you win. And"—she tilted her head back at the snake—"while I doubt it would've done anything, it could've bitten me if I got too close, so . . . thanks, Romeo. I guess I owe you dinner."

Chapter 11

Theo

It took another hour to flip the tractor, and another two to return Luke's, but by lunchtime, with Skye's persistence, he had mastered the act of driving a tractor five miles an hour on flat land. It was quite the accomplishment.

They spent the afternoon on their knees planting seedlings, and when the sun started to creep toward the horizon, with sodden pants and dirt crusted beneath every nail bed, Skye set the last seedling from the box into the hole Theo had dug and gave the small, fragile treetop an admiring pat. She stood, flyaways escaping from her ponytail, powdered by the rust-colored dirt. Looked up at him after a long day's work. Smiled.

She was breathtaking.

"You're up," she said, and Theo blinked, remembering he was still holding the shovel.

"Your father is an impressive man," Theo said, pushing the dirt back into its hole.

Skye, hands on both hips, tilted her head in his direction. "Yeah? How so?"

Theo shoveled another clod of dirt into the hole, his hands aching. "How *not* so? Apart from Christmas season, he's single-handedly managed this farm the whole of his adult life. I bet the work we did together today he could've done alone in the same span of time."

Skye laughed. "Theo. The work we did today *I* could've done in the same span of time." She waited a beat, pushed some flyaways from her eyes. "Anyway, yes, Dad keeps this place alive."

There was an undercurrent in her tone as she said it, something uneasy.

She kicked the dirt and looked up at him. "I don't think I realized how much he truly deserves for all his hard work until I moved back here. Back in Seattle, I went to a bakery beneath my studio every morning on my way to work. Spent ten dollars sliding my card through for a muffin and honey latte and didn't think twice. Why? Because I made three hundred times that on every piece and every commission and business was steady. But here it's different. Dad's hands crack and bleed for his living. I'd forgotten what that felt like until I came back."

She squinted as she looked at him, her brown eyes looking deep into his. "Isn't he admirable?"

Theo inhaled as he set the shovel on the ground. Exhaled as he heard the subtle accusation in her question.

There was so much she didn't know about her father.

He worked out the words before he spoke, careful to dodge the minefield. "I can honestly say I've never met a more loyal man—to the farm and to his family. And that, most certainly, is admirable."

Skye held his gaze, blinked.

Unspoken words danced in their eyes.

He kept the secret he'd promised not to reveal. But was he bound from sharing it even with her? He'd have to ask. Get clarification. Or not. After all, the news shouldn't come from him.

But what was she not saying?

As he opened his mouth, he thought he heard her almost imperceptible sigh. She returned her gaze to the receding sun. "Well, let's get to that dinner, shall we? I'm starving."

Theo's jaw tightened and he hesitated, trying to decide whether to let that shadowy topic slink away. But she clapped her hands and a cloud of dirt drifted into the air. She slapped a determined smile on her face. "And I'm sure you'll want a shower."

Another time then.

"I wouldn't complain," he said, well aware of the dirt covering every crevice of his body. At this point, he'd had the urge to itch something for a solid twelve hours.

"Fine. Pick me up when you're done?" Skye said. She seemed to realize how forward she sounded and shrugged. "It'd be silly to drive two cars into town."

"Actually, if it's all the same to you, I'll cook. I have a meal in mind." He smiled, catching sight of the mammoth tree in the center of the farm. "And a place. If . . . if it's okay with you. I figure, why not toast to good memories? Because . . . we did have them, don't you think?"

A questioning microexpression formed as her lips tilted, and she slowly followed his gaze over her shoulder.

He saw the merest twinkle come to her eyes.

He exhaled, truly exhaled, for the first time in years.

"Time?" Skye inquired.

He glanced to the sun melting into the trees, ran through the movements and motions that would need to take place in the next few hours. "Seven thirty."

"Dress?" she said, her brow raised.

He chuckled good-naturedly. "What else for a fine meal by a fine chef under the stars? Semiformal."

Skye looked into his eyes for one long moment before taking his shovel. "How could I have doubted you'd have it any other way?"

Chapter 12

Skye

*O*f course the man wanted semiformal.

Skye rummaged through her closet, each hanger scraping across the metal bar as she swiftly rejected every item. A white blouse she donned back in Seattle for gallery events. A sunflower dress at least a decade old. A pink number she bought half a dozen years ago and never wore.

The dress options were crammed between baggy sweaters and tank tops in the small closet barely larger than a coffin. Nothing fit for anything resembling the word *semiformal*.

Because she didn't *do* semiformal.

Back in Seattle, her favorite places to eat were local, hipster. Her favorite meal consisted of a vegan macro bowl coupled with a light brew. She could get away with wearing anything at those restaurants—anything except semiformal.

Skye pushed another hanger across the rack and stopped.

Touched the forest-green silk, trouser-leg jumpsuit.

Perfect.

She grabbed the hanger off the rack and threw the outfit on her bed before moving to the bathroom. She walked past the mirror and pushed open the curtain. Her face was worse than she'd imagined. The mascara she'd applied that morning had run far, far away from her eyelashes. And her hair . . . Skye frowned as she reached for a dirt clod clinging to the elastic band of her off-kilter ponytail. She looked like a wild, mud-covered minion.

Terrrrrific.

Theo had worn an orange flannel as conspicuous as an orange cone and managed to out-style her. He sported his share of dirt and sweat, but the effect was the opposite. While she went downhill by the hour, he became more masculine. Wiping the sweat off his forehead. Smiling with those ultrawhite teeth as they caught up on the past fourteen years. And that moment when he picked her up and ran like a wild man away from that snake . . .

A wild, ridiculous, very debonair man indeed.

Skye yanked the ponytail holder out of her hair. She gave herself a long look. Watched as her mud-crusty hair fell to her shoulders. Glanced down at her pathetic array of makeup options and irons, at the dried-up hairspray can in the bottom of the drawer.

She pressed her lips together.

Felt the childish impulse well within her.

Fifteen minutes later, her freshly showered hair dripped onto her robe as she shut the door of her house and crossed the road to her parents', the green silk jumpsuit draped over one arm.

An hour later, Skye glanced at the window as her eyes caught the headlights of Theo's Tesla passing on the road. She pulled the barrel out of her hair and let the last curl drift off the roll. Her mother stood in the doorway of the small bathroom, watching Skye with eyes bright as a baby doe's.

"I'm about to have to go, Mom. Thanks for this."

"Oh, honey, anytime. *An-y-time.*"

Skye felt like she was getting ready for prom.

Her mother didn't have to say it. It was as clear as the spotless glass on the bathroom window that she was pleased as punch about exactly everything that was happening in that moment. Her daughter going on a date with Theo. Her daughter walking across the road to ask to borrow her irons and makeup. Her daughter even *living* across the road so she could walk across it and ask for irons and makeup.

The smile on her mother's face was one of pure happiness. As it had been every day since her daughter had stepped off that plane three months ago.

It was moments like this that reminded Skye she'd made the right decision to move back. Not just to ensure her family was going to be okay financially, but to see her mother so happy.

Skye put the cap on her mother's lipstick tube and set it back in the neat row within the medicine cabinet.

"I think I know what I'll be getting you for Christmas," her mother said, nodding at the curling iron cooling off on the vanity. "And look at you. You look just *radiant.*"

"You should've seen me an hour ago," Skye said, deflecting

the compliment but still smiling. "Where's Dad? You guys have anything going on tonight?"

Her mother shifted in the doorway. "Oh. He went out an hour or so ago to run some errands. He said he'd be back soon."

"I thought he wasn't supposed to be driving with his shoulder."

"Yes, well," her mother said, her smile tightening as she smoothed down her robe, "you know your father. He's as stubborn as an ox."

"But you're more," Skye said, shutting the medicine cabinet and turning to her. "I have no doubt you could take the keys from him. You always win."

"But first one must know which battles to fight."

Skye saw the fiery twinkle in her mother's eyes. A moment later she patted her daughter's hand. "Now, you go off and enjoy your evening. I look forward to hearing all about it when you can."

"Right." Skye took a breath. Moved a curly lock out of her eyes. Glanced back to her mother. She couldn't say it. Couldn't ask the question about her father and Theo she'd been dying to ask since that day. So she said, "You really think this is a good idea?"

Her mother took Skye's hand. Squeezed it. "Honey, I've been waiting since the two of you toddled down the gravel road together at four years old, you holding his hand and tugging him through the fields to pick out your favorite Christmas tree, for precisely this moment."

Chapter 13

Theo

A frothy seascape in the paintings across the room watched over him as he cooked. Tie flipped over one shoulder, Theo stirred the pot and lifted a spoonful of the concoction to his nose. The savory scent filled his senses. He dipped a silver spoon in the pot and tasted. *Sublime.*

He turned to the kitchen sink, his back to the row of Seattle-coastline paintings.

It was remarkable how the day had transformed his emotions.

What had started that morning as a coffee mug full of nervous anticipation had become an uncontainable energy. It leaked out in the lightness of his step as he moved from stainless steel refrigerator to oven range. In the swiftness of his hands as he bounced from replying to a client's email to ripping open a bag. He was almost sure what he needed to do.

Almost.

Theo snapped the last container shut and placed it in the bulging cooler. He withdrew the chilled glasses from the freezer and set them carefully inside.

With one last glance at the centermost painting, a rocky boulder shrouded by mist and pines in the middle of the ocean, he picked up the cooler.

It was now or nothing.

Twenty minutes later, as he sat on a picnic blanket laden with plates and bowls beside the thirty-foot fir, he saw her emerge from the woods.

Green silk flowed gently from her capped sleeves to the cream high heels at her feet. A belt of the same fabric was knotted at her waist. Her dark locks, twisted in dramatic curls, matched her smoky eyes, and as she stepped silently along the path between ferns and mossy undergrowth, she resembled a fairy.

A vision.

He felt his breath stop. He stood there in his suit, gazing and waiting, beneath the giant fir.

When she stopped at the blanket, she moved a twisting lock out of one eye and behind her ear and gazed down.

"You are—you look . . ." He paused, unable to select a fitting word from all the synonyms running through his head. So he said simply, "Beautiful."

A rare shy smile crossed her lips, and when he saw the heat creeping up her neck, he waved at the spread. "Dinner is served."

The rosy blush around her ears faded as she peered down. When she saw what the blanket contained, she threw her head back and laughed. "You've got to be kidding me."

He smiled. "And by that you mean nothing but highest compliments for the chef?"

"Where's my caviar?" she said, slowly settling on the cream-colored pillow on the checkered blanket and adopting a cross-legged position. "I was expecting caviar."

He raised a brow as he opened the cooler and pulled out the chilled mugs. As he spoke, he filled her glass with authentic root beer. "Do you like caviar?"

"I'd rather eat crawdads." She raised a brow. "And in case you're momentarily confused and assume all hillbillies in these hills eat crawdads, the answer is no. Still, when you said semiformal . . ."

"You didn't expect ramen?" He handed her the chilled mug. "Skye, if we were going to eat out *here*, how could you possibly have expected anything different?"

She took a sip of the root beer, her cheeks glowing as the last rays swept across the horizon, then raised her glass. "I'll give you that."

He watched as she slowly took in the spread. Paper plates everywhere, featuring these items: Little Debbie cakes arranged like the Eiffel Tower, Swedish Fish candy arranged like one large piece of salmon. A New York–style cheesecake—the one thing he had made from scratch—with raspberry sauce dripping off its sides. Doritos piled on another plate. A pot of ramen noodles sat in the center of their blanket, two bowls empty and waiting in front of each pillow.

Snacks they'd hoarded throughout their childhood.

"You remembered it all," she mused. "Down to the last Swedish Fish."

"Sounds like you did too," Theo said, then raised his own

chilled mug. "To memories. I hope—" He paused. He felt words building up in him like water pressing against a dam. "I know what I did those years ago was unthinkable, but I hope in time you were able to forgive an old friend for his errors and re-member fondly the good moments in its stead."

Skye hesitated. Nodded. Raised her mug. "I forgave you for that a long time ago, Theo. But even so, to memories. The good ones."

She clinked her glass to his, then raised it to her lips.

Theo followed suit but frowned slightly as sassafras root and vanilla bean washed down his throat. It tingled. He had what he wanted: her forgiveness. She was here, sitting beside him, willing to eat this meal again. But if his error fourteen years ago wasn't the silent wedge still between them, what was it?

Even now, he could feel the tension.

But why?

Skye set the mug down and leaned back on both elbows. She looked up at the darkening sky. "Of all the pieces I've painted in my life, I've never been able to capture this view."

A warm breeze swept over the field, and Theo looked up to the sparkling gems above them.

"It taunts me," Skye continued, kicking her feet out so they rested one ankle over the other. "This view taunts me every night. In Seattle it wasn't so bad. I had light pollution to thank for that."

"Well," Theo said, rolling up both sleeves to the elbows, "on the bright side, you now reside in the best place to try again to capture it."

Skye let out a low chuckle. "Oh. I've tried. I've got a green-house studio full of trying. It'll be the death of me."

"I'd be . . . incredibly honored to see it."

For a long moment Skye didn't reply. Her clear eyes stayed focused on the stars, so long he began to doubt she'd heard him. But then she blinked. And before he knew it she was standing over him, reaching down to pull him up. "C'mon."

Minutes later, they were at the greenhouse, Skye reaching into her silk pocket for a small, single key.

A trail of bulbs flicked on down the center of the greenhouse as they stepped inside, illuminating the floor-to-ceiling glass and overflowing greenery. The air was thick with the scent of fresh dirt and flowers and turpentine. Rows of carrot tops stuck out of the nearest raised bed, kale and arugula behind and beside them.

Skye brushed aside a geranium from a hanging flower basket.

The greenhouse was crowded, and Skye squeezed between the trailing tomato vines and rows of peas to get to the center of the room. She didn't look back as he followed.

As the rows of vegetables cleared, she stopped at a wooden, paint-splattered stool. Put her hand on the seat that looked like it had been her sturdy companion for a decade.

"It's messy but . . . here it is. This is my life." Her tone held nervousness.

He smiled as he stepped out from the rows of vegetables. His gaze was steady on the canvas resting on the easel. "It's breathtaking."

She pulled a stray lock of hair behind her ear. "I've only just begun that one," she said, trailing her fingers along the row of freshly washed paintbrushes on the table. "It's just the underpainting, really."

"Nevertheless, those details—the juxtaposition of smooth and irregular forms in the fore- and backgrounds," he said, moving toward it, examining it closer. He reached out with one finger and she took a step forward, her breath hitching. "It's still drying," she said, but his finger had already stopped an inch from the canvas.

He turned and smiled, keeping it soft. Of course he knew better than to touch her work in progress. "I love this line of light here, along the tree line."

His gaze turned to her reference photograph. She'd taken that shot beneath the entrance of Evergreen Farm.

"Will this be a new series?" His gaze went to three completed canvases leaning against the greenhouse wall. All were different angles of Evergreen Farm. The rows of Fraser firs. Icicles dripping off the white pines. The Watkinses' cabin nestled against the ridge.

Her eyes flickered to his, as though she was surprised by his expression of familiarity with her pieces. As though it was not possible that he had followed her career since she left for the University of Washington to pursue fine art all those years ago. That it wasn't possible he knew the way she worked. Knew she always painted series.

But of course he had. He did.

"I—I don't know," she said at last, turning back to the painting. "If I can ever quit wasting my oils on half-finished skies, then yes. Maybe." Her gaze flickered to the other canvases of all shapes and sizes against the wall, all abandoned with stretches of black, blue, and silver paint streaked across them.

Theo stepped toward the painting on the easel. Carefully moved his eyes over the painting.

He felt her presence beside him. She crossed her arms over her chest, silently gazing at it as well.

"I never was able to cut it down," Theo said at last.

"I know," she said after a moment.

"You should've seen the lengths I had to go to to keep the family from doing so." Theo chuckled, recalling the number of times he had to make his case to the twelve brothers, parents, aunts and uncles, and cousins. "I almost resorted to making PowerPoint demonstrations. I was almost at the level of strapping myself to the tree in protest."

"The newspapers would've loved it," Skye replied. "That was your chance for front-cover exposure."

They both chuckled quietly in the vast room until their gazes slowly turned to each other.

Theo raised a brow. "Well, I suppose our ramen is getting cold out there."

Skye grinned. "Cold ramen. The only thing possibly less appetizing than warm ramen."

Tentatively, he extended his elbow. "Shall we?"

Tentatively, she took the crook of his arm. "We shall."

As they entered the field once again, the toads in the distance began to hum. For several minutes, they just listened, walking in step, Theo feeling her arm pressed against his side. The grass Skye's father mowed each week bowed beneath their feet with each step. Each fir shivered lightly in the breeze as they passed.

The world, in that moment, was perfect.

"I haven't been completely honest with you, Theo," Skye said, breaking the silence. But instead of feeling her pull away, she seemed to cling tighter to his arm.

A part of him didn't want to ask. The bigger part of him couldn't resist. "How so?"

"I said I got over it a long time ago. Up until three months ago I really believed I had."

"Until you moved back?" Theo said, raising a brow.

"Just before that. I was at my parents' house and found something that . . . that just made me believe the worst in you all over again."

He swallowed, the burn lingering in his throat. What had she found? An old picture? A memento?

"I need to talk with you about it," Skye continued. "I need to get this off my chest before I could even possibly take one step further."

"Of course," Theo said, pulling her tighter, not wanting to let her slip away. "Anything."

Their feet hit the gravel driveway and he stopped, letting go of her arm to face her properly and look her in the eyes. "What do you need to ask?"

Skye's eyes glimmered as she pressed her lips together and looked up at him. He saw the hope in her eyes and his tension eased. Whatever she was about to ask, he could see she *wanted* him to reply with the right answer. Whatever it was.

"When I was with my parents—" Skye began.

The sound of a car rolling onto the gravel cut her off. Skye stopped as they turned, blinking into the beam of two small headlights.

He knew that car.

Skye's voice was low. "Who is that?"

She withdrew her hands from his, already bracing for what she didn't understand.

The car hit the brakes twenty feet away.

Theo felt his jaw flex. "It's a woman I know. Ashleigh. It's not what you think—"

Skye started moving backward, spotlit like an actress onstage. Her hands were balled at her sides. "Why is she here?"

"I—" Theo squeezed his eyes shut. If Skye had found some trinket that reminded her of how he had broken her heart, and she was struggling to get over that, he couldn't imagine what reliving *this* horrible moment in their history might do. He pressed his hand against his temple. "I'm not sure. If I'm honest, I'm not sure. I broke it off with her today—"

"You have a girlfriend?"

But already Skye was waving him off, her bracelets banging against each other with the movement. "You know what? I don't want to know. I don't want to be a part of this."

The driver's door opened. Ashleigh set one high heel onto the gravel and stepped out. "Theo?"

"Skye, *wait*," Theo called, but it was no use. Skye, hiking up her pantlegs, was walking as fast as she could toward the woods.

He could hear Ashleigh's door slam shut, but Theo didn't turn his head. He called out to Skye. "What did you expect me to do? I only ran into you yesterday. I did everything I could to get things right here."

"See, now there's where you're wrong, Theo. You didn't do everything you could. Fourteen years ago, you didn't do everything you could. If you had, we wouldn't be doing this right now." Skye turned. For the first time, he saw Skye's eyes spark against the moonlight.

Theo's forehead creased. "But I did. I ran after you. I even got a *broken nose* running after you. And I called and apologized to your voicemail more times than I could count, until you flew all the way across the country and changed your number—" He halted. Threw out a hand. "What else could I have done?"

"What you *should've* done is flown out to Seattle and begged me to come back. You should've banged on my parents' door until they gave you my address. You should've given up UVA and flown out to Seattle and found some crappy apartment as close to me as possible and apologized every day of your life until I took you back. I gave you *everything*, Theo. I got into that Seattle school *two years before I went* and turned it down to stay near you. To be with *you*." Skye lifted her chin. "You should've put it all on the line for me too. Just like I put it all on the line for you."

Theo swallowed as Ashleigh took a step toward him. "But you told me to leave you alone. You said in no uncertain terms—"

Skye threw her head back in exasperation. "I was *lying*, Theo. I was angry and hurt and I was *lying*. And I blindly assumed you cared about us enough not to give up based on a few words."

"*Your* words," Theo said quietly, taking a step toward her. "I thought it was what you wanted."

For several moments they faced each other in silence, Skye's face drained of color. Finally, she waved an arm at Ashleigh, who was sliding back into her car. "Clearly you have some things to sort out. I'll leave you two to it."

She stalked three more steps before turning one last time.

"You know? All day I kept trying to *understand* how the person I knew could treat my father this way—"

Theo put up a hand. "Wait, what?"

The gravel sputtered as Ashleigh's car flew into reverse.

"I saw the letter, the one with your fancy letterhead detailing his salary." She shook her head. "Honestly, Theo, you treat *my father* as unfairly as a migrant worker straight out of the Depression. He's devoted his *life* to making an organic tree farm actually successful—which takes a lot of time and labor—and you can't give him more than minimum wage."

Theo squeezed his eyes shut as he tried to process what she was saying. Rubbed his temple. "You think that I would do that?"

She put her hands on her hips. "Isn't that what you're doing?"

He pressed his lips together, put his hands on his hips. Everything was becoming clear. The anger and distrust that had been hidden behind her eyes all along. This wasn't just about what had happened fourteen years ago. It was about now. Then and now.

All those comments about his organic Peruvian coffee beans and how her father worked so hard.

"You think I would pay your father so little—"

"That they would still be living in their double-wide driving that same thirty-year-old truck with the broken AC? Yeah, Theo. Yeah, I do. What evidence do I have to tell me otherwise?"

Theo pressed his hand to his chest. "Me, Skye. I would hope you'd know the truth because you know *me*."

They stared at each other wordlessly as Ashleigh's headlights fell between them and the car backed swiftly down the lane. By the time the lights swerved onto the road and dissipated through the trees, the moment held the feel of a punctured balloon, slowly deflating into a small mass on the floor.

He wasn't sure if he or she turned away first, but moments later they were moving in separate directions, each trudging slowly beneath a pale moon and its electric sky of stars.

Chapter 14

Skye

Skye's heels sank into the mossy ground with each step. Her fingernails bit into her closed palms as she marched through the small patch of woods and came out at the greenhouse on the other side.

She felt like she'd been tossed underwater. Like she'd been invited to a nice waterfront restaurant and was sitting on a fine patio drinking champagne one moment, clinking her glass with a man beneath a string of hanging lights, and the next was falling backward out of her chair into the water.

It was startling. Infuriating. Confusing.

But what rubbed her raw was a slimy feeling in the pit of her stomach she couldn't quite shake. The feeling that he wasn't entirely to blame for what had just happened.

And worse than the feeling of being furious at him for his mistakes was the feeling of being furious at herself for the possibility of hers. She had to know. Right then. She had to talk to her mother.

Skye marched through her side yard without stopping and walked across the bridge. Two knocks on her mom's door, and her mother appeared.

She took in Skye's expression and then opened the door wide. "Oh, honey. What happened?"

"Well, to cut to the chase," Skye said, peeling off her sodden heels at the threshold and stepping barefoot inside. "We were about to start a *lovely* meal when Theo's newly departed *girlfriend* showed up."

"Oh no." Her mother shut the door, her hand pressing against her chest and the faded stripes of her apron. The air smelled of sautéed garlic and onions.

Skye's fists tightened. "Yes."

She took Skye by the shoulder and guided her to the kitchen. "Let's get you something to eat."

Skye followed her into the yellow-wallpapered kitchen and sat in one of the three chairs surrounding the breakfast table. She put her elbows on the table. Raked her hands through her hair. Her mother set a glass of milk in front of her and moved back to the stove.

Skye picked up the glass numbly. "I don't even think I know what I'm supposed to *think* here."

"I'm sure it's all very confusing for the both of you," her mother said softly, sliding a bowl of soup in front of her. "But then, you both have had entirely separate lives until yesterday."

Skye frowned.

"Did he say how long he'd been detached from this other

woman?" her mother asked, setting a stainless steel spoon beside the bowl and slipping into the chair beside her.

"Hours." Skye exhaled, turning the glass in her hand. "Apparently somewhere in our day together he stole away long enough to break up with her."

"And then she came to see him, probably to try to make amends, and it threw a wrench in his well-planned date," she mused aloud.

Skye saw where this was going and frowned. "You're taking his side."

"Of course not," her mother said, taking her hand. "I'm on your side. I'm on both your sides. Although, I wonder . . ." Her mother stood and returned to the stove.

Skye watched her mother stir the pot, saying nothing more.

"What? You wonder what?"

"If you're not being a bit too hard on him."

That was it. She had to know.

"Why do you like him so much?" Skye set her glass down. "How can you stick up for Theo when he pays Dad what he does? How does that not infuriate you? Dad, you—you're both worth *ten times* this." She waved at the wallpaper. "And Theo *could* give that. Theo *should* give Dad a decent wage."

Her mother's ladle slowed to a stop.

"Where did you get this information?" she said quietly. "Did Theo talk with you?"

Skye pressed her lips. Shook her head. "No. I saw the letter in a drawer."

She saw her mother's expression and felt an inward quake. This was why she'd never brought it up. This shame that crossed her mother's face was the reason Skye had kept it to herself.

"I'm sorry," Skye continued, then waved at the counter. "It was lying in a drawer I looked through while I was making cookies. I didn't mean to pry."

Her mother nodded. "Well, I can most *certainly* understand why you're confused." She turned back to the soup. "There's a reason the Watkins family has agreed to pay your father that salary. A few reasons, actually, for why they agreed to my request to lower it."

"Lower it?" Skye said. "*You* requested to *lower* it?"

"Theo's letter was just confirming our verbal arrangement." Her mother nodded. "About this time last year, shortly after"—she hesitated, turned—"the Bristol casino opened. I realized I had no other choice. I drove down to Theo's office and spoke to him in person."

"*You* went down to Theo and *asked* him to lower Dad's salary? Why?"

Skye halted, felt her breath quake. "How bad is it, Mom?"

She hesitated. "Bad enough I needed Theo's help."

"But how does lowering his salary help anything? Shouldn't it be the other way around?" Skye looked around, realizing all too suddenly the television made no noise. "So is that where he is right now? The casino?" She gripped the corner of the table, her voice rising. "Is that the 'errand' he was talking about?"

Her mother didn't move. "That's where he said he wouldn't be. But time will tell."

Skye felt the punch in her gut as she stared into the face of her mother. Her peaceful, placid mother in her apron, soup ladle in hand. "And you're just going to stand there? And let him throw all your money down the garbage chute?"

At this, for the first time, her mother smiled. "Thankfully, honey, this house isn't fancy enough for a garbage chute. And yes, in my own way, I'm doing everything I can to help him."

"What are you doing?"

"Well, for starters, cutting his salary by 60 percent. And by becoming an employee of Evergreen Farm and making twice his salary myself. Theo made quite a sacrifice, convincing the rest of the Watkins family of my plan." She hesitated, then lowered her voice. "For a long time I've known that the Watkinses hold on to the tree farm for sentimental purposes. They spend any profit on their employees."

"So . . . Dad."

She nodded. "Your father, and the few part-time employees who come in for the harvesting season. So when Theo told me they'd agreed to essentially double our income, well . . ." She shook her head. "I don't think they agreed. I think he's paying me independently. He denied it when I pressed, but . . ."

Skye sat back, stunned.

Her mother cleared her throat. "And then, of course, I think hosting the Gamblers Anonymous group in our home once a week is starting to make an impression on your father too."

"Those are all *gambling* addicts?" Skye said, her world turned entirely upside down now. She'd seen the group coming to their double-wide every week, the average-looking men and women carrying potluck dishes. Laughing. Doing and looking as normal friends do.

"They're all *people* who struggle with gambling addiction," her mother replied. "Yes."

"And now *you're* working on the farm too?"

At this her mother looked absolutely smug as she lifted her

chin. "Maintenance supervisor, at your service," she replied. "A cute little title Theo and I thought up. I've always wanted to be a supervisor."

"In other words . . ."

"In other words, I do exactly what I've always done and nothing more. I keep your father in line."

Skye stared at her mother, at this woman who was twenty steps ahead of her. "So . . . does Dad know?"

"He's a proud man, Skye. He wouldn't ask if he did. He prefers to pretend none of this is happening." She shrugged. "So I pretend along with him."

"And you guys have enough money. You don't have to live here."

Skye's mother's smile softened. "Honey, this is our home. My daughter lives in a beautiful cottage across the road. My husband walks to work. And these walls carry the millions of wonderful memories of where I raised our family. Why would I ever leave?"

With her mother softly turning back toward the old stove, Skye finally felt like she had nothing more to ask or say. So instead she looked. Looked at the breakfast table where she'd talked with her mom and eaten every meal before jumping on the school bus. At the china cabinet in the corner carrying all the knickknacks and centerpieces her mother used around the dining room table every holiday. At the couch and recliner where her dad sat in the evenings with her mother, read the paper, and watched TV.

Her mother wasn't poor. She wasn't scraping pennies from her coin purse because she had no other option.

She was just content. And had enough healthy self-awareness to live out her contentment.

And Theo? Theo wasn't just the man who'd understood her mother, who'd kept her secret, who'd been there for her. He was the one who'd been saving her parents all along.

Chapter 15

Skye

THREE WEEKS LATER

Skye strolled down the herringbone brick sidewalk of Abingdon, gift bag swinging from her fingertips, the giant blue bow knocking her knees. She took her time, feeling the warm early-May breeze seize her hair and lift it momentarily, leaving a tingle along the back of her neck. Pink pansies in two hanging baskets cheered up the black streetlamp outside Katbird's Wine & Gourmet Shoppe, and her gaze drifted to the large windows and the display of cheese beside handcrafted Italian pottery. She stopped. Took a step toward the seafoam vase nestled beside crystal glasses. Her mother would love it.

She made a note to pop in on the way back from the shower and give it a closer look.

She walked past the Tavern, admiring the mossy slate roof. Another breeze swept her green silk jumpsuit softly across her skin. She slowed to read a couple lines on the plaque about its construction in 1779.

This was the third time she'd worn the jumpsuit in three weeks—the first with Theo, the second when she went to dinner with Luke and some of the old gang (where, sure enough, Luke had confirmed Theo's lasagna-making expertise). She could've bought or chosen another outfit for his wife's baby shower. But this was what she wanted to wear, she realized, as she looked through her closet this morning. And she was trying these days to practice doing the things she liked without regard for what anyone else might think. To be a bit more like her mother.

She walked past several more colonial-era buildings, taking in both the ancient architecture and the trees lining Main Street. Traffic went by, some tourists destined for the Barter Theatre with its flapping maroon and yellow flags, some citizens moving through town about their business. Skye lifted the Raven's coffee cup to her lips, no quicker or slower than before.

The moment was worth lingering over.

Her steps slowed just before a four-way crossing as a sign came into view. A brown sign with bold script written across it: *Theodore Watkins III, Financial Adviser.*

She stopped. Looked up to the redbrick, colonial-style office building. Considered taking a step toward the door.

But like the rest of the windows, the six glass panes revealing the foyer inside were dark, the office void of life. Just as well. She'd do best apologizing when her schedule was clear.

She knew what she wanted to say, and it could take a while.

Another three blocks and Skye stopped at the Barter. Turned left into the grand entrance to the historic building across from it. Smiled politely to the two teenage valets of the Martha Washington Inn and descended the steps. Garden art and quiet porticos greeted her as she walked along the winding brick path leading to one of the Martha's many entrances.

As she approached the door, she moved the baby shower gift to her left hand and opened the door with her right. She stepped onto the plush, olive-colored carpet and turned toward the spa, where Tracy, with stomach protruding, was finishing up a cut and color before her party started.

Skye stopped.

The baby rattle inside the gift bag jingled as it dropped to her feet.

Slowly, she took a step toward the first row of gilded paintings, her eyes wide. The waves crashed onto the sand of the Seattle coastline, the marine life beneath a seafoam green sea, the boulder and its crop of trees protruding just off the shore in the midst of the sea. She'd completed and sold this series years ago. Her finger traced her own signature along the bottom edge. The black plaque beside it with gold lettering announced: *Display Only.*

How?

She looked down the wall, counted. One, two, three, four, five.

At the end of the hall, Tracy turned the corner and grinned when she spotted Skye. "There you are! I just finished up. Ready to go?"

Skye drew up her finger at the largest painting, felt her mouth hanging open like that of a codfish. "How did these get here?"

Tracy raised a brow. "You didn't know? I assumed you knew. Theo brought them in two weeks ago."

"Theo?" Skye's throat was drying fast. "But how? How did

he have them—?" She squeezed her eyes shut for a moment, finding the questions coming faster than she could process.

Tracy shrugged. "All I know is that I saw him in here meeting with the manager with one of your paintings one day, and the next they were replacing all the old displays with yours."

Chapter 16

Theo

Theo rubbed his eyes, weary from hours of exposure to lamp-light and computer screens. The office had long closed up for the day, and yet he sat, logging in the numbers on the Excel sheet in the still room.

The Barter ticket sat on his desk, unused, while outside the street was lined with the parallel-parked cars of Barter visitors. It was opening night for *King Lear*, but tonight, like every night the past three weeks, he had work to do. Things to prepare.

Unbelievably, Ashleigh had returned to him that evening three weeks prior. Turned her headlights around. Listened and braved a conversation about mending fences. And for a milli-second, he had considered it. But as he did he realized he couldn't maintain a conversation about building their relation-ship while keeping one eye on the door, with one part of his heart hoping to hear Skye's knock. He couldn't do that to Ashleigh, who deserved much, much more. And despite his mistakes, he couldn't do that to himself. He couldn't let Skye go. Not again.

So he resolved then and there to do something about it.

To take that risk Skye needed.

Theo sighed and leaned back in his chair, back aching from the day's load of sitting through meals and meetings and reports. His legs ached with the desire to move, to pedal, to run. Perhaps he'd actually go on a run tonight before packing the last box. He glanced out the window to the dark street.

A light flashed into his eyes and he blinked.

He frowned, looked out the window again.

A light blinked again, this time covering the whole of his window with its light. A moment later it ceased, then flicked on again.

Was that . . . ?

Theo pushed back his chair. Stood.

The light continued blinking on and off as he moved to the foyer, then turned the knob on the front door. When he opened it, he was certain.

"Skye?"

Skye, standing on the brick sidewalk beneath the maple, clicked off the flashlight. Her hand fell to her side as he strode toward her.

She smiled slightly as he stepped onto the sidewalk.

He glanced down at the flashlight. "I hate to be cliché, but what are you doing here?"

"I, um . . ." Skye looked from his eyes to his jacket pocket and up again. "I wanted to apologize. I know everything about my dad and . . . I wanted to say I'm sorry. I thought you wouldn't do anything like that and yet . . ." She shrugged. "I was wrong to think it. I was wrong about a few things. And for what it's worth, I was wrong to expect you to take all the risks." She took a step toward him. "And maybe you have a girlfriend now—"

"I don't," he interjected.

"And if you do," she continued, though a smile was starting to rise, "I'm sure she's lovely, but I didn't want to let another day pass without taking a risk and telling you I know what I want."

Theo's eyes softened. The beating in his chest picked up its pace as he took another step forward. "And what is that?"

She blinked as he tentatively touched both of her elbows and took the final step. "Why, you. Of course."

A moment passed in silence as he let her words wash over him. Words he'd craved to hear for years. Decades.

Skye blinked again. "Unless . . . ," she began slowly, "you feel differently—"

But he was closing her lips with his, both hands on the tips of her elbows, gently pressing her to him. Time slowed as he slipped one hand to her shoulder, then cradled her neck as they stood there beneath the maple tree, the whispers of passing cars swirling around them.

He could live this moment forever.

As the world surrounding them came into focus again, Theo stepped back and gave his head a vehement shake. "Skye, you bested me again. I was going to woo you first."

Skye laughed, cheeks flushed as she pulled a strand back behind her ear. "Calm down, Romeo. You win in the wooing.

I saw my paintings up in the Martha this afternoon. What I don't understand, though, is how you found them."

He smiled and, keeping one hand on her elbow as though afraid to let go, turned them toward the office door. "They aren't hard to find when they've been featured in your living room for a decade."

Skye halted. Looked up to him as he locked the office door. "You've been hoarding my paintings here? In your house? You bought . . . that entire series?"

"No, I have the Spring of 2016 series in my house," Theo said, smiling wistfully as he turned toward her. "What I had in the living room at the cabin, however, my *new* home, were those. Now, how do you feel about lifting a few of my moving boxes?"

Theo felt Skye stop. She turned to him. Her eyes were as large and round as he'd ever seen. Her voice was nearly a whisper. "Are you telling me you want to move to the cabin?"

His smile was his reply.

"But, but what about your work?"

"I'll commute." Theo shrugged. "An hour commute is hardly anything. Citizens of the cities are offended by people who drive under an hour and claim they commute."

"And all the bugs? And snakes?"

"I plan on having to carry you out of a few shady situations, but I think you'll be safe with me."

"You'd do all that for me?" She glanced around. "You'd leave all this, for me?"

Theo's eyes softened. "Skye, whether or not you showed up tonight, I was going to be your neighbor, rapping at your door with a morning cup of coffee, swinging by with the offer of soup every time I hear you're sick, dropping off a card every Christmas, birthday, and holiday, until . . ."

"Until . . . ?" Skye said.

Theo smiled as he took her hand in his. "Why, of course, until you opened the door."

Epilogue

S he'll sell for ten thousand. Not a penny less!"

Skye picked up Luke's booming voice over the hum of the crowd.

Swiftly she handed her mother the small flute of champagne. "Excuse me. I have to distract a man who keeps parading around as my agent before my agent actually gets here and kills him."

Her mother and three of the visitors at Evergreen Gallery laughed lightly as they opened up the circle for her to depart into the crowd. As Skye slipped between the clusters of guests, her name popping up like iridescent bubbles by individuals merrily trying to get her attention, she couldn't help smiling.

A packed room of family, friends, patrons, and curious visitors.

The crisp white walls were so freshly painted the smell of latex still hung in the air.

Floor-to-ceiling windows showed off the herringbone brick

sidewalks of Abingdon and *Evergreen Gallery* in delicate green script on the outdoor signage.

Track lighting beamed neatly over each canvas, each one a new angle on the sparkling night sky.

Only one thing was missing. As she was just reaching Luke—who stood squarely in front of the largest canvas, a blue-eyed baby strapped to his broad chest as he haggled with an elderly woman dripping in pearls—she saw it.

Passing Luke, she moved to the open front door and stepped outside.

Directly across the street, Theo, just having turned the lock on his own office door, turned around. When he saw her, he stopped. Gave a little lopsided smile as he lifted one hand, the oversized scissors dangling from his fingers.

"Found the ribbon cutters!" he called out.

He dodged the oncoming traffic, jogged lightly across the street, and met her on the other side, eyes shining on the woman who'd turned from childhood best friend to lost love, to next-door neighbor, to wife, and now the latest: neighboring business owner and daily lunch date. And all it took was thirty-six years.

She took the scissors from his hand and reached on tiptoes for a kiss, her cheeks glowing like the soft pink rose petals on their wedding day. "Just in time."

He Loves Me; He Loves Me Not

Kathleen Fuller

To James. I love you.

Chapter 1

I'll be back in a minute. I'm going to pass out right now."

Sophie Morgan chuckled, knowing full well her mother wasn't serious. But she didn't doubt Mom was surprised by Sophie's announcement. She snipped the end of a rose stem and added it to the pink glazed vase on the table in front of her. "Very funny."

"I'm telling you the truth. My heart just stopped from shock."

Adjusting her earbud, Sophie rolled her eyes. "There's no need to be dramatic, Mom. All I said is that I'm going on a date." *As soon as someone asks me out, that is.*

"You can't expect me to take this news lightly." Her voice became muffled as she said, "Roger, our baby is *finally* getting married."

"What?" Sophie dropped the pink carnation she'd just picked up. "I never said that, Mom."

"Oh, but it will happen eventually. I'm sure of it."

For a brief second, Sophie wished she were as confident as her mother. Then again, sometimes her mother's confidence bordered on annoying, especially when she was being *helpful*.

"How's life in Arizona?" she asked, eager to change the subject. Her parents had moved away from Maple Falls, Arkansas, ten years ago to Tempe to be closer to the daughter who had fulfilled their mother's dream—Lis was not only married but also had two children.

"So, who's the lucky man?" Mom asked, ignoring Sophie's question. "Where did you meet him? How many times have you gone out?"

Sophie sighed, not surprised that her mother didn't take the bait. The woman had a one-track mind. Fortunately Sophie's two coworkers, Hayley and MacKenzie, were busy with customers up front and not back here to listen to what was turning out to be an embarrassing conversation. Then again, Sophie should have known not to call with such momentous news during work hours.

"Mother," she said in the same tone an irritated parent would use when calling a child by their first *and* middle names. "I only said I was ready to date. Not that I had a date. Please don't rush me."

"Rush you? When have I ever rushed you? When have I ever pointed out that you're thirty-six and it's high time you have a social life—"

"Thirty-five," Sophie corrected.

"Really? I thought you were thirty-six. You know how I am with dates and ages. Anyway, when have I ever put pressure on you to marry, er, date?"

Despite her mother's insistence on being exasperating,

Sophie couldn't help but smile. She had spent the last decade devoting her time and money to Petals and Posies, the floral shop she bought after saving for it for years. Keeping the shop afloat had been a struggle since the town had been in a steady decline for a long time. But things were changing in Maple Falls. She was busier than ever, and now that she could afford to hire help, she could also afford to take some time off. Which meant she was finally ready to go on her first date since high school. Maybe now her mother would quit bugging her about her social life, or rather, her lack of one.

"Let's just say you've been very insistent."

"You're exaggerating."

Sophie could practically hear her mother rolling her eyes. "Mom, I need some space. Dating takes time. It's not as if my future"—she almost said *husband* but caught herself—"date is going to walk into my shop in the next two hours."

"Then you don't have any prospects yet? That's wonderful."

"It is?"

"There are some lovely single men here at church. One of them is even a *doctor*."

Sophie snickered at her mother's reverent tone. "Ooh, a doctor. Let me book my ticket now."

"You joke, but I'm serious." Mom harrumphed. "It's not like Maple Falls is teeming with single men your age."

She couldn't argue with that. In fact, she knew only two— Landon Ferry, who didn't even live in Maple Falls anymore, but had moved to Malvern several years ago. For the past two weeks he had stopped by the shop three times, buying a bouquet each time. He was just as handsome as he'd been in high school, and although he was twice divorced, she knew through the grapevine—which consisted mainly of her friend April—that he was available. He was also in a profession her mother would get giddy over—a lawyer with his own practice.

The other single guy was Joe Johnson. The two men couldn't be more different, in both looks and occupation. Landon was tall, fit, an impeccable dresser, and he had the thickest black hair she'd ever seen. He always looked as if he'd walked right out of a high-end barber shop. Joe, in contrast, was on the short side, barrel chested, never without a worn-out baseball cap, and probably had no idea where to buy a suit, much less owned one. He was a high school history teacher and football coach, and excellent at both. None of those qualities were strikes against him. She had never been one to get hung up on looks or professions. She'd known Joe since kindergarten, and not a single time had she ever thought of him in a romantic way. Then again, she'd forgotten what it was like to think about romance at all.

"Sophie? Are you still there?"

"Yes, I am," she said quickly, going back to work on the bouquet she was making for an online order. She added the carnation, then picked up a few stems of baby's breath.

"Well, I was just saying that you should try online dating. Lis said it's all the rage now."

"How would she know?"

"Her friends tell her. I'm sure she can give you some helpful advice about dating."

No thanks. "That's okay, Mom. I'm sure she's busy with the kids and everything. How are they doing?"

Mom launched into a detailed explanation of everything Sophie's niece, Addison, who was in preschool, and her nephew, Sebastian, who was a toddler, had done for the last two days. Sophie interjected a "hmm" and "you don't say" at all the right moments as she finished the bouquet. She already knew everything the two kids had done since Lis never failed to post a social media update every day about her perfect family. Unlike other families, Lis's truly was perfect, and Sophie was glad she and her husband and kids were happy. She just wished her mother hadn't always held up her younger sister as the ideal Sophie consistently failed to meet.

"I think I should come for a visit," Mom said.

Panic shot through Sophie. "That's not necessary, Mom."

"I can give you support. Advice. Encouragement."

Interference. She never should have told her mother she was thinking about dating. She should have waited until she was engaged. Or had already eloped.

"I appreciate it, but Addy and Bash need you." Her niece and nephew hadn't been called by their full names since they were born.

"True. And Lis and Dan are leaving for their cruise in two weeks, so I need to prepare to keep the punkins."

"Exactly."

"But you'll keep me posted, right?" A note of desperation filled her tone.

"Of course." Her heart softened again. Mom meant well, and Sophie needed to remember that. "I have to go give Hayley this order so she can deliver it, and we're busy up front. Tell Dad I said hello."

"I will. Oh, I'm so happy for you, Sophie! You've worked so hard to make your store a success. Your dad and I are very proud of you. I'm glad you're taking some time for yourself."

She couldn't help but smile. Knowing her parents realized how hard she worked and what she had accomplished meant the world to her. "Thanks, Mom. I love you."

"Love you too. Oh, and dear?"

"Yes?"

"I realize that you're an independent woman, and I know that's important to you. But just remember that it's okay to want companionship."

"I have friends, Mom."

"I'm talking about *male* companionship." Before Sophie could protest, her mother said, "Talk to you soon!" Then she hung up the phone.

Sophie swiped her phone screen, then took out her earbuds and put them in her pocket, followed by her phone. She stared at the clear glass vase in front of her. Of course independence was important to her. But that wasn't what had kept her from dating. Up until this point her job had been all consuming. She'd made the choice not to date, and now she was choosing to date. She just hoped it wasn't too late.

Shaking off the depressing thought, she tied an emerald green ribbon around the vase, then picked it up to take out front to Hayley. She was determined to focus on work for the rest of the day. It wasn't like she'd be able to do something about her dating life immediately. Now that she'd told her mother, she would have to follow through with diving into the dating pool. Maybe that was the reason she called Mom in the first place—because more than once, she'd thought about chickening out, and she knew Mom would never let that happen.

She walked into the front of the shop, which was full of flowers, gifts, and, fortunately, customers. She smiled at Jasper

Mathis, an older man who stopped by at least once a week, mostly to look at the flowers and shoot the breeze with the customers. Every once in a while, he bought a single rose, though Sophie had no idea whom he gave it to. Not that it was any of her business.

What would it feel like to get flowers? And not just from friends who don't want me to be left out on Valentine's Day. She couldn't count how many flower bouquets, sprays, garlands, and gifts she had made over the years for all the Valentine's Days, weddings, and anniversaries. She'd even made a few for husbands who were trying to get out of the doghouse. How would it feel to be surprised with a vase filled with her favorite flower, simple pink roses, from a man she loved?

Maybe one day she would find out.

———

"Well, it's about time."

"Shh." Joe held his hand up and glanced around the Sunshine Diner. Even though it was late afternoon and the lunch rush had passed, a few people were still in the diner. More importantly, two of them were his students, although they were in the back of the restaurant washing dishes, probably since the moment school let out over an hour and a half ago. "If I wanted the whole town to know I would have told Gina."

His best friend and coworker, Travis, scoffed as he dug into a thick piece of cherry pie. "Your sister doesn't even live here anymore."

"She has connections," Joe said somberly. "Lots of them are people she talks to on the regular. Gina pounces on gossip.

Remember the time she told everyone you were afraid of the dark?"

"We were in fourth grade."

"She hasn't changed, trust me." Joe loved his sister, but he'd been thrilled when she announced she was moving from Maple Falls to Boise, Idaho, after meeting a potato farmer online. From all accounts she was happy, but she still had strong connections to Maple Falls, just like Joe did when he lived in Little Rock for ten years, teaching at Central High School and working as an assistant JV football coach. When the opening at his alma mater—tiny Maple Falls High School—appeared eight years ago, he jumped on it and never looked back.

"All right." Travis leaned forward. "But, hey, congrats on finally joining the living."

Joe frowned and used a white paper napkin to wipe the condensation off the glass of his double-thick banana shake. "I'm just going on a date, not coming back from the dead."

"Same thing, in your case."

As Travis scarfed down the rest of his pie, Joe pondered his friend's statement. He'd been plenty satisfied with his teaching and coaching, plus working with youth camps in the summer. Being able to positively affect young lives was gratifying and rewarding. But lately something had been missing in his life. Companionship. He wasn't sure why he'd changed his mind about staying single, but he had. Now he wished he'd kept that decision to himself.

"So, who's the lucky girl?" Travis pointed his fork at Joe. "And I mean that. You've been Maple Falls' most eligible bachelor for too long."

"When did you suddenly turn into a girl?"

Travis smirked. "Being concerned about you isn't girly. Look, I've known you all my life. You've always been a family man. I'm just sayin', it's time for you to have your own."

"My last attempt didn't turn out so well."

"Because you married the wrong woman at the wrong time."

Joe nodded. He and his ex, Jenna, had married right out of high school, ignoring everyone's warnings, including Travis's. The marriage lasted six months before Jenna asked for a divorce and moved to Florida. They hadn't kept in touch, and that was seventeen years ago. But the failure had been long lasting.

"Don't tell me you're still hung up on her," Travis said.

Joe shook his head. "Of course not."

"Good. She was all wrong for you."

"I know." Joe slurped his shake. "And she's in the past."

"Right. So, I'll ask you again, who's the lucky woman?"

Joe took another sip of his shake, stalling as he thought about the woman he had finally decided to ask out—he glanced at the clock on the wall—in about half an hour. He figured she wouldn't be too busy at work, but he didn't want to ask her in private, because if she turned him down, she would have to be polite about it if they were in a public place.

Chicken. His hands were starting to get damp just thinking about saying the words, *"Would you like to have coffee sometime?"* Yeah, he was definitely lily-livered when it came to this dating thing.

He chalked up his nerves to being out of practice with women and anything that had to do with romance. Which was why he had chosen this particular woman for his return to the dating scene. He wouldn't be too bent out of shape if she turned him down. If she didn't, he figured that going out for coffee would be their first and last date. But at least he would have had a date.

"Fine. I see you want to keep it to yourself." Travis grabbed the bill off the table. "I've got to run and get Layla from ball practice. Plus, there's a stack of English essays waiting to be graded." He let out a long-suffering sigh as he got up from the table. "Hopefully this time at least half of my students remembered to write a topic sentence."

"You're not fooling me. You love your job. Even the grading essays part."

Travis grinned, his white teeth contrasting with his mahogany skin. "I definitely do. Catch you tomorrow."

As Travis left, Joe polished off his milkshake, now more milk than shake, and glanced at the clock again. He had about twenty minutes to kill, and when he spied one of his former students and her mother walking into the diner, he decided to visit with them a little bit. By four o'clock, he knew he couldn't wait any longer. His nerves wouldn't allow him to.

He put a tip on the table, then walked out of the diner . . . and headed for Petals and Posies.

Chapter 2

At 4:00 p.m., Sophie told Hayley and MacKenzie they could clock out. Normally the two women would stay until closing, five or five thirty depending on how busy the store was. They weren't busy now, and Sophie knew the college students had finals at the end of the spring semester, which was next week. She wanted them to do well, and when she said they could leave, neither protested.

After the girls left, Sophie straightened up the store, then started sweeping the stray leaves, broken stems, and ribbon threads on the floor into a small pile behind the counter. When the front door chime sounded, she looked up, then forced herself not to stare as Landon strolled through the door, looking surprisingly casual in a light blue short-sleeved polo, khaki pants, and tan leather slip-on shoes. He also looked unsurprisingly handsome.

Not staring at Landon was an impossibility, especially when he flashed his charming grin at her. She leaned the broom against the wall but missed, and it clattered to the floor. She kicked it to the side and walked to the counter, hoping her smile matched his. She also hoped she didn't look like an idiot.

"Hi," she said, her voice catching. She cleared her throat. "Uh, what can I help you with today?"

Landon slipped his hands into his pockets and looked around the store. "I think this is the first time I've been in your shop when it's been empty." He turned to her and smiled again.

"It happens." Oh, that smile. It could melt a glacier. She found herself leaning forward, her waist pressed against the glass counter.

He stepped toward her until they were as close as they could be, considering the counter between them. "I'm not complaining."

A ripple ran down her spine. Had he lowered his voice? Made it husky on purpose? Or was she imagining—more like wishing—he had? Or hoping that the way his piercing gray eyes held hers meant something?

More likely, her thoughts about the possibility of romance in her future had made her lose her mind, because a man like Landon would never be interested in a woman like her. He seemed the type to want a trophy girlfriend or wife. One who looked as impeccably perfect as he did. *I'm not even in the ballpark*. She didn't think she was unattractive, but she wasn't high fashion either. More like serviceable. *Ugh*. That didn't sound appealing at all.

"Er, we have our spring bouquets on sale," she said, focusing on her job instead of her inane thoughts. "Do you like daffodils?"

He put his palms on the counter, leaning even closer. "I'm not here to talk about daffodils."

Sophie gulped. "Oh."

Landon reached over and tucked a loose strand of hair behind her ear. "You look pretty today."

She didn't know how to respond. She didn't look any different today than she did any other workday. She was wearing her pale blue denim work shirt over a red T-shirt, navy blue shorts, and comfortable shoes any granny would be proud to sport. That was her typical uniform. The only thing different was that she had a pink scrunchy holding back her long, curly hair instead of a blue one. Maybe she'd been mistaken about his preferences.

"Ah, thanks?" Why couldn't she stop sounding like an idiot?

"Then again, you look pretty every day."

Now she really didn't know what to say. When was the last time anyone had said she was pretty? Probably April, and probably on Easter when she splurged and bought a new dress for church. Flattered and unnerved, she started straightening her business cards, which were already neatly displayed in a clear acrylic holder.

"I wondered if you'd like to have dinner with me tonight?"

The cards flipped out of her hands just as the chime sounded over the door. Joe Johnson walked inside, then paused as Landon turned around.

"Hey, Soph." Joe waved as he strolled to the counter.

Sophie grimaced and grabbed at the cards littering the counter. No one called her Soph anymore, not even April. She wasn't sure why some of the kids in high school had started calling her that in the first place, including Joe. Of course, he wouldn't call her anything else, since they had rarely spoken to each other in the last fifteen years. "Joe."

Landon frowned as Joe walked up next to him. "We're kind of busy here."

"Oh." He took two steps to the side. "I'll wait, then."

Landon gave him a pointed look, then turned to Sophie. "Are we on for dinner tonight?"

For some reason, she was a bit embarrassed about being asked out in front of Joe. Which didn't make sense. Why should she care what he thought? But she couldn't help glancing at him and was surprised when she saw his easygoing expression turn dark.

"Sophie?"

She turned to Landon, then inexplicably to Joe again, struck by the contrast between them, and wondering why Joe was here. And why was he so upset?

"She can't go out with you tonight," Joe said.

"What?" both Sophie and Landon exclaimed.

"And why not?" Landon added.

"Because . . . she's going out with me."

———

To say his foray back into the dating world was going badly would be the world's biggest understatement. Joe couldn't believe the words that had flown out of his mouth. But he couldn't help it. When he heard Landon asking Sophie out, he lost all sense. Not because he'd missed his chance to ask her himself, but because of all the men in Maple Falls—or the greater central Arkansas area, for that matter—Landon Ferry was the last one she should ever consider dating. Or talking to. In fact, she'd be better off ignoring him altogether.

Now that Joe was starting to corral his brain cells and think clearly, he realized he had stepped into a pile of . . . *Oh boy.* Sophie did not look happy.

"Well, I guess I missed my chance tonight." Landon's fake smile remained plastered in place, but Joe could see the annoyance in his eyes as he shifted his gaze to Sophie's. "Another time, then." Giving her a wink, he turned on his heel and quickly headed to the door.

Sophie lifted her hand, still full of business cards. "Wait—"

But Landon was already gone.

"Good riddance," Joe mumbled.

Sophie tossed the cards on the counter. "*Why* did you do that?"

Joe turned to her, steeling himself against her anger, and she sure had a right to be angry. When he looked into her deep blue eyes, he was stunned by how furious she was. Her cheeks had always seemed to be rosy in high school and every time he'd seen her after that, but now they were the color of the Maple Falls Volunteer Fire Department's only fire truck. She seemed to be shooting flames at him with her eyes too. He involuntarily took a step back.

"I know you're mad—"

"*Mad* doesn't begin to cover it. How dare you come in here and sabotage my date with Landon?"

"Because you shouldn't be going out with him."

Sophie huffed and crossed her arms. "You have no right to say that."

He had every right and reason to say exactly that, but he

wasn't going to get into it with her. He also couldn't let her think it was okay to go anywhere near Landon Ferry. "I'm trying to stop you from making a terrible mistake."

She tilted her head at him, her cheeks turning an even deeper shade of red. "It was just a date."

Exactly what he'd been thinking on the way over here to ask her out. It was just a date. It didn't mean anything. It was practice for real dating. "It wouldn't be a simple date to Landon. He's got an ulterior motive. He always does."

Her arms dropped to her sides. "So you're saying he wouldn't want to go out with me unless he wanted something from me."

"That's exactly what I'm saying."

The anger in her eyes faded to something else. Sadness? *Oh no.* "That's not a reflection on you," he added quickly.

"Right." She didn't look at him as she gathered the business cards.

Her forlorn tone propelled him forward. "Sophie, I'm sorry."

"It's okay." She straightened the stack of cards. "I'm sure you're right."

"I am." When she kept her gaze down, he touched her hand. "You have to believe me, Soph."

She yanked her hand away from him. "No one's called me that in years." She finally met his gaze, a bit of the fire back in her eyes. "You would know that if you knew anything about me."

He nodded. She was right. He didn't know much about her, other than she was a good businesswoman and she was single. She was also generous, since she sponsored a girls' softball team every year, had donated equipment to the high school varsity team, and mentored a few of the senior girls who wanted to learn flower arranging. He hadn't thought about how she had served the community until right now. Turned out he knew more about her than he thought, but that didn't negate the fact that he didn't know her personally.

Unexpectedly, he wanted to. "Let me make it up to you," he said, surprising himself for the second time since he'd walked into Petals and Posies.

"Are you going to call Landon and tell him I'm free after all?"

"No."

She lifted her chin and put the cards neatly back in the holder. "Then I don't see how you can fix this."

"Let's have dinner tonight."

Sophie stared at him. If she rolled her eyes any harder, she'd have to pick them up off the floor. "Not funny."

"It's not meant to be. That's why I came here in the first place."

She frowned, her eyes filling with confusion. "To ask me on a date?"

"Yes." He put his hands behind his back and began rocking on his heels, a habit that showed up when he was nervous. And the nerves were hitting him like a tidal wave slamming into a tiki hut. He hadn't been this ill at ease a few minutes ago. Why was he anxious now? When she slowly nodded, he stopped rocking, his unease turning to happiness.

"I see," she said, still nodding. Then she pointed to the door. "Get out."

"What?"

"You heard me. Get out of my store. And don't bother ever coming back."

He opened his mouth to say something else, but clamped it shut, then turned and left, his nose filled with the scent of dozens of different flowers as he hurried past the displays. Strange he would notice that now. When he stepped outside, he made sure to move away from the front door and windows before face-palming himself.

"Stupid, stupid." He'd not only made Sophie mad but also managed to get kicked out of a flower shop of all places. And he was upset that she was upset. Really upset. He glanced back at the store and saw that she had turned off the light for the electric red Open sign.

There was nothing left for him to do but walk away. So he did, regretting how he'd handled the entire situation. His first jump into the dating scene had ended up in a giant belly flop.

But there was one thing he didn't regret—tanking her date with Landon. He hoped the smarmy lawyer wouldn't ask her out a second time.

Chapter 3

"I can't believe he did that."

Sophie nodded as April handed her a cup of chamomile tea. As soon as she drove away from Petals and Posies, she'd called her best friend, who immediately told her to come over. When Sophie arrived, she discovered that April had sent her husband, Darren, out for the evening. Now she and April were in the couple's modest den, sipping chamomile tea and snacking on sugar cookies.

Sophie was feeling a little better, but not enough to let go of her anger at Joe. "Trust me, he did," she said, brushing a crumb off the corner of her mouth.

April shook her head and curled her feet under her as she leaned against a gray-and-white checkered throw pillow. "He seems like such a nice guy. Why would he act like a jerk?"

Shrugging, Sophie took a sip of her tea. "I have no idea. He's never set foot in Petals before, at least as far as I know. And it's not like we talk or anything."

"But he asked you out." April's thick brown eyebrows lifted. "And you're not surprised by that?"

"Of course I am. I go from not having a date in forever to two men asking me out at the same time." She stilled, the reality of her words hitting her. She'd been so mad at Joe for lying about their date that she hadn't fully realized he had asked her to dinner. She frowned. "I'm confused."

"So am I," April mumbled.

"One thing is for sure, though. Joe does not like Landon."

April nodded. "That's obvious." She sat up straight and looked at Sophie head-on. "But the bigger question is—what would you have said to Landon if Joe hadn't butted his nose in your business?"

Butterflies suddenly ramped up in her stomach. "I don't know. I was so shocked that he asked me."

Grinning, April said, "Then you would have said yes."

"Maybe?" Sophie set down her mug. "It was so sudden. I didn't have time to think it over."

"You mean *overthink* it over." April's grin faded into an annoyed frown. "Don't tell me you would have turned him down because it was too spontaneous."

The thought had crossed her mind. She didn't like surprises, which was another reason she was mad at Joe. But then again, when Landon asked her to dinner, she'd gotten that giddy feeling she hadn't experienced since high school when Peter Lewis, the captain of the basketball team, had asked her to senior prom. Of course, those feelings faded quickly when she found out he asked her as a favor to her sister, Lis, who was on the cheerleading squad. Still, she and Peter had enjoyed the prom, even though there was nothing romantic between them.

"Good grief, you're overthinking as we speak." April moved from the love seat where she'd been sitting and plopped herself next to Sophie on the couch. "The next time a man asks you out, you say yes. Do you hear me?"

"Except for Joe." She scowled. "I will never, *ever* go out with him."

"Never say never."

April's singsong tone irritated her. "I can't believe he asked me out," Sophie muttered. "The nerve—after what he'd just done?"

"I guess he really wanted to go out with you." She tapped Sophie's arm playfully. "Not that I blame him. You're a real catch."

"That's what all my *friends* say." She picked up her tea again. "I'm not sure Joe really did want to go out with me. Like he said, he wanted to make up for wrecking my potential date with Landon."

"*Or*," April said, giving her a pointed look, "he wrecked your potential date with Landon so *he* could go out with you."

Sophie thought about what Joe had said—that he'd come to the shop to ask her out. But he was acting weird when he said it, rocking back and forth, his gaze darting around the store. Which made her think he was lying.

"I wonder what he has against Landon," April mused.

"Don't know, don't care." Well, that wasn't exactly true. She was curious why Joe—who, as far as she knew, was an upright guy—would lie to Landon, then turn around and lie to her. But she was still too irritated with him to find out, because that would mean she would have to see him again.

"That doesn't sound like you." April frowned. "Neither does kicking someone out of your shop."

Now that she'd had some time to cool down, she felt a little bad about that part. She let out a sigh. "I shouldn't have kicked him out," she admitted. "But I was so angry."

April nodded, her expression sympathetic. "Maybe you should try online dating after all."

Sophie groaned and tapped the back of her head against the couch cushion. "No way. I'm thinking about dropping this entire romance thing."

"After just a little bit of drama?"

"A little bit? That was more drama than I've had in an entire year."

April laughed. "But isn't it just a little bit exciting too? I've never had two men want me at the same time."

"Joe doesn't want me."

"Mm-hmm." April grabbed the plate of sugar cookies from the coffee table. "Keep telling yourself that."

I will. Besides, even if Joe had been serious about wanting to go out with her, after today he'd never come near her again. She should be glad about that, but for some reason she wasn't. She didn't like having loose ends, especially when she was in the wrong.

"I'm going to end up apologizing to him, aren't I?"

"Yes," April said, handing her a cookie. "Because you're a woman of integrity."

Sophie snatched the cookie out of her hand. "Just this once, I don't want to be."

Joe leaned his chin on his palm and stared out at the class full of students in front of him. Study hall had started thirty minutes ago, and he'd barely made a dent in the stack of history quizzes he brought to work on. He'd been lucky with his study hall class this year—the students were mostly upperclassmen and mature enough to keep quiet and at least pretend they were studying. He also didn't have a problem with them closing their eyes for a minute or five. There was enough pressure on these kids as it was, and if they wanted to snooze a little, he wasn't going to stop them.

"Mr. Johnson?"

He blinked and sat up straight, looking at the young woman waving her hand in front of him. "Yes, Mandy?"

She got up from her seat and walked over to him. "Can I go to the restroom?" she whispered.

Joe nodded and quickly scribbled a pass for her on a sticky note. Only after she left the room did he realize she'd already been to the bathroom once this period. She was one of the students who always tried to see what she could get away with, and usually he told her no when she asked to leave the room a second time.

He glanced at the rest of the students, and a couple of them smirked, knowing exactly what had happened. He ignored them and looked down at his papers. Soon, however, his mind was drifting again, back to Sophie and what happened yesterday at Petals and Posies. He inwardly cringed for the dozenth time.

He'd made a mess of things, and now he wasn't sure how to handle it. Should he go back to the store and try to apologize again? But she'd told him not to come back, so that wouldn't work. Should he forget it ever happened? That would be the easiest tack, since their paths rarely crossed anyway. Still, he would know he'd made a mistake and hadn't rectified it, and that didn't sit well with him. Maybe he could call the shop, since that would technically not be going to the store. But he didn't relish the idea of her hanging up on him—

"Bye, Mr. Johnson!"

He gave his head a hard shake as the students filed out of the classroom. Oh boy, this wasn't good. Not only had he not heard the bell, but he had no idea if Mandy had returned. Not that it mattered now, since she would be on her way to her next class anyway. He gathered up his papers and walked back to his classroom, determined to focus on the last two classes of the day. They were both about civics, which he enjoyed, and at least when he was teaching his mind wouldn't get away from him again.

At the end of the school day, Joe shut his door and sat down at his desk, determined to finish grading the quizzes. He plowed through them, recorded the grades in the gradebook on the computer, then shut down the machine for the day. He headed for home, still unsure how he was going to apologize to Sophie. He'd even thought about writing her a letter but nixed that idea too. What could he say, other than "I'm sorry"? She would probably tear it up anyway.

He needed to burn off some steam, and his favorite way to do that these days was to go to the driving range. His football-playing days were long behind him. During the season he helped coach the team, worked out with the guys in the school workout room, and tossed the ball with them before practice began. As much as he still loved football, he'd really settled into golf and played as much as he could in his free time. There was nothing better than whacking a few balls to work out his frustration. He kept his clubs in the back seat of his extended cab, so he headed straight to the nearby range.

An hour later he was feeling much better and headed home. He pulled into his driveway and stopped his truck like always to grab the mail from the mailbox. When he pulled out the stack, he was surprised to see a small envelope with only his name on it. He climbed back in the truck and opened the envelope, then pulled out a small note card.

Dear Joe,

 I shouldn't have lost my temper yesterday. I apologize for that and for kicking you out of my shop. You're welcome to come back anytime.

Sophie

Joe grinned. They'd had the same idea, only she'd had the courage to go through with it. He put the card on top of the envelope, parked his car in the garage, closed the door, and went inside.

He walked through the small alcove that housed his laundry room, ignoring the pile of towels on top of the dryer that needed to be folded, and went to the kitchen. He set the mail on the counter and glanced at Sophie's note. Then he looked around the house. The only sound was the buzz of the refrigerator. No one was there to welcome him home, or to eat dinner with, or to talk to about his day.

In the past he'd been too busy to notice. Or he'd ignored the loneliness. Probably some of both. But lately he couldn't ignore the fact that he hadn't expected to be single and without a family of his own at thirty-five. When he married Jenna, he'd intended to be married to her for the rest of his life. *Look how that turned out.*

He picked up the note card again and reread it. She didn't need to apologize to him, since he was the one in the wrong. Not only did she say she was sorry, but she'd also invited him back to the store. Okay, *invite* was a strong word, but still—maybe he was getting a second chance with her.

A feeling that had long lay dormant traveled through him. Attraction. Anticipation.

Joe tapped the card against his lips, then set it down, the courage he'd been searching for all day appearing full force. He grinned. Sophie Morgan had opened the door for him, and he was going to walk through.

Chapter 4

By four o'clock the next day, Sophie was exhausted. The flow of customers in her shop had been nonstop, and she'd fretted all night about the note she left in Joe's mailbox.

After leaving April's she had gone home, fully intending to spend the rest of the evening watching TV and forgetting that Joe Johnson existed. Instead, she went straight to her junk drawer, pulled out the pack of note cards she'd tossed in three months ago, and wrote him a quick apology note. Before she lost her nerve, she searched for his address in the church directory, then drove over and dropped off the note. She assumed he wasn't home because there was mail still in the box, but she sped off just in case.

When she got back to her apartment, she took a long, soothing bath, which normally helped her sleep. It hadn't worked last night. Why didn't she just write "I'm sorry"? Why did she have to add the part about him being welcome in her store? He wasn't, of course, but what if he took her seriously instead of realizing she was just being polite?

Fortunately, there hadn't been much time to ponder that during the workday. Hayley and MacKenzie were busy in the back filling a last-minute order for one of their best customers who would be picking it up first thing in the morning. She leaned against the counter, glad that for at least a few minutes the shop was empty. She was thankful for the brisk business, of course, but right now she wanted to sit down and put up her aching feet.

The phone rang, and she let out a big yawn as she picked up the receiver. "Petals and Posies. How may I help you?"

"Hi, Sophie."

A tiny thrill traveled through her. "Hi, Landon," she said, unable to keep the surprise out of her tone.

"I was wondering if you were free for dinner tonight?" he asked.

Inexplicably, she paused. She hadn't expected him to extend the invitation again so soon. Actually, she hadn't expected him to ask her out again at all. It struck her as strange that he was expecting her to be able to drop whatever she was doing at a moment's notice. Then again, her social calendar wasn't exactly full, either.

"*I'm trying to stop you from making a terrible mistake.*"

Joe's words came to her mind unbidden. Great, he was interrupting her thoughts now. Still, she couldn't help but wonder why he thought her going out with Landon was a mistake. Did he know something about Landon that she didn't?

"Sophie?" Landon said, impatience in his tone. "Are you there?"

The chime above the front door rang, and she looked up to see Joe walking into her store. Unbelievable. How could this happen twice? Then again, it was her fault. She shouldn't have been so polite.

"Sophie, I'm waiting for your answer."

Landon sounded even more impatient now. When Joe reached the counter, she said, "Yes. What time do you want to meet?"

"I'll pick you up at five." The charming tone was back. "At the shop."

She tried to smile but couldn't with Joe staring at her. She met his gaze, surprised that he was back so soon. When her eyes locked with his, she froze. Had she ever noticed the gold flecks in his hazel eyes? Had she ever noticed he had hazel eyes? Gorgeous eyes, now that she was paying attention. And there was something in his gaze that made her mouth go dry. *Oh my.*

"Is that all right?" Landon's voice sounded in her ear.

"What?"

"Five o'clock. Does that time work for you?"

"Yeah. Sure." She blinked, and whatever trance had held her disappeared. "I mean, yes. I'll be here."

"See you then. And Sophie?"

She turned away from Joe. "Yes?"

"I can't wait to see you."

Click. She looked at the phone receiver for a minute. Shouldn't his words excite her? A handsome, successful man was asking her out. She couldn't ask for a more perfect launch back into the swing of dating. Instead, she felt a tiny bit uneasy.

"Hey, Sophie."

She hung up the phone and turned to Joe, her guard back

up. Thankfully when she looked at him this time, she felt nothing but annoyance. "Joe."

His slightly crooked grin vanished. "Uh, I got your note."

"Good." She crossed her arms.

"You didn't have to apologize."

"I know." She wasn't going to give an inch with him. Just because her good Southern manners forced her to apologize didn't mean she trusted him. Or even liked him. *Then what was that feeling a few seconds ago?*

"I need to apologize, though. I'm really sorry. I shouldn't have butted into your business like that. You were right to be upset."

Her tense shoulders relaxed a little. "Apology accepted," she said, her tone less sharp.

"I liked the note card." He touched the brim of his baseball cap, then thrust his hands behind his back again and started rocking on his heels. "What kind of flower was that?"

"A gerbera daisy."

"Are they all red?"

She was surprised he was asking questions about flowers. Then again, he was probably making small talk, which she didn't have time for. *Because I have a date.* She had a date! She glanced down at her work uniform, which consisted of her usual denim shirt, this time with a navy blue T-shirt underneath. She couldn't go out with Landon looking like this.

"Did you want to buy something?" Sophie asked, the words shooting out in a rush as she tried to calm her nerves. Did she have time to run home and change? She glanced at the clock. If she left in five minutes, she'd be back just in time for Landon's arrival. "If not, you can show yourself out."

Joe stopped rocking. "You're still mad at me?"

"I'm not mad." Which was true. She was panicked, but not mad. "I have things to do, that's all."

The phone rang again, but Sophie ignored it.

"Don't you need to get that?" Joe tilted his head in the direction of the phone.

"The girls in the back will answer it." She tapped her foot. They would also have to close the shop for her, but they had done that before, so she wasn't worried. What she wanted was for Joe to leave. "You didn't answer my question," she said, glancing at the clock again.

"What was it?"

"Do you want to purchase something?" She couldn't keep the annoyance out of her voice.

"Well, I—"

"Sophie?"

She turned to see MacKenzie poke her head around the doorjamb to the back room. Her auburn ponytail hung over her shoulder. "Yes?"

"That was Mr. Ferry. He said he might be a few minutes late picking you up tonight."

Sophie's cheeks burned. She didn't miss the curious glint in MacKenzie's eyes, and she ignored it. "Thanks, Mac." When the girl disappeared into the back room, she turned to Joe, flinching at his dark expression.

"You're going out with him?" he asked, his hands now hanging stiffly at his sides.

She looked at him straight on. "That's none of your business."

"Even after what I told you yesterday?" He took a step toward the counter.

"You didn't tell me anything!" Realizing she was almost yelling, she lowered her voice and leaned toward him. "You *ordered* me not to go out with him. For no reason at all."

"I didn't order you." He leaned closer to her. "I strongly discouraged it, that's all."

Her gaze didn't move from his. "What I do with my dating life is none of your business."

"What if . . ." He paused, his eyes holding hers. "What if I want it to be?"

———

Joe couldn't keep his eyes off Sophie. Somehow they'd ended up with only the counter between them, and for some crazy reason he wanted that counter gone. He couldn't believe he'd ever thought Sophie Morgan was quiet and prim. This woman was fiery. *And beautiful.* She smelled so good, like a mix of flowers and sweet-scented shampoo, the combination heady instead of clashing. Her red cheeks looked so soft, her mouth so kissable—

"What are you talking about?" She scowled, but she didn't move away. Instead, it seemed like she had inched a little closer.

What had he been talking about? Oh, he'd said something about wanting her dating life to be his business. And he did, just not like this, with them at odds with each other. Although it was kind of sexy, he had to admit. He grinned at her.

Finally, she pulled away from him. "You're nuts," she said. "And I have a date to get ready for." She turned and started walking toward the door to the back room.

"Go out with me," he said.

Not stopping, she let out a short laugh. "Right. Like I would ever do that."

"I'm serious."

This time she stopped and turned to face him. "Why should I?"

"Because . . ." He wanted to tell her something casual, like he thought they would have fun together, or it was something to do, or they were both single so why not. But while all of that was true, it wasn't the main reason. "Because I like you."

Was that surprise flickering across her face? Then again, he probably imagined it because now she was eyeing him with suspicion. "Since when?"

Good gravy, why was she asking all these questions? "Does it matter? I like you and I want to go out with you. Is that so hard to comprehend?"

"Not when you put it so *romantically*," she said, sarcasm dripping from her words.

He had to admit his game needed some work. *A lot of work.* But that didn't change how he felt. "Sophie, please go out with me." Great, now he sounded like he was begging.

Her stance softened. "You are serious."

"I am." For once he stood still, even though his nerves were in high gear. "We can go out for dinner tonight."

"I have a date, remember?"

"Cancel it."

Her thin light brown eyebrows shot up, along with her chin. "No. I want to go out with Landon." She gave him a derisive look. "I don't want to go out with you."

Ouch. Double whammy. Not only had she rejected him, but she was also still going to see that slime bucket Ferry.

Joe quickly regrouped. Fine, she didn't want a date with him? He could accept that. He hadn't exactly presented himself in the best light to her. But he couldn't abide her seeing Ferry. The determined set of her chin told him she was going no matter what he said.

Then an idea came to him. "Do you like to golf?"

She frowned, looking surprised. "I've never played before."

"I can teach you. It's a fun game, and a great way to work off steam."

"I'm not steamed."

He smirked. "You weren't until I showed up."

"What if I don't want you to teach me?"

She wasn't going to make this easy on him, and he respected that. But he had made some headway—her frown had disappeared. "I've been a jerk, I know that. And I understand that you don't want to go out with me on a date. But I still want to do something to make up for making you mad. I'm not a bad guy, I promise. I want to prove it to you."

"By teaching me how to play golf?"

"Not the whole game. We'll just hit some balls at the driving range. If you hate it, you can blame me, and we won't do anything together again." That wasn't the result he wanted, of course, which was a complete change from how he felt yesterday afternoon when he was talking to Travis. Sophie was supposed to be an icebreaker. A way to ease back into dating. Now, and he still couldn't explain why, everything had changed. Even so, being with Sophie as friends was better than nothing—if she accepted his offer, of course.

"I guess you won't leave until I give you an answer." She let out a heavy sigh, as if he'd asked her to build a brick wall with him. "Fine. I'll hit a few golf balls with you. But that's it, and only if you promise to leave me alone afterward."

"Deal," he said quickly.

"Wonderful. Now can you please leave? I have to tell the girls to close the shop."

"I'm outta here." He pointed his thumb toward the front door. "I'll see you tomorrow night after work. I can pick you up at—"

"I'll meet you there at six."

He gave her the address, then beat it out of the shop. As he got in his truck, he couldn't help the smile taking over his face. One way or another, tomorrow night was going to be interesting.

Chapter 5

Sophie pulled into the parking lot at Ace's Driving Range, which was just outside of Maple Falls. The gravel crunched beneath her tires as she pulled into a parking space next to an older-model black pickup truck. She realized she had no idea what Joe's car looked like. As she turned off the engine, she paused, asking herself for the dozenth time why she had agreed to Joe's invitation. More importantly, she asked herself why she was looking forward to it.

She thought about her date with Landon last night. She'd never tell Joe, but it was a disappointment. She'd managed to rush home and change into something presentable, then run a brush through her hair and arrange it into a loose ponytail at the nape of her neck. She only wore makeup to church on Sundays, but she added a little mascara to her sparse eyelashes before hurrying back to the shop in time for Landon to pick her up in his white Mercedes with genuine leather upholstery. How did she know it was leather? He had mentioned it twice on the way to the steak house in Hot Springs.

The meal was delicious, the conversation anything but. She'd had no idea someone could talk about himself for an hour straight, but Landon had. After she stopped gaping at his looks, she realized he was boring and tuned him out about fifteen minutes in. That's when she started thinking about Joe's warning. Surely he hadn't gotten upset because he knew Landon was a dud when it came to interpersonal communication. But why had he been so insistent about wanting her to stay away from him?

It was only when Landon started inquiring about her shop, the history of it, and how she ran the business that she felt remotely engaged. Some of his questions were a little too nosy, especially the ones about the day-to-day management of her business, but then again, he was a lawyer. They were used to asking questions. She had evaded the more detailed ones, but at least she'd had the chance to get a word in edgewise.

When he dropped her off at home, she had hurried inside, not inviting him in. She wouldn't have even if things had gone well. She wasn't ready for that step yet. The date had been such a letdown she wasn't even sure if she wanted to go out with anyone else at that point.

Knowing she couldn't keep Joe waiting, she got out of the car. At least tonight would be over quickly. She fully intended to humor him for a few minutes, then go back home and spend Friday night on her couch, like she always did.

The sudden sensation of butterflies in her stomach as she approached the range surprised her. They'd been absent last night with Landon, but now they were flitting around with a vengeance.

Sophie touched her stomach, as if the gesture would settle

them down, then she looked out at the range. A long strip of fake grass was divided into several spaces, and two golfers were already hitting balls into a large field. To her right stood a brightly painted blue-and-yellow clubhouse. She assumed she needed to go there for instructions.

"Hey, you made it." Joe appeared at her side.

She turned and looked at him. For once he wasn't wearing his baseball cap. His black hair was almost military short, but the style looked good on him. He was dressed in a navy blue collared, short-sleeved shirt, and instead of shorts he wore trim khaki pants. She barely noticed those, since she couldn't keep her eyes off his biceps. They were huge and accentuated by his tight short sleeves.

Quickly she turned away from him and said, "Uh, yeah. I'm here. What do we do?"

"Don't sound so excited." He chuckled, and she released an inward sigh of relief that he seemed relaxed. She didn't like being uptight, and lately she'd been wound up tighter than an old-fashioned alarm clock.

He led her to the clubhouse, asked for something called a driver for her, then pulled out his wallet.

She held up her hand. "I'm paying," she said and pulled her own wallet out of her crossbody bag. She handed the money to the teenager behind the counter, then turned to Joe. "What are you going to play with?"

"My driver is over there." He pointed to one of the stalls where a golf club leaned against a wall next to a white bucket. "I got here a little early to get a few balls in."

Sophie nodded and followed him to the stall. "I really don't know what I'm doing," she said, suddenly feeling nervous. She wasn't the most athletic person.

"That's okay. I do." He flashed her a confident grin, which somehow managed to settle her nerves. "I'll demonstrate what to do first, then I'll show you the steps involved."

She watched, the cracking sound of golf clubs hitting balls surrounding her. Joe lined up in front of the ball, and she listened as he explained everything he was doing.

"When you're ready to hit the ball, you bring your club back while bending your elbows." He drew his arms back and then connected with the golf ball, hitting it high and far until she couldn't see it anymore.

"Wow," she said, forgetting that she was supposed to be disinterested in the activity. She moved closer to him. "How far did it go?"

"Almost three hundred yards." He looked pleased.

"Is that good?"

"Decent enough." He turned to her. "Are you ready to try?"

She shook her head, her nerves popping up again. "I don't think I'll be good at this."

Joe's expression was encouraging. "You won't know unless you try." He motioned for her to stand in front of him as he stepped back from the tee. He gave her verbal instructions on how to grip the club, how to stand, how to place the club next to the ball, and then how to bring the club back before striking the ball. "Time to give it a shot," he said, moving away from her.

Sophie tried to integrate all the steps, but her mind and body wouldn't cooperate, and she ended up hitting the ball barely a few feet.

"Hey, that's not bad," he said.

She turned to him and smirked. "We both know it was bad."

"All right, so it wasn't good." He approached. "But it wasn't bad. You made contact with the ball, which is half the battle." He put another ball on the tee and stepped back again.

Again she tried to remember everything he'd said, but when she missed the ball twice, he moved to stand behind her.

"You're overthinking it," he said.

"Of course I am," she mumbled. When didn't she overthink things?

"Try to relax."

She stiffened. "I am relaxed." She felt him move closer to her, and the tickling in her stomach started up again.

"It might be better if I show you," he said, his voice close to her ear. He was only a few inches taller than she was, and his chin hovered over her shoulder. "Is it okay if I do this?"

When his arms circled around her and his hands covered hers as she held the golf club, she could barely manage to nod. He smelled wonderful, like fresh soap and a light, woodsy-scented cologne. Nothing like the overpowering scent Landon must have bathed in before he picked her up.

"You want to draw the club back like this." He gently coaxed her arms into a swinging motion. After doing that a few times, he let go of her hands and stepped back. "Do you think you have it?"

She had something, that was for sure. She couldn't breathe, and once again her mouth turned to cotton. She was tempted to ask him to give her one—or twenty—more personal demonstrations. Whatever happened to hitting a couple balls and hightailing it back home? She couldn't deny the pleasant feeling coursing through her, or her surprise that she had such a strong reaction to Joe.

Before she could overanalyze all that, she swung and hit the golf ball. This time it went a decent distance, and she was thrilled. She spun around and looked at Joe, grinning. "How was that?"

"Well done." He beamed. "You might be hitting them farther than me by the time we're finished."

Sophie's gaze drifted to his impressive biceps again. *Not when you have those guns.*

This time he noticed she was looking at him, which made him grin wider.

Cheeks flaming, she grabbed another ball from the bucket, almost knocking it over, and quickly set it on the tee. Without hesitating, she swung at the ball . . . and missed.

"Want me to show you how to hit it again?" he asked.

She glanced at him, irritated at the teasing tone of his voice, not to mention his stance—arms crossed over his broad chest, emphasizing those biceps. Knowing he was doing that on purpose, she shook her head.

"I'm fine." She grabbed another ball, and this time she went through the paces before hitting it. There. She'd hit a few balls. Now it was time to go home, although she had to admit she was having fun. What wasn't fun was this strange attraction she was experiencing, and the sooner she left, the better.

"How about I get us some drinks?" Joe asked, sticking his golf glove into the back pocket of his pants. "Do you like lemonade?"

"Yeah, but—"

"Great. I'll be right back."

She watched him walk away and noticed that he looked just as good from the back as he did from the front. Ugh. She didn't need to be noticing anything about him. But she couldn't just leave, not when he was nice enough to get her a drink.

Grabbing another ball, she figured she might as well hit one more while he was gone. Then she would thank him for the lemonade and the golf lesson and leave. And this time she would keep her word.

———

"Who's the pretty lady?"

Joe frowned. He should have known Claude, the owner of the golf range who was also running concessions right now, would comment on Joe bringing a woman with him. He'd never brought one before.

"A friend," he said, glancing at Sophie as she hit another ball off the tee. She was actually pretty good for her first time driving. He wasn't really paying attention to her golf form, though. It was *her* form he couldn't stop noticing, especially after he'd been so close to her. It had taken every ounce of willpower he had to step away from her.

Claude raised one bushy gray eyebrow. "A friend, hmm?"

"Yeah."

"What can I get you two?"

"Two lemonades, along with an order of mind your own business." Joe intended the words in jest, but he didn't want the old man asking any more questions.

Raising his hands, Claude stepped back from the counter.

"You're a mite touchy for just a friend," he said in his slow Southern drawl. Before Joe could respond, the old man snuck off to make the lemonades.

As he waited, Joe turned and watched Sophie again, and for the first time since he'd seen her tonight, he wondered about her date with Landon. He'd wondered about it plenty during the day, but once she stepped out of her car and he saw how pretty she was in her white T-shirt, gray shorts, and white tennis shoes, his focus had been entirely on her. So much so that he was having his worst day on the driving range in a long time. That would normally bother his competitive spirit, but right now he didn't care.

Claude brought out the lemonades and set them on the counter. When Joe reached for his billfold, the man held up his hand again. "On the house."

Joe shook his head. "I'll pay for these."

"You're one of my best customers, so the drinks are on me today. I'm just glad you didn't order beer."

"We live in a dry county."

"Exactly." Claude grinned and pushed the drinks toward him. "Don't keep your *friend* waitin'."

"Thanks." Joe took the drinks and hurried back to the range, in as much of a hurry to get back to Sophie as he was to get away from Claude's good-natured ribbing. Sophie had just finished hitting a drive that shanked left when he arrived at their stall.

"Ugh," she said. "I'm getting worse."

Joe handed her a lemonade. "That happens sometimes, especially when you're not used to an activity. I think you're doing great."

She looked at him from beneath her lashes. "Thanks," she said softly, taking the lemonade from him.

He took a swig, the sweet beverage cooling his throat but not his thoughts. Then again, he probably shouldn't be surprised. Fifteen years was a *long* time to go without a date. Then he had to remind himself this wasn't a date. He was making up for being a heel about her and Landon.

"How was your date last night?" he blurted, unable to keep himself from asking the question, even though he had vowed not to bring the jerk into their conversation.

After a pause, she said, "It was okay." She set the lemonade down on a small table flanked by two chairs, then quickly picked up her club and grabbed a golf ball out of the wire basket.

That was uninformative. Did she mean it was okay in a good way? Or was she just being polite?

When she swung at the ball three times and missed, he placed his lemonade next to hers on the table and walked over to her.

"Relax," he said, gesturing to her shoulders, which were lifted close to her neck. Apparently he'd struck a nerve, and he wished he'd kept his big mouth shut.

"I *am*," she said through gritted teeth, and pulled back and swung again. This time she barely nicked the ball, and it fell off the tee.

"Hey." He moved closer to her and took the club from her hand, afraid she might start swinging it again. "I'm sorry I asked about you and Landon."

"It's all right." She waved her hand at him and sighed. "To be honest, the date was awful. He's incredibly boring and likes to talk about himself constantly."

"What a surprise," Joe mumbled, trying not to smirk.

"It was a waste of time." She met his gaze. "You were right, I shouldn't have gone out with him."

The breeze from the fan in the corner of the stall lifted a strand of loose hair from her ponytail. He fought the urge to tuck it behind her ear. "I'm sorry," he said again, meaning it.

She scoffed. "I'm waiting for the 'I told you so.'"

He shook his head. "I'd never say that to you." He handed her back her club. "We've got five balls left. Would you like to hit the rest?"

After staring at him for a moment, she nodded. "Yes. I would."

"Good. You can pretend they're Ferry's head."

Sophie smiled, and his knees nearly buckled. Oh boy, he was in trouble here. *So much for a friendly outing.* At least on his part.

⌒

Sophie had never experienced anything as satisfying as getting out her frustration by driving golf balls. *Why haven't I done this before?* But she knew the answer. It was the answer for everything she'd missed out on during the past fifteen years. Work. Work, work, work. For once she hadn't thought about Petals and Posies since she'd left the shop.

How could she when her attention kept flip-flopping from golf to Joe, focusing mostly on Joe the past twenty minutes. While she had gotten out her frustration over Landon being a bust, Joe had sat there drinking his lemonade and calling out a few pointers that were actually helpful. When she saw that only one ball was left, she grabbed it from the basket and walked over to him.

"You can hit the last one."

He looked at the ball, then up at her. "Are you sure?"

She nodded. "Positive." Truth was, she needed a break. Her arms were sore from swinging the club, not to mention the way her body had tensed when Joe mentioned Landon. She'd hoped he wouldn't, but when he did, she couldn't be dishonest about the date. She'd also genuinely thought Joe would gloat, but he didn't. If anything, he looked sympathetic. Strange, since he had been so insistent that she not go out with Landon.

"All right." He took one last drink and stood up, then took the ball from her hand and walked to the tee.

Sophie sat and grabbed her lemonade, the plastic cup slick with condensation. It was a warm night, but not too humid. Very pleasant for hitting golf balls. As she took a drink, she realized it was also pleasant to watch Joe. More than pleasant, she realized, taking in how good he looked as he squared up in front of the tee. His forearms were tan and muscular, but they didn't compare to those biceps. *Who knew I was such an arm girl?*

She gave her head a hard shake, nearly spilling her lemonade on her lap. Where were these thoughts coming from? This was Joe, a man she hadn't paid a lick of attention to in fifteen years. But for some reason, tonight she couldn't keep her eyes off him. More importantly, he hadn't rubbed her nose in the failed date. He'd also introduced her to a game she knew she was going to play again.

Friends, remember? We're here together as friends.

Thwack! The sound of the driver hitting the ball brought

her out of her thoughts, and she watched the white sphere fade into oblivion. Was it possible to hit a ball past the range? If so, Joe would be the one to do it.

He was grinning as he walked over to her. "Now that was a good drive." He sat in the chair on the other side of the table. "Want to hit another bucket?"

She shook her head, then tugged the errant strand of hair that had been bugging her all evening behind her ear. "The muscles in my arms say no."

Joe chuckled, resting one ankle over his knee. "Then we should listen to your muscles. You don't want to injure yourself."

Her gaze went to his biceps again, then she quickly took another sip of her lemonade. He'd caught her staring at him once; she didn't want him to see her doing it again.

They sat in silence for a moment, then Joe uncrossed his legs. "I'll take your driver and the bucket back to the clubhouse."

Disappointment suddenly coursed through her. Their evening was over. They would get into their cars, and she would go back to her house. Alone. Like she always had. She glanced around the range and saw two empty stalls and no one at the clubhouse. The stall next to them had three teenage boys making the usual ruckus teen boys make.

"Do you mind waiting until I finish my lemonade?" she asked, a little embarrassed she was using such a weak excuse to extend their time together.

"Sure." He leaned back in his chair. "I don't want to rush you."

She nodded, taking another sip, a tiny one this time. "Do you coach the golf team at school?"

He shook his head. "Nah. Football keeps me plenty busy.

It's my first sports love. Besides, the golf coach is excellent. His short game leaves me in the dust."

Sophie had no idea what a short game was, but she would make sure to google it when she got home.

"Hold still," Joe said, turning toward her.

"What?"

"There's a bee hovering over your head."

She looked up and saw the bee. She wasn't afraid of them, but she also didn't want to get stung. She remained still, only to cast a look at Joe, his placid expression transforming into fear.

"Sophie!" he suddenly yelled.

Before she knew it, they were overrun with bees. He grabbed her hand and she dropped her lemonade, then together they ran toward his pickup. He had the key out before they got there and quickly unlocked then opened the door, shoved her inside, scrambled in next to her, and slammed the door shut.

Chapter 6

*A*re you okay?"

Sophie looked at Joe, who was only an inch or two away from her. She nodded, breathing heavily from the exertion of running across the parking lot. She couldn't remember the last time she'd run anywhere.

"You didn't get stung, did you?" Joe's gaze roamed quickly over her body.

Her face heated and her breath caught in her throat. "N-no," she said, trying to regain her composure.

"Good." He scooted back on the bench seat.

"What happened?"

"I'm not sure. I heard the kids next to us throwing golf balls against the roof earlier. I have no idea who they are—they don't go to Maple Falls High School. I bet they disturbed a nest when they were goofing off."

Sophie looked out the windshield and saw the kids running toward a white SUV and flailing their arms in the air. As soon as they were all inside, the car's engine roared to life and the teens peeled out of the gravel lot.

Joe shook his head. "Kids," he said in a frustrated tone. Then he winced.

"Did you get stung?" Sophie leaned closer to him and saw several stings on his forearm. "Oh no."

"It's fine. Just a couple bee stings."

She looked at his face and saw one on his cheek. Without thinking, she touched the spot right below the sting. "Does it hurt?"

His gaze held hers. "I can barely feel it."

Did his voice sound huskier, or was that her imagination? She didn't care. She also couldn't move, and then he covered her hand with his.

"Sophie, I—"

"Ouch!" She yanked her hand away and started batting at a bee buzzing in the truck's cab.

"That's it." Joe jammed his key into the ignition, turned it, and they flew out of the parking lot. As soon as they were on the road, he rolled down the windows. Two bees flew out.

"Are there any more?" he asked over the wind rushing through the cab.

Sophie looked around, then shook out the hem of her T-shirt. "I think they're gone."

"I'm keeping the windows open just in case."

"Where are we going?"

"Back to my place. I have some calamine lotion in the medicine cabinet." He glanced at her. "If that's okay."

She nodded, and when he faced forward, she winced. Hopefully he didn't see it, because the bee had stung her on the cheek, too, but unfortunately not the one on her face. She shifted on the truck's bench seat and leaned as much as she could to her left without drawing attention to herself.

When she glanced at Joe's forearm and saw red welts forming, she knew he was making the right decision by getting some medicine as soon as possible. "You're not allergic to bees, are you?"

"Fortunately, no. At least, not much. I don't go into anaphylactic shock, but my skin reacts." He looked at her. "What about you?"

"No allergies."

"You're lucky, then." He turned into the entrance of one of the two modest suburbs on the outskirts of Maple Falls, then pulled into the second driveway. He shut off the engine.

"I'm going to leave the windows open," he said. "In case more are hiding out."

"Good idea." She looked at Joe's house in front of her. A beautiful hedge of pink azalea bushes lined a concrete front stoop. The house was sand-colored brick with cream shutters and a brown front door, which matched the brown door of the garage.

Joe got out of the truck, and before she could pull the latch, he'd jogged around and opened the passenger door for her, then held out his hand. She took it, inwardly smiling, appreciating that he was such a gentleman.

He paused, letting go of her hand. "Uh, do you want to come in? Or I can bring the lotion out here."

She hesitated. *This is not a date, remember?*

"I'll come inside." She followed him down the sidewalk to the front door.

When she crossed the threshold, she was immediately impressed. The house was not only tidy but nicely decorated too.

"I'll be right back. Make yourself at home." He gestured to the brown leather couch in the living room.

Sophie winced. "I think I'll stand."

He gave her a puzzled glance, then disappeared down the hallway. A few seconds later he came back. "Brand-new bottle," he said, taking off the cap. He held it out to her. "You first."

She threaded her fingers together. "I don't have as many stings as you do. You go ahead."

"Are you sure?" When she nodded, he dabbed the pink lotion on the swollen bites on his arm. "I need to get some ice on these too," he said, putting the bottle down on the kitchen counter. "Do you need some?" When she shook her head, he asked, "You got stung in the truck, right?"

Nodding, Sophie felt her cheeks flame, and she frowned. She hated that she blushed so much. "I did."

"Where?"

"On my backside."

His lips twitched. "You're on your own with the lotion, then. The bathroom is down the hall."

She caught his grin as he turned to the refrigerator and opened the freezer. She couldn't help but smile as she took the bottle and went to the bathroom, which was just as tidy as the rest of the house she'd seen. It was also neater than her place. Housekeeping was always last on her list of things to do. If they had gone to her place, she would have been even more embarrassed than she was now.

Sophie applied the soothing lotion to her sting, wondering

how she managed to get stung there in the first place, then walked back into the kitchen. Joe was sitting on a barstool next to the kitchen counter, an ice pack resting on his forearm. She set the lotion on the counter.

He moved to get up. "Do you want something to drink? I've got Coke, water, tea—"

"I'm fine." She moved a little closer to him. "You didn't put any lotion on the sting on your face."

He touched it. "Is it bad?"

"Not too bad." The welt was red, but not as angry and swollen as the ones on his arm.

Still, it needed tending to before it got that way. She picked up the lotion, took off the cap, then put a little on her index finger. She leaned over and dabbed it on his cheek.

"There," she said, surprised at the softness in her voice. "Feel better?"

His eyes didn't move from hers. "Much."

The swirling of butterflies in her stomach was now at a fever pitch. When his gaze dropped to her mouth, she could barely breathe.

He's going to kiss me . . . and I'm going to let him.

———

If Sophie knew how badly Joe wanted to kiss her, she'd probably slap him. At the very least she'd walk right out of his house and call a friend or an Uber to come get her. Having made several mistakes already, he was determined not to screw up now. He yanked his gaze from hers and stood, the movement almost painful—and not because of the bee stings.

"Uh, it's probably safe back at the range now," he said, turning his back to her as he tried to get his wits together. "Claude probably has the exterminator on the premises by now."

"Oh. Right. I'm sure it is."

He turned back to her, wondering if he was imagining that she sounded disappointed. Of course, he was, because now she wasn't even looking at him. She was scanning the room, and he was thankful the cleaning service he'd hired to come by twice a week had decided to come out today instead of yesterday. Usually his place, while not dirty, was messy, mostly due to him being so busy, which was why he'd hired the service.

Why was he thinking about cleaning, anyway? *Because it's better than thinking about kissing Sophie.* He pressed the ice pack to his arm, but what he really needed was a cold shower. If he couldn't keep his focus on something other than Sophie, he'd end up kissing her, and that would be strike three in her book.

He tossed the ice pack on the counter and headed for the front door. "I'll make sure the truck is empty of critters," he said as he opened the door, then walked out without waiting for her response. When he got outside, he drew in a deep breath. *Get it together, man!*

Serious about making sure his truck was clear of bees, he checked everything, including the engine, which not only bought him time to collect himself but also proved that they were finally free of the pesky insects. He walked back to the house and poked his head inside the front door.

"It's safe now," he said, then nearly laughed out loud at the irony. His emotions were definitely not safe, and the sooner he got her back to the range, the better.

He opened the truck door for her, barely thinking about

the gesture because he'd always done it. He even opened the door for his sister, although she, being the independent woman she was, always pitched a fit. Which was why he never failed to open the door for her. He climbed in the driver's seat, and a few minutes later they were headed back to the range.

The silence in the cab was overwhelming. Why weren't they talking? Everything had been easy until . . . *Until you almost kissed her.* Had she sensed that he'd wanted to? He had no idea. If he'd learned one thing this evening, it was that he couldn't trust his emotions.

Joe turned into the parking lot, which was now empty except for Sophie's car and Claude's classic Crown Victoria. The old man was holding a can in each hand and spraying them around the stall where the teenagers had been. When he saw Joe pull up next to Sophie's car, he hurried over to them. Joe rolled down the truck window.

"What happened?" he asked when Claude reached them.

"Idiot kids." Claude scowled, looking like he was ready to exterminate some teenagers. "They saw a hole in the roof and started throwing balls at it, trying to see if they could get one in. I was going over there to tell them to knock it off when bees started coming out of the hole. You know the rest." He shook his head. "I guess I should thank them. At least we weren't busy, and now I know I need to inspect for more nests. Anyways, I'm closed for the night, obviously. Did you two leave anything?"

"The club I used and the golf ball bucket," Sophie said. "I can get them for you."

"I'll put them up." Claude lifted the cans. "Back to work I go."

Joe rolled the window back up as Claude took off. He

frowned, wondering if he needed help. As soon as he said goodbye to Sophie, Joe decided to find out. He turned to her, prepared to see that she'd opened the door and was already half-way out.

But she remained in her seat, looking at him.

"Joe," she said, her tone serious. "I need to ask you something."

He was surprised. "Sure."

"Why didn't you want me to go out with Landon?"

~

Sophie had spent the ride back to the golf range trying to stem her disappointment.

She'd been so sure Joe was going to kiss her, then felt like a fool for being completely wrong. Then again, what did she know about men? When was the last time she'd actually kissed one? Never, since the last kiss she'd experienced was a per-functory one from her date at the senior prom, and that didn't count. How pathetic. Thirty-five years old and never been kissed. How humiliating. At least by the time Joe pulled into the parking lot, she had disabused herself of the kissing idea.

But there was one thing she wanted to know. She hadn't planned to ask him, but now that their friendly evening was over and he'd made up for interfering in her life, she wasn't sure if she'd have the opportunity again. She needed to know why he had been so against her going out with Landon.

He was quiet for a long moment, then he rubbed his palms on the legs of his pants before turning to her. "You knew I was married before, right?"

She nodded. "To Jenna." She'd been surprised to hear that they had gotten married, because they were so young and the first couple in their graduating class to do so.

"And you know we divorced six months later." When she nodded again, he let out a bitter chuckle. "The perils of small-town living. Right after the divorce, Jenna moved to Malvern. I wasn't sure why, since one of the reasons she wanted a divorce was because she didn't want to live in Maple Falls anymore, and she was afraid of getting stuck here." He frowned. "I told her we could move to Hot Springs if she wanted. I just needed to be within commuting distance of Henderson State, where I was attending. But that wasn't good enough. And it wasn't like Malvern was a big city." He blew out a breath. "I'm sure you're not interested in all those details."

Actually, she was. Not for the gossip factor, but because Joe was revealing a part of his past, one she suspected he rarely revisited. He was trusting her enough to explain things, and she appreciated that. "I don't mind."

"I'll give you the short version anyway." He looked directly at her. "Jenna was having an affair with Landon."

Sophie's jaw dropped. "What?"

A dark look crossed Joe's handsome face. "Yeah. It started about a month after we got married. I never asked her how, and she didn't tell me, other than she thought married life was boring. Or more accurately, I was boring."

Sophie couldn't think of anything further from the truth. Joe Johnson was anything but dull. He was kind, considerate, an excellent coach and teacher, and good-looking. Jenna had to be nuts to throw him away like that.

"I guess she thought Landon was boring, too, because a

few weeks after she moved to Malvern, she left for Florida. I haven't talked to her or Ferry since." He lifted his gaze to her. "Then when I saw him asking you out, I . . . Never mind. You know what I did."

He'd wanted to protect her. That was what he'd been doing, and in turn she kicked him out of the shop. Granted, she had no idea, but did it matter? Sophie shivered at the thought that she'd had dinner with someone so vile.

"Anyway, that's the reason," Joe continued. "But I promise I won't do it again."

"You won't have to. I won't be seeing him again."

Joe's face brightened, only to turn serious again a moment later. "Good." A pause. "Well, I guess I'd better see if Claude needs help. I don't think two cans of bug spray will protect him if there's another nest around here."

It was as if he couldn't wait for her to leave. Of course, he probably couldn't. They had nothing else to do or to say.

"All right." She reached for the passenger door latch, expecting him to jump out and finish opening the door for her, like he had at the house. Instead, he remained in place.

"Goodbye," she said, getting out.

"See ya."

Heaviness settled over her heart as she shut the truck door and made her way to her car. There wasn't a bee in sight, and the calamine lotion had done its job soothing the sting on her backside. She was tempted to look over her shoulder, to get one more look at Joe before she never saw him again. It might be overdramatic, but considering how infrequently their paths crossed, she was sure it was close to the truth.

Even so, she kept her focus on her car and her thoughts in

perspective. There hadn't been anything between her and Joe in the past, and there wouldn't be in the future. It wasn't like he was the only single guy in the world.

There's always internet dating.

Defeated, Sophie groaned as she opened her car door.

Chapter 7

Feeling like a heel for not opening the door for her, Joe waited for Sophie to drive off. He hadn't wanted to face her after telling her about Jenna and Landon. He might've tried to stop her and ask for another date.

Instead, he pushed all that away, reminding himself that he and Sophie didn't exactly run into each other very often. And even if she had been interested in another date, he was sure he'd squashed her interest after revealing his past. The pain still haunted him, although it wasn't because he missed Jenna. She had made a fool out of him, and that was what hurt. He'd been in love, or thought he was anyway, and she had said she loved him. Yeah, she loved him so much she was in another man's bed a month after their honeymoon.

He banged his fist against the steering wheel as the memories he'd shoved deep down coursed through him. Then he sat back in his seat. That was the past, and he needed to keep it there. He had owed Sophie an explanation, and he was grateful to see sympathy instead of pity in her eyes. But that didn't mean they were meant to go out again, much less be together. The fact that he was even thinking about that right now made a new, confusing ache appear in his heart.

Joe flung open the truck door and walked toward Claude. He needed to do something to get his mind off the past, and especially off Sophie. The last thing he wanted to do was go to an empty house and stew, so he approached Claude, who was shaking one of the cans of insecticide. It sounded empty.

"Do you have any more?"

Claude nodded. "In the storeroom." Then he turned to Joe. "Where's your girl?"

Joe almost chuckled that Claude would consider a woman in her thirties a girl, much less *his* girl. "She went home."

"Oh. I'm sorry. Hey, bring her back tomorrow. I'll give you both two buckets. On me."

Shaking his head, Joe said, "I won't be seeing her anymore."

"She's that upset about the bees?"

"It's not the bees. It's me. She's not interested in me like that."

"That's not what I saw."

Joe frowned. "What?"

"I pay attention to things around here." Claude smiled, revealing a gold bottom tooth. "My friend, she couldn't keep her eyes off you."

"She was probably looking at the bee stings." He gestured to his arm.

"Trust me, she wasn't lookin' at that part of your arm."

Joe stilled, remembering how he had caught her looking at him shortly after she arrived at the range. He'd kept in good shape since he'd stopped playing football, and he liked to lift.

Still, the feeling he'd gotten when he saw she had noticed his biceps—

"Earth to Joe." Claude clucked his tongue. "When was the last time you were on a date? Not counting tonight."

"Tonight wasn't a date—"

"Yeah, yeah. Whatever." He looked at the nozzle on the can. "The time before that?"

Joe paused. "Jenna. My ex-wife."

Claude's head snapped up. "You were married?"

"Don't look so shocked." Man, his ego was taking some hits tonight.

"I don't mean it like that. I just never pegged you for being divorced."

It's not like Joe had wanted to be. Over the years he'd realized that even though it hurt and he'd been humiliated, Jenna's divorcing him had been for the best. The marriage would have been miserable because he never would have been able to please her. He knew that now, thanks to hindsight.

"Let's get back to the date thing. So, you haven't been on a date since your divorce, which was . . ."

"A long time ago," Joe muttered.

"Okay. Makes sense." Claude gestured toward the club-house with a nod. "Let's get the rest of that spray. I think I got them all, but I want to be sure."

"You didn't call an exterminator?"

"Oh I did, and she's coming out in the morning. But I want those things *dead* dead."

Joe couldn't argue with that. He followed him, unsure about Claude's earlier point. "What do you mean it makes sense?"

"That you wouldn't see that—what's her name?"

"Sophie."

"Ah, Sophie. Lovely name for a lovely girl." He gave Joe a side-look. "There it is."

"What?"

"A little jealous spark."

Joe laughed as they walked into the storeroom behind the clubhouse. "Me, jealous? Of you, old man?"

"Hey, at least I can see what's right in front of my nose." He opened the door. "Now where's that bug spray?"

"Here." Joe grabbed a can off the shelf nearest to the door. As he handed it to Claude, he thought about the man's words. Was he right, that Sophie was interested, and Joe couldn't see it? Nah, that couldn't be it. Could it?

Claude took the can, then found two more and handed them to Joe. They went back to the tees, and he helped spray them down and look for more holes. After emptying the cans, Claude declared they'd done everything they could do for the night.

"Thanks for your help," he said as he threw the cans away.

"No problem."

"Now, what are you going to do about Sophie?"

Joe thought the old man had dropped the subject. "Nothing," he said. "There's nothing I can do."

Shaking his head, Claude walked over to Joe and clapped him on the shoulder. "You're going to ask her out again."

"But—"

"What have you got to lose?"

A pause. "She could turn me down."

"True. And would that be the worst thing in the world?"

Joe shook his head. What Jenna had done to him was. So

why did the thought of Sophie rejecting him make him feel almost as bad? Less than two days ago, he'd been fine with asking her out. *Because I didn't know I cared for her then.*

"Look, son. You can spend the rest of your life protectin' yourself because of what happened in the past, or you can let all that go and find out what you've been missin'. I can see you like this girl. You're not any better at hiding your feelings than she is. Problem is, you're both afraid."

"And you figured that out after seeing us together for a couple hours?"

Claude laughed. "You forget, I've been married over fifty years. I have six kids, and they're all married too. I've learned a few things."

Joe considered his words. "I'll think about it," was all he managed to say.

Clapping him on the shoulder again, Claude said, "That's all I'm asking you to do."

After Joe left the range, he headed straight home. He saw the bottle of calamine lotion on the kitchen counter, then thought about Claude's words again. They had been all he could think about on the drive home.

The next day, which was strangely slow for a Saturday, Sophie let Hayley and MacKenzie off for the afternoon. The day was bright, sunny, and warm, and she was sure everyone was out enjoying the beautiful weather before summer bore down and made it too hot to do much of anything outside. She went to the back and straightened up the workroom. When she spied a daisy on the floor, she picked it up. The stem was bent but the petals were still in place. Even so, the flower couldn't be used. She glanced around, as if worried someone might see her, then she started to pluck the petals.

He loves me . . .

He loves me not.

By the last petal, she not only felt stupid for playing such a dumb game, but she'd also landed on *he loves me not.* Frustrated, she tossed the empty stem into the trash. She hadn't been able to get Joe off her mind all night or today. What he told her about Jenna and Landon had broken her heart. How could that woman be so callous to a kind man like Joe? She knew there were two sides to every story, but she couldn't imagine Joe doing anything to cause Jenna to treat him so badly.

She didn't doubt his version of what happened either. She could easily see Landon having an affair with a married woman and not caring about the consequences. She now despised him instead of merely thinking he was an egocentric bore. How many men out there were just like him, only concerned with themselves and not caring whether they hurt someone or not?

The idea of going out with anyone except Joe Johnson made her uneasy.

Meeting men she didn't know beyond a picture and profile on the internet didn't appeal to her either. She knew April would set her up with someone if she asked, or her mother would try to, but Sophie didn't want that.

I want Joe. And she couldn't have him. *Maybe I'm not ready to date, after all.*

The chime sounded over the entry door, and for once she didn't rush to the front of the store. She sighed as she trudged out of the workroom, then gasped when she saw the man standing there.

"What are you doing here?"

Landon—looking like he'd just stepped out of a men's style magazine with his perfect hair, perfect outfit, and perfectly fake smile—walked to the counter.

"Hello to you, too, Sophie."

She crossed her arms over her chest. "How can I help you?" she asked, fighting for a polite tone, but failing. All she could see was the man who had played a part in wrecking Joe's marriage.

"We need to talk."

"No, we don't. And if you're not here to buy flowers, you can show yourself out." On second thought, she wasn't sure if she would sell him so much as an empty stem after finding out about him and Jenna.

The perfect expression slid from Landon's face, changing to anger. "I'm not leaving until we have this conversation."

A chill ran down Sophie's spine. "I'm not going out with you again, Landon," she said firmly.

"Oh, don't worry. I won't be asking."

"Then we have nothing to talk about."

"Except your business. I have a proposition for you."

Against her will, Sophie listened as Landon launched into a lengthy explanation about how beneficial it would be for her to sell Petals and Posies.

"I have a buyer already lined up. He's willing to pay you more than this place is worth."

"Why?" Sophie crossed her arms again. "What's so valuable about my property?"

"That's not for me to disclose."

She lifted her chin. "I'm not interested."

"You haven't heard the off—"

"I don't care what the offer is. This is my shop, and I will never sell it." When she saw him flinch, she added, "Did you really think you could wine and dine me a few times and I would fold and sell my business? Do you have any idea how long and hard I've worked to make it successful?"

"I'm sure I can convince you that selling is in your best interest," he said, regaining his composure, clearly not caring that she had put her heart and soul into her shop. "Listen, I'm not supposed to tell you this, but I know I can trust you. My client is *very* interested in revitalizing Maple Falls."

"By buying up all the businesses?"

"Most of them are hanging by a thread anyway."

She squared her shoulders and leveled her gaze. "Not mine."

"With what my client is willing to pay, you can buy a shop twice as large in Hot Springs if you want. Just think how successful you would be if you had a larger shop in a well-populated city."

Although she couldn't dispute his point, she still wasn't interested. "I suppose you'll get a nice bonus if you convince me to sell."

Landon held out his hands, palms up. "Hey. I've got to make a living. Just like you." He leaned forward again, faux charm oozing from every pore. *What a snake.* "C'mon, Sophie. Think about your future. Maple Falls is like every other small town around here. It's been swirling the drain for years. It's only a matter of time before you go down with it."

He might be right about the town having gone through some rough years, but that was changing. Price's Hardware down the street and Knots and Tangles, the yarn shop across from her store, were legacy businesses that were doing well. Just like her shop.

"Does your client want to buy all the businesses on Main Street?"

A pause. "If he can."

"Then I'm definitely not selling." The thought of some rich venture capitalist taking over the Main Street properties and razing the old buildings that had existed since the late nineteenth century infuriated her. She couldn't let that happen. "You can tell your client where to shove it."

Landon's calm facade disintegrated. "For crying out loud, Sophie, if you'll just listen to me—"

The chime sounded over the door, and Sophie almost sank with relief when she saw Joe walk in.

"Not again," Landon muttered.

"Joe!" Sophie rushed around the counter and went to him. "Landon was just leaving."

Landon looked at Joe, and Sophie saw the glint of superiority in the man's eyes. He was worse than a snake and she couldn't stand him. She was about to tell him exactly that when he turned toward the door. "I'll be back to finish our conversation."

Before Sophie could respond, Joe moved between her and Landon. Then he looked at Sophie. "Is that what you want?"

A million thoughts went through her mind, and none of them were about Landon. "No," she said, keeping her gaze on Joe. "That's not what I want."

Joe turned to Landon. "You heard her. She doesn't want to talk to you."

Landon scoffed. "Stay out of this, Johnson. You know who's going to win here." He lowered his voice. "Me. Just like I won Jenna."

Without hesitating Joe grabbed Landon by the collar with one hand and by the waistband of his pants with the other, then rammed him out the door.

"Not this time, Ferry." He shoved Landon down the sidewalk. The man stumbled but regained his balance.

Sophie rushed to lock the door in case Landon tried to get inside.

Instead, a woman and her daughter walked by, gaping at him. He straightened the collar of his expensive casual shirt, then turned and walked away.

———

Joe felt the adrenaline drain from his body. Uh-oh. He shouldn't have manhandled Landon the way he did. Having the element of surprise helped, but the fact was, Landon wasn't a strong man to begin with and never had been. And not just physically. Landon still believed he was the victor in an imaginary battle Joe hadn't known he was waging. Maybe Landon just liked collecting women, the way some people collected stuffed animals or stamps. Either way, the man was despicable.

He had to admit, taking out the weasel had felt good, but he wasn't proud of that fact.

"Joe?"

The furious haze cleared, and he saw Sophie leaning against

the door of her shop, a shocked look on her face. Once again, his plan had gone up in smoke. After mulling over what Claude said, he'd decided the old man was right. Joe had to stop living in the past. He wanted to take a chance with his heart, and even though it would probably sound crazy to Sophie, he had to tell her how he felt, and he'd deal with whatever came next.

Instead, he'd thrown Landon out of her shop.

Real smooth.

"Sophie, I'm sor—"

"That was awesome!" She pumped her fist as she walked up to him. "You picked him up like he weighed nothing." Her gaze went to his arms, and she looked at them appreciatively.

Joe was glad he'd worn the short-sleeve Maple Falls football T-shirt.

She stood in front of him. "I'm so glad you're here."

"Did he do anything to you?" Joe could feel the adrenaline pumping through him again at the thought of Landon hurting her.

"No."

He listened as she told him about Landon's client wanting to buy the shop.

"I told him to forget it, of course. I realized that was the only reason he paid attention to me in the first place. He's a user and a jerk. I can see that now." She smiled, her eyes never leaving Joe's. "Thanks to you."

Now was the time. He had her undivided attention and the shop was empty. It was the perfect moment to tell her how he felt. "Sophie, I . . ."

"Yes?"

Her softness undid him. Forgetting his words, he grabbed

her in his arms and kissed her. A thrill ran through him when she encircled her arms around his neck and returned the kiss . . . and the next one . . . and the next one.

Finally, they both pulled away, Joe keeping his arms around her.

"Wow," he said, leaning his forehead against hers.

"Yeah," she replied, sounding as breathless as he did. "My thoughts exactly."

"I've been wanting to do that since last night."

"I wanted you to kiss me last night." Her cheeks turned rosy.

Joe laughed. "Claude was right after all."

Sophie frowned, brushing her fingertip over the almost nonexistent bee sting on Joe's cheek. "About what?"

"I'll explain later. Sophie, I know it's strange and we haven't known each other that long—"

"Only since kindergarten," she said, a wry smile on her lips.

"Right. But I'm talking about more than that. I want to get to know you, Sophie. I want us to date. I can show you how to play golf, and you can show me how to, uh, arrange flowers."

"I wouldn't put you through that torture," she said. "But I'd love to play golf. I want to spend more time with you too."

"How about tonight?"

She grinned. "Definitely."

He finally released her and took a step back. "At least we got the first kiss over with."

Doubt crossed her features. "Was it okay?"

Joe grinned. "It was perfect."

Epilogue

Sophie adjusted the crown of daisies in her hair and checked her makeup in the mirror, then sighed with happiness. Back in May when she decided to take a chance on dating, she had never expected to find a man like Joe Johnson, much less fall in love with him. And now here she was, standing in a beautiful hotel room in the Dominican Republic, waiting to marry a man she had known all her life, and who had unexpectedly turned out to be the man of her dreams

She frowned slightly at her reflection. Her mother was going to kill her for this. Not just her mother, but April and her other friends, Hayley and MacKenzie, and probably half of Maple Falls. When she'd called her mother and told her she was seeing Joe, Mom had peppered her with so many questions Sophie's head was spinning by the time she hung up the phone. Why she wanted to know what brand of spaghetti sauce Joe preferred, Sophie had no idea. When she told Mom he made his own, she said, "You're dating a man who can cook? Now that's a keeper! I can't wait to meet him."

Mom and Dad would meet him all right . . . after the honeymoon.

Soon after she talked to Mom, she'd called her sister. Like everyone else, Lis was happy for her and told Sophie she had dibs on being matron of honor, which was only fair because Sophie had been her maid of honor.

Of course, April had approved of Joe, too, and of how he had thrown Landon out of the shop.

"I shouldn't be surprised that he's so slimy," she'd said. "But do you think his client will be able to buy up Main Street?"

"Not if I can stop it. I told Hayden and Riley what happened, and Hayden is going to spread the word to the other businesses about what's going on. We have to preserve Maple Falls."

"Agreed." Then April had switched subjects, insisting that she and Darren double date with Sophie and Joe soon. They'd all gone out together several times, as well as with Travis and his wife. Sophie overheard Travis hinting about being Joe's best man the last time they came over for dinner.

Sophie cringed at the memories. She never intended to hurt anyone's feelings, and she would apologize to everyone when they returned to Maple Falls. But she had to be true to herself. Today was her day, and there was only one person she wanted to spend it with. Then there was the practical angle of getting married and honeymooning in the same place, and she couldn't think of anything more romantic than that.

She stepped back from the mirror in the hotel bathroom and looked at the simple sleeveless white dress she slipped into a few minutes ago. The hem hit above her knee, and she wore flat-soled white sandals. A strand of pearls completed her outfit and she nodded with satisfaction as a knock sounded at the door.

"Sophie?"

"Coming." She hurried to open the door. Joe stood there, dressed casually in tan shorts, slip-on shoes, and, at her insistence, a short-sleeve polo shirt.

Very nice.

He took a step back and whistled. "You look gorgeous."

"So do you."

He grinned. "Are you ready to do this?"

She nodded.

"No regrets?"

"About eloping? Absolutely not."

He started rocking back and forth on his heels. "Good, because there's still time to have a wedding if that's what you want."

His words surprised her. "What about football season? Teaching? It's July. Even a small wedding would take several months to plan."

"I can find someone to sub for me." He walked into the room and closed the door behind him. "If you want a regular wedding with your family and friends, just say the word."

Sophie paused, but not because she wanted to go through the trouble of planning a wedding. Eloping had been her idea, and two weeks after she mentioned it to Joe, they made the arrangements together and arrived yesterday. Even if they wanted to get a refund they couldn't. Knowing he would let all that go to make her happy touched her deeply.

I am so in love with this man.

Then she wondered if he was having second thoughts. "You

don't mind that Travis and your sister and parents aren't here, do you?"

"Definitely not. Weddings are about the bride anyway. The groom is just along for the ride, and I like it that way."

She walked over to the bed and picked up the ordinary bouquet of daisies, matching the ones on her head, along with five pink roses. Surprising herself, she had decided to keep the flowers to a minimum. Despite being involved in many elaborate weddings over the years, including her sister's, she'd realized after Joe proposed almost a month ago that she didn't want that for herself. Her wedding would be about her and her future husband, not the spectacle.

She turned to him and smiled. "I love you, Joe. And this wedding, with just the two of us, is exactly what I want."

"Good. Because it's exactly what I want too." He put his hands on her waist. "Then again, anywhere you are is where I want to be."

"Corny." She tapped him on the arm, then let her hand linger over his muscles before pulling away. *There will be time for that later.*

He shrugged. "It might be corny, but it's the truth."

"Do you have the rings?" she asked.

"Can't forget those." He pulled two bands out of the pocket of his shorts, the smaller one gold and the larger one black, and held them in his palm.

She touched his band. "Perfect."

Nodding, he returned the rings to his pocket. When he leaned forward to kiss her, she placed her finger on his lips. They'd stayed in separate rooms last night, and while in many ways she was flaunting tradition, she was firm on this point.

"Not until after we're husband and wife."

He groaned, dropped his hands to his sides, and took one small step back. "You drive a hard bargain, Mrs. Soon-to-Be Sophie Johnson."

Sophie laughed. "But you put up with me anyway."

He snuck a peck on her cheek, then grazed her earlobe with his lips.

"I love you, Sophie," he whispered. "Let's go get married."

She slipped her hand in his, and they left the room to start their new life together.

He loves me.

Acknowledgments

A Summer Detour

B ringing a book to market takes a lot of effort from many different people. I'm so incredibly blessed to partner with the fabulous team at HarperCollins Christian Fiction, led by publisher Amanda Bostic: Jocelyn Bailey, Matt Bray, Kimberly Carlton, Nekasha Pratt, Jodi Hughes, Margaret Kercher, Becky Monds, Kerri Potts, Savannah Summers, Marcee Wardell, and Laura Wheeler.

Not to mention all the wonderful sales reps and amazing people in the rights department—special shout-out to Robert Downs!

Thanks especially to my editor Kimberly Carlton. This collection was her brainchild, and I'm so thankful to have been included in it. Kim, thank you for your incredible insight and inspiration. You not only help me take the story deeper but also make the process enjoyable, and for that I am so grateful! Thanks also to my line editor, Julee Schwarzburg, whose attention to detail makes me look like a better writer than I really am.

Author Colleen Coble is my first reader and sister of my heart. Thank you, friend! This writing journey has been ever so much more fun because of you.

I'm grateful to my agent, Karen Solem, who's able to somehow make sense of the legal garble of contracts and, even more amazing, help me understand it.

To my husband, Kevin, who has supported my dreams in every way possible—I'm so grateful! To all our kiddos: Chad, Trevor and Babette, and Justin and Hannah, who have favored us with two beautiful granddaughters. Every stage of parenthood has been a grand adventure, and I look forward to all the wonderful memories we have yet to make!

A hearty thank you to all the booksellers who make room on their shelves for my books—I'm deeply indebted! And to all the book bloggers and reviewers, whose passion for fiction is contagious—thank you!

Lastly, thank you, friends, for letting me share this story with you! I wouldn't be doing this without you. Your notes, posts, and reviews keep me going on the days when writing doesn't flow so easily. I appreciate your support more than you know.

I enjoy connecting with friends on my Facebook page, @authordenisehunter. Please pop over and say hello. You can also visit my website DeniseHunterBooks.com or drop me a note at deniseahunter@comcast.net. I'd love to hear from you!

Pining for You

Where else could I start, but with everyone at Thomas Nelson? From the amazing efforts of the sales team to gorgeous designs of my cover designer, I am appreciative of you all *every single day*. Special hugs and cheers to: Kim Carlton, Jocelyn Bailey, Kerri Potts, Amanda Bostic, Becky Monds, Nekasha Pratt, Matt Bray, Marcee Wardell, Savannah Summers, Laura Wheeler, Jodi Hughes, and Margaret Kercher.

Special thanks to Kim Carlton: supremely intelligent, witty, insightful, and an overall joy and balm to the soul to be around. I love our little lunches that surprise us both by turning into something more—like this!

To Erin Healy for your perennial wisdom that continues to grow me into the writer I want to be. I *love* working with you.

To Halie Cotton, thank you for making the cutest cover for this collection!

To Nathaniel Pellman of Swinging Bridge Farm, thank you for answering all my questions about Christmas tree farms.

To Ashley Hayes, dear friend and marketing genius. You get zero points for the actual writing of this book, but you get approximately 1,000 points for keeping me sane. Where would I ever be without you? Why would I even need a phone if I didn't have you and our FaceTimes?

To Christine Berg, for always reading my books and brainstorming with me . . . even when my books are *far* from ready to be seen by anyone.

Acknowledgments

To Kimberly Whalen, agent extraordinaire! Thank you for always being so open and available and encouraging; it means a lot to me.

To the ACFW community, fellow Thomas Nelson authors, and dear writer friends. I love growing together.

To my patient husband, for all those nights you put the kids to bed so I could work, for all the times you read my drafts, and the thousands (millions?) of hours you've listened to me talk through my books. I love all our memories riding the Creeper Trail in this town, camping on Whitetop Mountain, and that one notable Sunday we accidentally walked 17 miles up the trail with nothing but $2 for a Pepsi and a candy bar. I love you and our never-ending adventures.

To The Martha Washington Inn, The Barter Theatre, and the incredible areas of Whitetop, Damascus and Abingdon I've been privileged to enjoy as a Bristolian all these years. Thank you for being the most Hallmark-worthy communities in all creation. You are a world of inspiration, and I can't wait to show readers our wonderful town through this book and my other rom/com, *The Cul-de-Sac War*!

To those bookstagrammers and bloggers who have shared my books in the most gorgeous of ways.

To my Creator. This book was about mistakes and forgiveness, and I'm so thankful you are quick to forgive all of ours.

And thanks to every *single* reader who encourages me on social media, replies to my newsletter emails, shares my books, writes reviews, tells your book clubs, and just makes me feel like I'm part of a cozy community. I appreciate everything you do more than I can say.

He Loves Me; He Loves Me Not

A big thank you to my editors, Kimberly Carlton and Jodi Hughes for their expert help and guidance as I wrote Sophie and Joe's story, and as always thank you to my agent, Natasha Kern, for her amazing support. Everything I know about golf (which isn't much!) is due to my husband, James. Thanks for showing me how to drive a golf ball. Next time we'll work on our putting. ☺

Discussion Questions

A Summer Detour

1. What was your favorite scene? Why?
2. Allie was determined to prove her competence by driving the restored Chevy for her parents. Have you ever tried to change someone's opinion of you? Discuss what happened as a result.
3. Years ago Luke was so afraid of losing Bill and Becky's love that he sacrificed his relationship with Allie to preserve it. Has fear ever caused you to make a bad decision? What was the outcome?
4. How did you feel about Becky's treatment of Allie versus her treatment of Olivia? Did you relate most to Becky, Olivia, or Allie? Did your parents favor a sibling? What outcome did that have on your relationship with your siblings and your parents?
5. Luke took the blame for the stolen Chevy, sparing

Allie her parents' disapproval. How does this show Luke's growth?

6. In the end Allie didn't allow Luke to take the blame for the stolen car. How does this show her growth?

7. "Maybe it was time to stop clinging to the unrealistic hope that his parents would become what he needed and just be grateful for what he already had." Are you clinging to unrealistic expectations in some area of your life? Discuss.

8. Who would you most like to take a road trip with? Who would least like to take one with?

Pining for You

1. Skye Fuller ran away from her relationship with Theo in her younger years and pursued becoming an artist in Seattle. She ultimately succeeded, but also lost her relationship with Theo. Do you think she should've left?

2. As it turns out, Theo had subtly given very much in efforts to support Skye's family. Have you ever met someone with quiet integrity? Who were they and what were they like?

3. Theo is a "city" mouse whereas Skye is settled in the country. Do you like how they compromised in the end? Have you ever experienced differences of opinion with a loved one on where and how to live? How did you resolve them?

4. Theo settled on a mountaintop without enough town

residents to fill a grocery store in order to be with his love. Would you do this? What city conveniences would you miss most? (Answer: Mine would be drive-thru coffee ;)).

5. Skye had to learn a thing or two about the danger of making assumptions without seeking clarification of the truth. Have you ever made an assumption that turned out to be wrong? What happened?

6. Skye left Seattle in order to be near her family again and, sometimes the importance of being close to family changes with time. How close do you live to your family? Why? Has this changed over the years?

7. Though Theo loved Skye, there were real challenges and temptations during his long-distance relationship with Skye while at college. Do you think his fall was understandable? Have you ever experienced anything like this? How did it turn out?

8. Theo, a bachelor of thirty-five years, was so desperate for companionship and marriage that he very nearly settled down with Ashleigh, despite a few flaws. What do you think he should've done, had Skye never turned up? Do you think it's right to settle for someone who may be great but isn't quite the person you dreamed?

9. Who is your favorite character and why?

10. Who is your least favorite character and why?

11. Poor Ashleigh has been through quite the ringer, having lost her relationship with Chip in *The Cul-de-Sac War* and now Theo in *Pining for You*. Do you think she should have her own story? (Please email me personally your thoughts on this at melissa@

melissaferguson.com! I'd love to get feedback and decide about what to do with poor Ashleigh ;)).

He Loves Me; He Loves Me Not

1. Sophie is reluctant to try online dating. Have you ever dated someone you met online, or know anyone who has?
2. Joe had to put the past behind him so he could move on with Sophie. Have you ever had an event in your past keep you from moving on?
3. What advice would you give to someone who was trying to let go of the past?
4. Sophie and Joe took a chance on love. Has there been a time in your life when you had to take a risk?

The Riverbend Romance Novels

Don't miss this new series of love stories from bestselling author Denise Hunter!

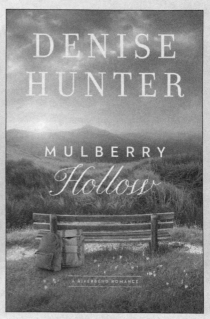

AVAILABLE IN PRINT, E-BOOK, AND AUDIO OCTOBER 2021

COMING APRIL 2022

THE THIRD AND FINAL BOOK, *HARVEST MOON*, COMES OUT IN OCTOBER 2022.

THOMAS NELSON
Since 1798

Two more hilarious, heartwarming romances from bestselling author Melissa Ferguson

"Melissa delivered a book that is filled with both humor and heart!"

—DEBBIE MACOMBER, #1 *NEW YORK TIMES* BESTSELLING AUTHOR, FOR *THE CUL-DE-SAC WAR*

AVAILABLE IN PRINT, E-BOOK, AND AUDIO

THOMAS NELSON
Since 1798

The Maple Falls Romance Novels

Welcome to Maple Falls, a small town where love and life collide.

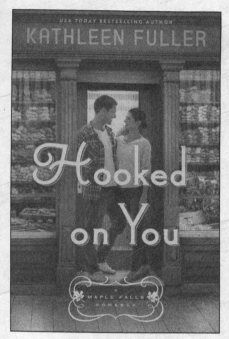

Available in print,
e-book, and audio

Coming January 2022

"Sign me up for a one-way ticket to Maple Falls. If you love small towns, charming characters, and sweet, swoony romance, *Hooked on You* is your next favorite read. Kathleen Fuller has knit one wonderful story yet again."

—JENNY B. JONES, AWARD-WINNING AUTHOR OF *A KATIE PARKER PRODUCTION* AND *THE HOLIDAY HUSBAND*

THOMAS NELSON
Since 1798

About the Authors

Denise Hunter

Photo by Neal Bruns

Denise Hunter is the internationally published bestselling author of more than thirty books, three of which have been adapted into original Hallmark Channel movies. She has won the Holt Medallion Award, the Reader's Choice Award, the Carol Award, and the Foreword Book of the Year Award and is a RITA finalist. When Denise isn't orchestrating love lives on the written page, she enjoys traveling with her family, drinking good coffee, and playing drums. Denise makes her home in Indiana, where she and her husband are currently enjoying an empty nest.

Visit Denise online at DeniseHunterBooks.com
Instagram: @deniseahunter
Facebook: @authordenisehunter
Twitter: @DeniseAHunter

Melissa Ferguson

Taylor Meo Photography

Melissa Ferguson lives in Bristol, Tennessee, where she enjoys chasing her children and writing romantic comedies full of humor and heart. Her favorite hobby is taking friends and acquaintances and turning them into characters in her books without their knowledge. She is confident you should read all her novels, starting with this one.

Connect with Melissa (and prepare for the possibility of becoming her next character) at:

MelissaFerguson.com
Instagram: @melissafergusonwrites
TikTok: @melissafergusonlife
Facebook: @MelissaLeighFerguson

Kathleen Fuller

Photo by Kathleen Fuller

With over a million copies of her books sold, Kathleen Fuller is the author of several bestselling novels, including the Hearts of Middlefield novels, the Middlefield Family novels, the Amish of Birch Creek series, and the Amish Letters series as well as a middle-grade Amish series, the Mysteries of Middlefield.

Visit Kathleen online at KathleenFuller.com
Instagram: @kf_booksandhooks
Facebook: @WriterKathleenFuller
Twitter: @TheKatJam